悦读丛书

浙江省社科普及全额资助项目

浙江省社科规划一般课题
——14KPCB06YB——

西湖传说文化探微

Exploring the Culture of the West Lake Legends

（汉英对照）

Written and Edited by Li Yingying
李莹莹 编著

浙江工商大学出版社
ZHEJIANG GONGSHANG UNIVERSITY PRESS

图书在版编目(CIP)数据

西湖传说文化探微：汉英对照 / 李莹莹编著. —
杭州：浙江工商大学出版社，2015.8
ISBN 978-7-5178-1216-6

Ⅰ.①西… Ⅱ.①李… Ⅲ.①民间故事－文学研究－
杭州市－汉、英 Ⅳ.①I207.7

中国版本图书馆 CIP 数据核字(2015)第 166546 号

西湖传说文化探微

李莹莹 编著

责任编辑 沈 娴
封面设计 王好驰
责任印制 包建辉
出版发行 浙江工商大学出版社
(杭州市教工路 198 号 邮政编码 310012)
(E-mail：zjgsupress@163.com)
(网址：http://www.zjgsupress.com)
电话：0571－88904980，88831806(传真)
排 版 杭州朝曦图文设计有限公司
印 刷 杭州五象印务有限公司
开 本 710mm×1000mm 1/16
印 张 14
字 数 237 千
版 印 次 2015 年 8 月第 1 版 2015 年 8 月第 1 次印刷
书 号 ISBN 978-7-5178-1216-6
定 价 39.80 元

浙江工商大学出版社营销部邮购电话 0571－88804970

内容简介

《西湖传说文化探微(汉英对照)》一书主要内容分为五章,分别为:1.名胜传说; 2.物产传说;3.人物传说;4.爱情传说;5.附录。全书共选取了21个传说。每个传说包含四个部分:简介、传说中文读本、传说英文译本、文化注释。在附录部分,提供了传统西湖十景、1985年新西湖十景和2007年最新西湖十景的简介,并介绍了西湖列入世界文化遗产名录的相关内容。

本书为中英双语读本,可用作外籍游客的导游读本、外籍人士学习汉语的读本、对外汉语教学的辅助教材、英语学习者的阅读材料以及英语教师的教学辅助材料。

Brief Introduction to This Book

This book falls into five chapters: 1. Legends of Places; 2. Legends of Products; 3. Legends of People; 4. Legends of Love; 5. Appendices. The book covers 21 legends of the West Lake. In each legend, there are four parts, that is, brief introduction, the Chinese original story, the English version and cultural notes. In Appendices, brief introductions to the traditional Ten Scenes of the West Lake, New Ten Scenes of the West Lake (1985) and the Latest Ten Scenes of the West Lake (2007) are given respectively. In addition, the information about the West Lake inscribed on the Heritage List by UNESCO (2011) is also provided.

Being bilingual, this book can be used as a guide book for international tourists, reading material for international readers interested in learning Chinese, teaching aids for teaching Chinese as a foreign language, reading material for English learners as well as teaching material for English teachers.

序(一)

被列入浙江省社会科学界联合会社科普及课题成果的《西湖传说文化探微(汉英对照)》一书,很快将付梓出版。作者李莹莹女士邀我为该书做序,我欣然同意,原因有二:一是我是土生的杭州人,从小在西湖边玩耍长大,有浓浓的西湖乡情;二是作为一名从事文化的工作者和研究者,我与作者有着共同的志向和爱好。

西湖已有两千多年的发展历史,它秀美的湖光山色、丰厚的文化内涵、包容的人文品格,成为世界上第一个以“文化名湖”申遗成功的世界文化景观遗产。俗话说:“一方水土养一方人。”世世代代的杭州人民,围绕西湖创造出了千姿百态的传说和神话,蔚然成为西湖由来已久的一种风俗文化。这是一种相沿积久而成的风气、习俗,被世人所称道和青睐,给杭州这一座城市和本地区历史文化的发展带来了机遇,促进了繁荣。

作者独具匠心、深入研究,将西湖的名山、名水、名人作为主要表现特征,分别在名胜传说、物产传说、人物传说、爱情传说四章与附录中,随不同历史、不同场景、不同气象,以仪态万方之意境,完美地将西湖风俗文化展现出来,且又制成双语读本,使中外读者能品吟西湖的无穷魅力。

《西湖传说文化探微(汉英对照)》,像一颗璀璨的明珠,深深地扎根于中华文化之核心,将发挥“存史、释义、育人”的作用,具有很强的历史穿透力与空间辐射力,对于传承杭州这座城市的历史文脉,具有很大的意义。这给我们伟大中华民族的文化又增添了许多丰富多彩且又生动活泼的地域人文记录。这就是本书对中华民族历史文化的贡献。

风俗文化要求与社会、时代结合,扑向人文科学的怀抱。在21世纪的中国的文化创作领域,我认为存在着三大趋势:一、只承认结果,不承认过程;二、只承认原则,不承认克隆和模拟;三、只承认亮点,不承认平淡无奇。这就要求作者适应新常态,要有新思维。期望本书的出版能使天下更多的读者受益。

是为序。

徐海荣

2015 年元月 12 日

PREFACE I

The book *Exploring the Culture of the West Lake Legends*, sponsored by Zhejiang Federation of Humanities and Social Sciences Circles, will be published soon. The author of this book asked me to write a preface to this book and I readily agreed. There are two reasons for that: Firstly, being a native of *Hangzhou* and growing up by the West Lake, I am deeply attached to the West Lake; Secondly, as a research worker of cultural activities, I shared the same ambition and enthusiasm as the author.

The West Lake, with a long history of over 2000 years, has become the World Cultural Landscape Heritage Site due to its beautiful natural landscapes, profound cultural connotations and inclusive humanism character. As the Chinese saying goes, "human beings are shaped by the land around them", people in *Hangzhou*, from generation to generation, have created various legends and myths and contributed to a particular folk culture of the West Lake, which brings both opportunity and prosperity to *Hangzhou*.

The author shows great originality in her in-depth study of the West Lake Legends, focusing on not only famous mountains and water but also influential people. The book involves five chapters, which are made up of legends of places, legends of products, legends of people, legends of love and appendices. These chapters collectively explore the key cultural elements related to the West Lake from various aspects. The book is written in both Chinese and English, which meets the needs of readers from home and abroad.

The book *Exploring the Culture of the West Lake Legends*, like a bright pearl, deeply rooted in Chinese historical culture, performs the functions of "recording history, interpreting meaning and educating readers". It has a strong historical penetrating power and spatial radiating capacity, which plays a significant role in inheriting *Hangzhou*'s history and enriching the regional records of Chinese traditional culture. The book aims to preserve and look after the Chinese historical culture so that these legends can continue to be enjoyed and live on in the future.

Folk culture is supposed to be integrated with the society and the era and embraced by social sciences. From my point of view, three main trends of cultural creation dominate the 21th century, namely, focusing on the outcome rather than the process; focusing on the principle rather than cloning or simulation; focusing on highlights rather than plainness. Accordingly, authors are expected to adapt to the new normal and develop new mode of thinking. We anticipate that this book will entertain and benefit readers all over the world.

This is the preface.

Xu Hairong

January 12th, 2015

序(二)

杭城之美,美在“半城山色半城湖”。西湖不仅以其“浓妆淡抹总相宜”的美丽自然风光享誉世界,更以其蕴含的深厚文化底蕴为世人称道。西湖文化滋长于源远流长的吴越文化中,是吴越文化的一张名片。丰富多彩、雅俗共赏的西湖传说,正是西湖文化的集中体现。

为了扩大西湖的影响力,浙江省、杭州市相关部门采取了西湖不收门票、关停西湖边的高档会所、还湖于民等各种举措,这些举措对于把世人“请进来”是非常必要和有益的。但如何使西湖真正“走出去”,还有许多工作要做。李莹莹女士的《西湖传说文化探微(汉英对照)》,正是在此方面做出的一个有益的尝试和探索。

作为该书作者的研究生导师,我有幸最早读到这部书稿。该书稿重点突出、脉络清晰、构思新颖、文化感深厚、翻译严谨,读后有耳目一新之感。

一是重点突出。西湖传说林林总总。在一本书里,不可能将所有西湖传说全部加以介绍,必须要把握与突出重点。本书将西湖传说分为四大块,即名胜传说、物产传说、人物传说、爱情传说,并由这四个方面扩展开去。如,名胜传说部分,该书重点译介了明珠、金牛湖、玉泉、飞来峰、虎跑泉、白堤、六和塔等传说,首先是关于西湖来源的两个传说,然后选取了代表西湖的泉、峰、堤、塔等经典景点的传说,可谓慧眼;又如,古往今来,与西湖传说有关的文人、政治家不胜枚举,该书重点译介了苏轼、岳飞、秦桧、康熙、乾隆,可谓匠心。全书译介了与西湖相关的传说二十一种,脉络清晰,条理分明。

二是构思新颖。一部书稿的成功,不仅取决于它有突出的重点、清晰的脉络,更取决于它有新颖的视角。创新是一切理论体系的灵魂,是一部书稿取得成功的关键。本书的可贵之处,就是作者在构思上大胆新颖。从宏观上讲,虽然已有不少的关于西湖传说的中文研究成果,但立足于对外宣传译介的并不多见;少量的关于西湖传说的英文研究成果中,又大都略去了西湖传说中所蕴含的博大精深的中国文化底蕴。作者将书稿定名为《西湖传说文化探微(汉英对照)》,并以此为核心,谋篇布局、展开研究,这无疑是一次创新性的探索。从微观上讲，书中很多具体内容的安排都独具匠心。如，人物传说方面，作者依次译介了苏轼、岳飞、秦桧、康熙、乾隆等人与西湖相关的传说，既体现了时间上的先后顺序，反映了自古以来西湖的影响连绵不绝；又通过历史上最著名的文人、政治家与西湖的亲密关系，揭示了西湖对社会各阶层的深刻的影响。

三是文化感厚重。统观书稿，既含有与西湖相关的景观文化、食文化、茶文化等，更含有与西湖相关的内涵丰富的精神文化。作者对西湖传说的译介，不是简单的翻译和介绍，而是将山水风光与历史人文有机结合，从文化的角度对各种景观、物产和历史人物加以审视与取舍，赋之以文化内涵与文化价值。每个传说后随附的“文化注释”部分，共收录了八十余条，涉及中国传统文化的方方面面。书中译介的西湖传说，反映了杭州人民对真善美的弘扬与追求、对假恶丑的惩抑与憎恶，彰显中华儿女的传统美德。如，在“金牛湖”传说中，金牛一方面破土而出，及时解救老百姓旱灾之苦，另一方面又把媚上压下、欺压百姓的县官、衙役统统卷入巨浪中去。“西湖醋鱼”的传说，反映了杭州人民不畏强权的独立精神。

四是翻译严谨而准确。作者在每一个传说、每一个景点的中文介绍之后，均附上对照的英文翻译，这着实难能可贵，体现了作者的学术自信。这种自信源于作者严谨的翻译。在作者之前，也有外国学者对西湖传说进行了译介，但受历史传统、文化背景等方面的限制，往往丢掉了传说中的文化精髓。作为中国学者，为了更好地向世人包括西方朋友推介西湖传说与西湖文化，译者在翻译的严谨性方面是下了功夫的。

当然，由于是科普读物，该书稿在理论研究的深度上还有待进一步加强，但是，瑕不掩瑜，仍不失为一本值得一读的好书。

孙迎春

2014 年 3 月

PREFACE II

The beauty of *Hangzhou* lies in the landscape that hills and lakes are all in sight. The West Lake attracts visitors from all over the world not only through its beautiful scenery but also by its profound culture. The West Lake culture originates in the long-standing and well-established *Wu-Yue* Culture and even becomes its representative. The colourful West lake legends appeal to all and are the main embodiment of the West Lake culture.

To raise awareness to the outside world of the beauty of the West Lake, *Hangzhou* municipal government as well as *Zhejiang* provincial government have tried different ways to make the West Lake as inviting as possible, such as free admission, closing the exclusive clubs, returning the lake to the public, etc. Despite these efforts, much remains to be done to attract people to the West Lake. Ms *Li Yingying*'s book *Exploring the Culture of the West Lake Legends* is a worthwhile piece that attempts to address this dilemma and encourage more people to discover the elegance and charm of the West Lake.

As the graduate supervisor to the author of this book, I have the privilege of being the first reader of this book. It gives prominence to main points and abounds in cultural connotations, with original perspective and precise translation.

Firstly, this book gives prominence to main points. There is a vast pool of the West Lake legends and there is no way they can all be covered in one book. The legends covered in this book falls into four categories, namely, legends of places, legends of products, legends of people and legends of love. The stories chosen in each part are quite representative. For legends of places, legends related to the origin of the nicknames of the West Lake are given top priority, followed by legends related to typical scenic spots around the West Lake, i.e. Jade Spring, *Feilai* Peak, *Hupao* Spring, *Bai* Causeway and *Liuhe* Pagoda. As for the people, *Su Dongpo*, *Bai Juyi*, *Yue Fei*, *Qin Hui* as well as the two emperors *Kangxi* and *Qianlong*, are both influential and well known.

Secondly, the book deals with the West Lake legends from an original perspective. Innovation is the soul of any theoretical system and the key issue to a successful book. On the macro level, the book intends to introduce the West Lake culture to international readers from the perspective of Chinese traditional culture, which is of great significance; on the micro level, the great originality lies in the layout of the specific contents. Taking the part about legends of people as an example, the stories are listed in the order of *Su Dongpo*, *Yue Fei*, *Qin Hui*, Emperor *Kangxi* and Emperor *Qianlong* for a number of reasons: firstly, they are arranged chronologically, from the *Song* Dynasty to the *Qing* Dynasty; secondly, from men of letters to statesmen, representing the deep influence of people from all classes.

Thirdly, the book contains sufficient cultural connotations. Cultures from landscape, food, tea to spiritual qualities are all covered in this book. Cultural notes are attached to each legend, with over 80 notes in all, touching various aspects of Chinese traditional culture. Stories in this book reveal the traditional virtues of the Chinese people. For instance, in the story of "Golden Buffalo Lake", the golden buffalo stood out and spewed out a large quantity of water to save people from the drought, while it rushed towards the Magistrate as well as his men and buried them down into the lake by huge waves. The story of "West Lake Fish in Vinegar Gravy" reflects *Hangzhou* people's spirit of defying the political power and pursuit of personality independence.

Fourthly, the author does well in producing accurate translation. The English version is provided after each story and note. The author's aptitude and self confidence in academic research derives from her accurate translation. Some previous versions translated by non-native scholars ignored the cultural essence due to the limit of their understanding of the historical traditions and cultural backgrounds of the source text. As a Chinese scholar, the translators of this book have made efforts in achieving accuracy in their translating work.

Admittedly, as a popular science book, there is still room for improvement in theoretical exploring. However, the defects cannot obscure the virtues. The book is definitely worth reading and strongly recommended.

SunYingchun

March, 2014

前　言

西湖传说，是老百姓口头的文学创作，是对西湖及杭州地区特定的自然风光、名胜古迹和历史人物等的脍炙人口的描述，是杭州人民智慧和创造力的集中体现，为杭州的风景名胜增添了艺术的主题和情节，赋予了西湖深厚的文化底蕴，形成了独特的西湖文化。2008年6月7日，西湖传说被列入第二批国家级非物质文化遗产名录。2011年6月，西湖文化景观被联合国教科文组织正式列入世界遗产名录。

本书主要内容包括名胜传说、物产传说、人物传说、爱情传说四个部分，选取了最具影响力的传说二十一个，每个传说附上相关的文化背景注释。全书提供文化注释八十余条，涵盖了大量的文化信息。附录部分还包括传统西湖十景、1985年新西湖十景和2007年最新西湖十景的简介，收录了西湖列入世界文化遗产名录的相关文件。本书所有内容都提供英汉对照。

西湖传说内容丰富，意蕴深远，其中蕴涵的许多中华文化元素、具有中国特色的语言表达，都给翻译带来了很大的挑战。在翻译西湖传说的过程中，译者尽可能地保留西湖传说中的语言和文化的原汁原味，并提供注释，帮助英文读者理解传说中特有的文化现象。译文语言采用口语表达方式，力求通俗易懂。

本书以文化的视野，对西湖传说进行系统的梳理和译介，具有重要的理论意义与现实价值。

一是有利于弘扬西湖文化、吴越文化、中华民族文化。西湖传说以多样的形式表现了中华文化精髓。如西湖传说中所倡导的勤劳勇敢、平等友爱、自强不息、人格独立等道德或精神，所提倡的忠孝之道，所体现的对真善美的追求等，都是西湖文化、吴越文化、中华民族文化的优秀内容；又如西湖传说中所表达的劳苦大众对美好生活的向往和追求，是中国古代老百姓朴素的幸福梦，说明了“中国梦”有着深厚而悠久的历史文化底蕴。因此，西湖传说的文化探微有利于弘扬西湖文化、吴越文化、中华民族文化。

二是有利于促进中西文化的平等交流。在经济全球化形势下，不同文化之间相互交流与碰撞，并呈现出鲜明的输出与接受的不平等性。西方发达国家凭借经济与科技优势，把持着文化交流的主动权，控制着文化交流中的流量、流速和流向，包括中国在内的广大发展中国家在文化交流中处于弱势和守势。面对这种境遇，保持和发展本民族文化的优良传统，大力弘扬民族精神，积极吸收世界其他民族的优秀文化成果，实现文化的与时俱进，是关系广大发展中国家前途和命运的重大问题。因此，对西湖传说进行系统的文化观照，用英文向西方世界展现中华民族文化的魅力，有利于西方世界了解并尊重中华民族文化，有利于促进中西文化的平等交流。

三是有利于发展西湖文化旅游产业。文化是旅游的灵魂，旅游是文化发展的重要途径，文化旅游现已成为国民经济支柱性产业。欧美游客来中国旅游，大都会首选北京、西安这样的古都，这无疑是由于其蕴含的深厚的中国传统文化底蕴。2011 年 BBC 制作杭州宣传片投放欧美，从中我们可以看到欧美游客的偏好，他们所关注的，可能不只是桃红柳绿的白堤苏堤而更是其背后白居易、苏轼所代表的中国古代文人的踪履，可能不只是古朴雅致的灵隐亭榭而更是晨钟暮鼓的僧侣。欧美游客更注重寻求的是一种文化的差异，他们喜欢的是东方文化的独特魅力。因此，发展西湖文化旅游产业，创新对外宣传，打造西湖文化品牌，有利于提升杭州城市的国际知名度和影响力，从而使杭州成为真正的国际重要的旅游休闲中心。

当然，弘扬西湖文化、促进中西文化的平等交流、提升西湖文化的国际影响力、发展西湖文化旅游产业，任重道远，还有许多工作要做。拙作只是努力体现上述几方面的价值，并希望以此吸引更多的人士加入到这一领域的工作中来。

本书为 2013 年浙江省社科联科普重点课题“西湖传说中英双语读本”(课题编号为 13ZD08)，2013 年度杭州市哲学社会科学规划课题“杭州旅游文化的多模态国际传播策略研究”(课题编号为 C13YY01)，以及 2014 年浙江省社科规划一般课题“西湖传说文化探微”(课题编号为 14KPCB06YB)的课题研究成果。该书同时是浙江工商大学“走出去战略与文化传播协同创新中心”的研究成果。

李莹莹

2014 年 5 月

FORWARD

The West Lake legends, the oral folk literature created by the working people, is a vivid description of the natural scenery, places of interest and historical figures, which adds artistic flavour to *Hangzhou* scenic spots and contributes to the unique West Lake culture. In June 2008, the West Lake legends were listed among the first collection of the State Level Intangible Heritage of China. In June 2011, the United Nations Educational, Scientific and Cultural Organization (UNESCO) announced that the World Heritage Committee had inscribed the West Lake Cultural Landscape of *Hangzhou* on its World Heritage List.

Legends in this book fall into four categories: legends of places, legends of products, legends of people and legends of love. The book covers 21 legends in all, and cultural notes are attached to each legend. In Appendices, brief introductions about the traditional Ten Scenes of the West Lake, New Ten Scenes of the West Lake (1985) and the Latest Ten Scenes of the West Lake (2007) are given respectively. In addition, the information about the West Lake inseribed on the Heritage List by UNESCO (2011) is also provided. Both Chinese and English versions are provided for each part.

Translating the West Lake legends, which involve many Chinese cultural elements, poses great challenges to the translators. The translators of this book have strived to keep the original flavour of the source language and culture and tried to make the translated version as coherent as possible.

This book intends to introduce legends to English readers from the perspective of Chinese culture, which is of great significance in many ways.

Firstly, this book helps to carry forward the West Lake culture, the *Wu-Yue* Culture as well as Chinese culture. The West Lake legends manifest the essence of Chinese culture in various ways, such as industry and courage, equality and fraternity, unremitting self-improvement and personality independence, loyalty and filial piety, and the pursuit of Truth, Good and Beauty, etc. The stories indicate that working people in ancient China cherished dreams of happiness, which is the key principle and symbolization of China Dream.

Secondly, this book helps to promote the equal communication between Chinese and Western cultures. Under the situation of economic globalization, Western developed countries dominate the process of mutual exchanges and collisions among different cultures, while the developing countries including China are in the weak position and on the defensive. Under this circumstance, maintaining and developing the cultural tradition of developing countries, and carrying forward their national spirit have an important bearing on the future and destiny of the developing countries. Translating the West Lake legends into English will play a positive role in helping people in Western countries to have a better understanding of the Chinese culture and accordingly promote the equal communication between Chinese and Western cultures.

Thirdly, this book helps the development of the cultural tourism industry of the West Lake. Culture is the soul of tourism, and tourism offers an important channel for cultural development. Cultural tourism has become the pillar industry in national economy. Tourists from Europe and America often choose ancient cities like Beijing and Xi'an as their first destinations mainly because those cities represent Chinese traditional culture. The advertising video program produced by BBC in 2011 targeting Western market reveals that tourists from Western countries are more interested in men of letters in ancient China like *Bai Juyi*, *Su Dongpo* than the scenic spots like *Bai* Causeway and *Su* Causeway lined with red blossoms and green willows; more fascinated with monks who ring the morning bell and beat the evening drum compared to the architecture itself of *Lingyin* Temple. Western tourists are more attracted by the cultural differences and the uniqueness of Eastern charm. Developing cultural tourism industry helps to make *Hangzhou* an internationally well-known tourism and leisure center.

Admittedly, there is still a long way to go to carry forward the culture of the West Lake, to promote the equal communication between Chinese and Western cultures and to develop cultural tourism industry of the West Lake. This book is just a tentative attempt in this area, hoping to bring more people to work together in this field of study.

This book is the research result of "The West Lake legends bilingual readings", popular science key research project supported by *Zhejiang* Federation of Humanities and Social Sciences Circles in 2013 (Grant No. 13ZD08); "Multimodal international communication strategy of *Hangzhou* cultural tourism industry" of *Hangzhou* Philosophy and Social Sciences Planning Project in 2013 (Grant No. C13YY01); "Exploring the Culture of the West Lake Legends"of *Zhejiang* Social Sciences Planning Project (Grant No. 14KPCB06YB). Additionally, this book is also the research result of *Zhejiang Gongshang* University's "Going Global Cultural Strategy and Cultural Transmission Collaborative Innovation Center".

Li Yingying

May, 2014

CONTENTS | 目录

第一章
名胜传说

Chapter I
LEGENDS OF PLACES

西湖水秀、山青、亭美、塔多情、桥浪漫，其本身就是一幅天然图画。每一个景点几乎都有比景色更动人的传说，像磁铁一样吸引着万千游客。

West Lake boasts of a number of green mountains, clear water, charming pavilions, sentimental towers and romantic bridges, like a natural drawing. There are touching legends behind almost each scenic spot, which attracts hundreds and thousands of visitors like a magnet.

壹◎明珠
The Bright Pearl

【简介】

杭州风景秀丽，气候宜人，有人间天堂之美誉。举世闻名的西湖就像一颗明珠镶嵌在这美丽风景中。西湖旧称明珠、武林水、明圣湖、金牛湖、龙川、钱源、钱塘湖、西子湖等。每个别名,各有来历。关于"西湖"这个名称,最早出现在唐朝。说起西湖的来历,有着许多优美的传说和故事,这篇传说尤为经典。

【Brief Introduction】

Hangzhou enjoys beautiful scenery and agreeable climate, which is regarded as a paradise on earth. The world-famous West Lake is like a brilliant pearl embedded in the beautiful view. West Lake used to have other names such as Bright Pearl, *Wulin* Water, *Mingsheng* Lake, Golden Buffalo Lake, Dragon River, *Qian Yuan*, *Qiantang* Lake and *Xizi* Lake, to name a few. There are fascinating stories behind each name. The name of West Lake originated in the *Tang* Dynasty. As for the origin of West Lake, it has a number of beautiful folklore and stories, among which the following story *The Bright Pearl* is one of the best-known.

【传说读本】

相传很久以前,在天河东边的石窟里,住着一条雪白的玉龙;在天河西边的大树林里,住着一只彩色的金凤。

玉龙和金凤是邻居,每天早晨,他们一个钻出石窟,一个飞出树林,打个照面就忙着各做各的事儿去了。

有一天,他俩一个在天空飞,一个在天河游,不知不觉来到一个仙岛上。在仙岛上,他们发现了一块亮闪闪的石头。金凤很喜欢,就对玉龙说:"玉龙玉龙,你看这块石头多好看呀!"玉龙也很喜欢,就对金凤说:"金凤金凤,我们把它琢磨成一颗珠子吧。"

金凤点头答应,他俩就动工了。玉龙用爪子抓,金凤用喙子啄。一天一天,一年一年过去了,他俩真的把石头琢成了一颗滚圆滚圆的珠子。金凤飞到仙山上衔来许多露珠儿,滚到珠子上,玉龙游到天河里汲来许多清水,喷到珠子上,慢慢地这颗珠子就变得明光闪亮了。

从此以后,玉龙喜欢金凤,金凤也喜欢玉龙。玉龙和金凤都喜欢他们的明珠。玉龙不愿回天河东边那个石窟去了,金凤也不愿再回天河西边那个树林。他俩就住在天河当中的仙岛上,日夜守着自己的明珠。

这颗明珠真是一颗宝珠,珠光照到哪里,哪里的树木常青,百花齐放,山明水秀,五谷丰收。

一天，**王母娘娘**走出宫门，一下就看见这颗明珠的宝光，心里非常羡慕。到半夜辰光(时候)，她就派一个天兵，趁玉龙和金凤睡熟的时候，悄悄地把这颗明珠拿走了。王母娘娘得到明珠，喜欢得不得了，连看也舍不得给人家看一看。她把明珠藏到仙宫里头，外面关起九重门，上了九道锁。

玉龙和金凤一觉醒来，发现明珠不见了，他俩真着急呀！玉龙找遍了天河底下的每一个石窟，没有找到；金凤寻遍了山上的每一个角落，也没有寻着。他俩伤心极了，可还是日日夜夜地到处寻找，一心想把心爱的明珠找回来。

王母娘娘生日的那一天，四面八方的神仙都赶到仙宫来祝寿。王母娘娘摆下盛大的蟠桃会请众神仙。神仙们喝着美酒，吃着蟠桃，齐声祝贺王母娘娘福如东海，寿比南山。王母娘娘一时高兴，就对众神仙说："各位仙长，我请你们看一颗珍贵的明珠，这可是天上难找、地下难寻的宝珠啊！"

说着，就从衣带上解下九把钥匙，打开九道锁，走进九重门，从里面取出那颗明珠，用金盘端着放在厅堂中间。明珠亮晶晶、光闪闪，神仙们看了都啧啧叫好。

这时，玉龙和金凤正到处寻找他们的明珠。金凤发现了明珠放出的亮光；就忙叫玉龙："玉龙玉龙快来看，那不是我们的明珠放出来的亮光吗？"玉龙从天河里钻出头来，一看："是呀，一定是我们的那颗明珠，快把它找回来！"

玉龙和金凤立刻朝着明珠的亮光找去，一直找到王母娘娘的仙宫里。那些神仙正在伸头探脑围着明珠叫好。玉龙上前说："这颗明珠是我们的！"金凤也说："这颗明珠是我们的！"王母娘娘一听火了，冲着玉龙、金凤，张口就骂："胡说！我是**玉皇大帝**的亲娘，天上的一切宝物都该是我的。"

玉龙和金凤一听也来了火气，一同向王母娘娘说："这颗明珠不是天上生的，也不是地下长的，是我俩辛辛苦苦，一天一天、一年一年琢磨出来的！"

王母娘娘一听，又羞又恼，脖子气粗了，脸也涨红了，伸手护住放着明珠的金盘，喝叫天兵天将把玉龙和金凤赶出去。金凤见王母娘娘不讲理，扑过去就抢明珠；玉龙见王母娘娘不讲理，也冲上去抢明珠。三双手都抓住金盘，谁也不肯放松。你拉我扯，金盘一摇晃，明珠滚了下来，滚到阶沿边，从天上掉到地下去了。

玉龙和金凤见明珠往下掉，急忙翻身跟下来保护。玉龙飞着，金凤舞着，他俩一忽儿在前，一忽儿在后，一忽儿在左，一忽儿在右，保护着这颗明珠，慢慢地，慢慢地从天空降落到地面上。这颗明珠一落地，立刻变成了清清的西湖。玉龙舍不得离开自己的明珠，就变成一座雄伟的玉龙山来守护它；金凤舍不得离开自己的明珠，就变成一座青翠的凤凰山来守护它。

从此，凤凰山和玉龙山就静静地卧在西湖的旁边。直到今天，杭州还流传着两句古老的歌谣："西湖明珠自天降，龙飞凤舞到**钱塘**。"

【English Version of the Original Story】

Once upon a time, there lived a snow-white Jade Dragon in a rock cave on the east bank of the Celestial River. Across the river was a great forest, where there lived a colourful Golden Phoenix.

As they were neighbours, the dragon and the phoenix met each other every morning before going their different ways.

One glorious day, the phoenix flew in the sky, while the dragon swam in the Celestial River. Together, they stumbled across a fairy island. There they found a shining pebble, which fascinated the Phoenix.

"Look, look, Jade Dragon, how beautiful this pebble is!" Golden Phoenix said to Jade Dragon.

Jade Dragon liked the pebble too and had a great idea. Jade Dragon said to the phoenix, "Why don't we polish it into a pearl!"

Golden Phoenix nodded in agreement. Then they started working on it, Jade Dragon with his claws and Golden Phoenix her beak. As the days became years, they at last made it into a perfect round ball. Golden Phoenix flew to the sacred mountain to gather dewdrops and sprinkled them onto the ball, while Jade Dragon carried vast amounts of clear water from the Celestial River and sprayed the water onto it. By and by the ball turned into a dazzling pearl.

From that moment on, they fell in love with each other and both of them were attached to their pearl. Jade Dragon did not want to go back to his cave; neither did the Golden Phoenix want to go back to her forest. So they settled down on the fairy island in the middle of the Celestial River, guarding their pearl day and night.

What a magic pearl it was! It became so gloriously radiant that wherever its rays were cast, trees turned evergreen and flowers all bloomed, with mountains green, waters clear and earth fruitful.

One day the **Heavenly Queen Mother**, who governed the West Heaven, left her palace and caught sight of the brilliant rays shed by the pearl. She was so overwhelmed with the pearl that she could not wait to have it. That night she dispatched one of her guards to steal the precious stone away while Jade Dragon and Golden Phoenix both sounded asleep. Having the pearl in her hand, the Heavenly Queen Mother was so thrilled with it that she would not let anybody else even have a look at it. She hid it in the innermost room of her palace, with nine locked doors to protect it.

To their great surprise, Jade Dragon and Golden Phoenix found the pearl gone when they woke up the next morning. Frantically, Jade Dragon looked into every rock cave at the bottom of the Celestial River, while Golden Phoenix combed every inch of the mountain, but in vain. Though broken-hearted, they continued searching day and night, hoping one day they would recover their cherished pearl.

On the birthday of the Heavenly Queen Mother, all the gods and goddesses in Heaven came to her palace to offer their congratulations. She prepared a grand feast, entertaining her guests with nectar and celestial peaches, the fruit of immortality. The gods and goddesses all proposed a toast to her,

"May your fortune be as boundless as the East Sea and your life last long like the South Mountain!"

The Heavenly Queen Mother became so excited that she, on a sudden impulse, declared,

"My immortal friends, I'd like to show you a precious pearl, the equal of which cannot be found either in Heaven or on Earth!"

With that, she unfastened nine keys from her girdle and unlocked the nine doors one after the other. From the innermost room of her palace she took out the bright pearl, putting it on a golden tray and, holding it carefully to the centre of the banquet hall. The pearl became gloriously radiant, dazzling the whole hall. The guests were all fascinated by its radiance and greatly admired it.

At this exact moment, Jade Dragon and Golden Phoenix were still searching for their pearl. Suddenly Golden Phoenix saw the familiar dazzling light from the pearl, and said to Jade Dragon, "Come on, Jade Dragon. Look, isn't that the light from our pearl?" Jade Dragon stuck his head out of the Celestial River and looked, "Yes! It must be ours! Let's go and get it back."

They flew towards the light, which led them into the palace of the Heavenly Queen Mother, where the immortals were clustering around the pearl and praising it lavishly.

Amid the pushing, Jade Dragon shouted, "This pearl is ours!"

Golden Phoenix shouted, too, "This is our pearl!"

The Heavenly Queen Mother was so enraged by their claim that she snapped, "Shut up! I'm the mother of **Jade Emperor**. All treasures in Heaven should be in my possession!"

Both Jade Dragon and Golden Phoenix were infuriated by her remarks. They protested in unison,

"This pearl was not produced by Heaven. It was not manufactured by Earth, either. It was all carved and polished by the two of us, day after day, year after year!"

Shamed and annoyed, the Heavenly Queen Mother clutched the tray tightly while ordering her army to drive away Jade Dragon and Golden Phoenix. Seeing the Heavenly Queen Mother so unreasonable, Golden Phoenix went to snatch the pearl from her. So did Jade Dragon. The three struggled over the golden tray with all their might, with neither party giving in. As the tray shook amidst the tussle, the pearl fell off, rolling to the edge of the stairs and then dropping into the air.

Seeing the pearl dropping, Jade Dragon and Golden Phoenix rushed out of the palace, trying to save it from being smashed into pieces. They flew next to the falling pearl, clinging to both sides, trying to protect it, until it slowly landed onto Earth. Hardly had it touched the ground when the pearl turned into a clear lake. Jade Dragon and Golden Phoenix could not bear to part from it, so they turned into two mountains, guarding the lake ever since. The two mountains still exist today, and are called Jade Dragon Mountain and Phoenix Mountain.

Since that time the Phoenix Mountain and the Jade Dragon Mountain have been lying there side by side on the southern shore of the lake in tranquility. Till this day, an old folk song has been widely circulated in Hangzhou as follows:

West Lake, a dazzling pearl, dropping from the heaven,
With the flying dragon and the dancing phoenix all coming to **Qiantang**.

【文化背景】【Cultural Notes】

▶ **王母娘娘**：传说中的女神，拥有至高权力。相传王母娘娘住在昆仑仙岛，她的瑶池蟠桃园种有蟠桃，食之可长生不老。

Heavenly Queen Mother: A goddess in the folklore with supreme power. It was said that she lived in *Kunlun* Fairy Island. She had a garden in the Jade Pool with celestial peaches, and people who ate these fruits would be immortal.

▶ **玉皇大帝**：道教认为玉皇为众神之王，神权最大，管理宇宙万物的兴隆衰败、吉凶祸福。居住在玉清宫。

Jade Emperor: According to Taoism, Jade Emperor is the King of all gods with the greatest power. He is in charge of everything in the whole universe. He lived in *Yuqing* Palace.

▶ **钱塘**：指的是钱塘湖，曾是西湖的别名。杭州城古称之一为钱塘郡，其管辖区内的湖就被称之为钱塘湖。

Qiantang: West Lake used to be called *Qiantang* Lake. *Hangzhou* city used to be called *Qiantang* County. So the lake, located in this area, was called *Qiantang* Lake.

贰 ◎ 金牛湖
Golden Buffalo Lake

【简介】

金牛湖是古代西湖的旧称，西湖位于杭州市区西面。唐朝后期开始称西湖。古时原与杭州湾相通,后来因泥沙堰塞而成。环湖一周约 15 公里,面积约 5.2 平方公里。湖周围有南高峰、北高峰、玉皇山等。湖中以孤山、白堤、苏堤分隔为外西湖、里西湖、后西湖、小南湖及岳湖。湖光山色,风景绮丽。古时人们对西湖水永不枯竭之谜产生好奇,故有"金牛出水"一说。现在涌金门涌金池有一座"金牛出水"雕像。

【About the Place】

West Lake, located in the west of *Hangzhou* City, used to be known as Golden Buffalo Lake in ancient times. West Lake has been named since late *Tang* Dynasty. In ancient times, the lake used to be connected with Hangzhou Bay, and later it became a barrier lake with sedimentation. The lake covers 5.2 square kilometres and is 15 kilometres in circumference. Along the lake, there are Southern Peak, Northern Peak and Jade Emperor Hill, etc. With the Solitary Hill, *Bai* Causeway and *Su* Causeway, the lake is divided into Outer Lake, Inner Lake, Back Lake, Little South Lake and *Yue* Lake. The lake and hills add radiance and beauty to each other, and create a unique sight. In ancient times people were perplexed by the phenomenon that West Lake has never dried up, and invented the image of a golden buffalo who spewedout water. Now there is a statue of "Golden Buffalo Emerging from West Lake" in *Yongjin* Pool near *Yongjin* Gate.

【传说读本】

从前,西湖上一片白茫茫的,沿着湖岸是黑油油的肥沃田地。周围的老百姓都在地里种着庄稼,用湖水灌溉。稻穗儿长得沉甸甸,谷粒儿长得圆溜溜,像一串一串的珍珠,真叫人喜欢。农闲了,大家就到湖上打鱼捞虾。人们和睦相处,过着安乐的日子。

在这湖底,住着一头金牛。只要天晴久了,湖水慢慢浅下去,湖里的金牛就会出现。老远就能看见它那金晃晃的背脊,昂起的头和翘起的双角,嘴里吐出一口口清水。这样,湖水立刻又涨得满满的了。

有一年夏天,算起来已经九九八十一天没有下雨啦,直旱得湖底朝天,四周的田地都硬得像石头,缝裂得有几寸宽,嫩绿的秧苗都枯黄了。老百姓干渴得眼睛凹进去,浑身没劲。他们天天盼望金牛出现。

这天早晨，大家正在湖边盼望着，突然传来“哞”的一声。哈，果然看见金牛破水而出。它摇摇头，摆摆尾，大口吐水，霎时间湖水又涨满了。

老百姓见了，个个喜得拍手叫好，流出了泪水，感激金牛。又见那头金牛抬起头，闪着亮晶晶的眼睛，“哞”的叫了一声，慢慢地没入湖中。

这事很快就传开了。钱塘县官听到后，捧着肚子笑呵呵他说：“这真是件活宝贝呵，要是把它拿来献给皇帝，一定能升官发财！”当下就吩咐手下人，赶紧去把金牛捉来。

那些**衙役**、**地保**一个个都急匆匆地跑到湖边，抬头望望，眼前却是一片白茫茫的湖水，哪儿还有金牛呵？问问附近百姓，大家见是**衙门**里的人，不是说没见着，就是悄悄地避开啦。

衙役们只得回报了县官。县官心里生气，拈着八字胡须，想啊想，想出了一条绝招。他对手下人说：“既然金牛不见了，沉入湖底，那你们就把老百姓都叫去，把湖水车干。谁不去，就斩谁！”

住在湖边的老百姓，男的、女的、老的、少的，都被赶到湖边。他们在县官的威逼下，只得架起水车车湖水。

车啊车，一连车了九九八十一天，累得大家精疲力竭，到了最后那一天，终于把湖水车干了。果然，金牛卧在湖底，它那身上的金光照得天明地亮。

县官走去看看，也被金光照得连眼睛都张不开，他还吆喝着衙役们赶快下湖去抢金牛。说也奇怪，那金牛好像生了根似的，掀也掀不起，抬也抬不动。老百姓都暗暗打心里高兴。

县官一看搬不动，就对百姓说：“谁能抬起金牛，赏白银三百**两**！”

可是老百姓都站着不动，气呼呼地不睬他。县官见老百姓不理，就大声怒吼道：“今天若不把金牛抬起，就将你们统统杀头！”

这县官的话刚说完，只听那头金牛大叫了一声，真像晴天炸了个霹雳。但见飞沙走石，地动山摇，那县官吓得面如土色，双腿发软，心想逃走，可是一步也挪不动。

这时，那金牛立了起来，仰天长啸一声，从口中吐出一股白花花的大水，直冲县官、衙役而去，一下子把他们全都卷入巨浪中去啦。立刻，湖水又满了起来。从此以后，湖中的金牛不再出现了，湖水再也没干过。

人们忘不了金牛，就在湖旁边的城墙上筑起了一座高高的城楼，天天爬上城楼去盼望金牛。这座城楼，就是后来的“涌金门”。

【English Version of the Original Story】

Long ago, West Lake was shrouded in mist. Along the banks was rich black soil. Crops grew in fields and were irrigated with the lake water. Ripe ears of rice hung heavy on the stalks, and when fully ripe the grains looked like charming strings of pearls. During slack farming seasons, people would go fishing and catch shrimps at the lakeside. They enjoyed happy and harmonious lives.

On the lake bottom there lived a golden buffalo, who emerged during drought days when the lake water diminished. The buffalo's golden-coloured back could be seen in the far distance, with its head lifted up and its two horns high in the air. It spewed out clean water and the lake became full of water again.

One summer, the lake got extremely dry. There had not been a drop of rain for months. All the farmland around the lake dried up like stones and cracked widely. Young green rice seedlings withered and turned yellow. People were hollow-eyed and feeling weak from the lack of clean drinking water. Day and night they prayed for the return of the golden buffalo.

One morning, when all the people were expecting the buffalo, there came a sudden loud "Moo". The golden buffalo rose up from the bottom of the lake as anticipated. Shaking its head and tail, it spewed out water from its big mouth. Instantly the lake became full of water again.

Amazed at the miracle, people were overjoyed and clapped their hands, while tears ran down their cheeks. They were very grateful to the buffalo. The animal lifted its head, blinked its bright eyes and slowly submerged into the lake water again, with a loud "Moo".

News of the miracle spread quickly. Hearing about it, *Qiantang* County Magistrate gave a great belly laugh,

"What a precious living treasure! If I can get it and send it to the emperor as a gift, I'll surely be able to get promoted to a higher position with a bigger fortune."

At once he ordered his men to capture the golden buffalo and bring it to him.

The *yamen* **runners** and **local constables** all hurried to the lake. They looked at the water which was completely covered in mist, but there was no sign of the golden buffalo. They inquired about it, but the people knew they were *yamen* runners and either said no or avoided them.

The *yamen* runners had to report to the Magistrate; who became very angry. Then he worked out an unexpectedly tricky move. He gave an order to his men,

"Since the golden buffalo has disappeared and sunk into the lake bottom, order all the people to go to the lake and drain out the water. Anyone who refuses to do so will be beheaded! "

All the people living around the lake, regardless of age or gender, were driven to the water's edge. Under the local officials' threat and force, they had no choice but to set up a water wheel to drain water out of the lake.

They worked for months without any rest. They were all exhausted. At last there was no water left in the lake. Sure enough, the golden buffalo was seen there lying on the lake bed with its golden colour lighting the whole area.

The Magistrate went up to it and wanted to have a closer look, but the golden buffalo's bright colour made him unable to keep his eyes open. He ordered his men to hurry down to the lake bed to catch the golden buffalo. Oddly enough, the buffalo stood firm and remained still, as if he was rooted into the earth. People felt so relieved.

Seeing that the buffalo refused to move, the Magistrate said to people there,

"Whoever can lift the golden buffalo will be rewarded with three hundred ***liang*** of silver!"

People stood still and ignored him, although they were very angry. The Magistrate roared,

"All of you will be killed unless the golden buffalo is lifted!"

At that point, the golden buffalo cried out like a thunder from the sunny sky. Sand and stones began flying around in the air. The Magistrate was frightened out of his life and his face turned as white as a sheet. His legs trembled uncontrollably. He wanted to run away, but was unable to move.

At this moment, the buffalo stood up, yelled to the sky and spewed out a large quantity of water, which rushed towards the Magistrate as well as his men. All of them were gulped down into the lake by huge waves. Immediately the lake became full of water again. Since then the golden buffalo has never appeared again and West Lake has never run dry.

The local people missed the buffalo so much that they set up a tall tower on the city wall near the lake. Every day they climbed up the tower with the hope of seeing the buffalo. The gate tower was later named "*Yongjin* Gate."

【文化背景】【Cultural Notes】

▶ **衙门**:衙门是封建中国的官邸。地方衙门通常具有相似的结构要素:一个前大门,一个庭院,一个大厅(通常是升堂审判场所)和办公房、牢房、储藏室各若干,以及任职官员及其家属、员工居住的房宅。

Yamen: A *yamen* was a government office in feudal China. At local level, it generally had similar features: a front gate, a courtyard and a hall (typically serving as a court of law); offices, prison cells and store rooms; and residences for the bureaucrat, his family and his staff.

▶ **衙役**:衙门里的差役。

***Yamen* runners**: Local officials in a government office.

▶ **地保**:清朝和民国初年在地方上为官府办差的人。

Local constables: Persons who worked for the government among the common people during the *Qin* Dynasty and the early period of the Republic of China.

▶ **两**:数量词,古代衡量金、银、铜的计量单位,1 两等于 50 克。

Liang: a measure to weigh gold, silver and copper, etc. in ancient China. One *liang* is equal to 50 grams.

叁◎玉泉
Jade Spring

【简介】

玉泉位于西湖西北面玉泉山麓,植物园以北,杭州三大名泉之一。泉池呈长方形,长 14 米,宽 10 米,深 3 米。泉水从地底涌出,砌石为池,清澈见底。池内蓄大鱼,浮沉荡漾,有"鱼乐园"之称。自宋朝以来,已吸引无数观鱼爱好者和游客前来,成为杭州最佳观鱼点已有七百多年历史。

【Brief Introduction】

Located at the foot of Jade Spring Hill, in the northwest of West Lake, near the Hangzhou Botanical Garden, Jade Spring is one of the three best springs in Hangzhou. The spring is a rectangular pool about 14 metres long, 10 metres wide and 3 metres deep. The spring water intermittently emerges from the ground to feed the pool and its water is as clear as crystal. With large fish swimming in it, the pool is known as "the World of Frolicking Fish". Since the *Song* Dynasty, it has attracted countless fish watchers and other visitors and remained the best location to view fish for more than 700 years.

【传说读本】

早先,钱搪江口有一条深不见底的地沟,叫作"天开河"。在天开河里,住着一条草龙。草龙能翻江倒海,腾云驾雾,本领很大。但他粗里粗气的,不懂得世事,整天在江里钻进,海里钻出,和大小鱼虾们嬉戏。

一天,有只官船押着两条驳船从钱塘江口经过。官船鸣锣开道,神气十足,驳船上却是一片哭声。草龙见了很奇怪,左右一打听,才知道人间有个皇帝，皇帝手下有许多官儿。这两只驳船上的人是皇帝派官儿抓老百姓到京城去做苦工。

草龙知道了这事，十分气愤，他把尾巴一甩，“哗啦啦”一个大浪头扑过去，打翻官船，救下了两船百姓。草龙想：“官船是给我打翻了啦，可皇帝还在京城呢。皇帝这么坏，我应该收掉他，换个好的。”于是，他便驾起乌云，冲出天开河，向京城飞去。

皇帝正在宫廷里和大臣、妃子们饮酒作乐。宫娥彩女们吹的吹，弹的弹，唱的唱，舞的舞，好不快活！冷不防天色霎时变了：狂风刮得大树折腰，倾盆大雨哗哗落个不歇。只见草龙驾着乌云，气势汹汹地闯了进来。这一下，吓得三千**御林军**抱头乱窜，皇帝更惊得目瞪口呆。幸而有个胆大的侍卫，拉开弹弓，朝草龙打了一弹丸。这一弹弓凑巧打中草龙的右眼，疼得他大吼一声，扭过头，“哗啦啦！”尾巴扫坍宫殿一只角，飞走了。

草龙逃回钱塘江口的天开河里，越想越恼火，咬牙切齿地发誓要报仇。

那时，**清涟寺**里住着一个会看病的老和尚，医术很高明。草龙打听到有这么一个和尚，便变化成一个粗黑结实的大汉上门求医。老和尚看他形状怪异，心里很疑惑，就问：“哎呀，哎呀，你这只眼睛怎么会弄成这个样子的呀？”

草龙编了个谎话，说是上山凿石头，不小心被碎石子爆的。

老和尚用钳子钳出草龙眼睛里的东西，一看是弹丸，就往地下一摔，说：“明明是颗弹丸，为啥说是碎石子呀？你到底是什么人？不讲明白我不医！”

草龙见老和尚发了脾气，怕他真的不给自己医治，就把怎样被射了一颗弹丸的经过，老老实实地说出来。末了还说：“等你把我的眼睛医好了，我就去报仇！”

老和尚听了草龙的话，大吃一惊。心想：“我这寺院是皇帝造的，我享的是皇帝福，如今他要去损害皇帝，这还了得！”便想了个计策，假意向草龙笑笑说：“要我医好眼睛不难，不过，你拿什么来谢我呢？”

草龙说：“只要你能医好我的眼睛，你要什么奇珍异宝，我都给你。”

老和尚听了摇摇头说：“奇珍异宝我不要。这寺院里缺水，你先替我钻个泉眼吧！”

草龙不知是计，便满口答应了。老和尚选定一块地，草龙就一个跟头扎进泥土里去，清清的泉水便从他扎进去的洞口汩汩地涌上来。草龙越钻越深，井水也越涌越大，很快汇成了一口大池。这时老和尚急忙将佛前供奉的玲珑石塔移过来，在泉眼当中一竖，这样就把草龙牢牢地压在地下啦。

草龙上了老和尚的当,被压在地下再也出不来了。可是草龙钻出来的那个泉眼,因为涌出来的泉水像碧玉一般清洌,人们就把它叫作“玉泉”。在玉泉附近还有两个水池,一个叫“珍珠泉”,一个叫“晴空喜雨泉”。据说草龙的头伏在珍珠泉下面,所以地面上一有震动,草龙惊醒过来,在地下舒舒气,水面上就咕噜噜地冒出许多小小的气泡。晴空喜雨泉底下,正好盘着草龙的尾巴,因此在大晴天里,上面总是雾蒙蒙的。

【English Version of the Original Story】

Long ago, at the mouth of *Qiantang* River, there was a fathomless trench, called “Heaven-Built River”, where a folk dragon lived. The dragon had tremendous power and could overturn rivers and seas, and could walk on clouds. However, he was rough, rash and quite ignorant of worldly affairs. He idled in rivers and seas. He played all day with fish and shrimps.

One day an official boat was passing along the mouth of *Qiantang* River, with two barges under escort. The officials in the boat were very arrogant and beat gongs to clear their path, while people on the two barges were wailing and whining. The dragon inquired about it and was then told that on the earth there was an emperor with lots of officials working for him. The people on the two barges were common people caught by those officials, and were sent to do physical work in the capital city.

Learning this, the dragon got so furious that he shook his tail and a big wave rolled by and overturned the official boat. The people on the two barges were rescued. Then an idea occurred to the dragon. He thought to himself, although the official boat was upside down, the emperor was still in the capital. Since the emperor was so evil, the dragon planned to subdue him and bring him under control, and then a better qualified emperor could be nominated. So he mounted the clouds, rushed through Heaven-Built River and flew towards the capital.

At that point, the emperor was enjoying wine and making merry with his ministers and concubines at the Imperial Court. All his maids and concubines were fully occupied with a variety of performances. To everyone’s surprise, the sky suddenly darkened. Terrible storms cracked tall trees and heavy rain kept pouring down. The dragon stalked defiantly into the court. This made three thousand **Imperial Guards** lose their heads and scurry away in panic, not to mention the horrified and dumb-struck emperor. Fortunately for the emperor, a brave guard used his catapult and shot the dragon. The shot struck the dragon's right eye. He uttered an agonized yell, turned back his head, slammed his tail over a corner of the palace and flew away.

The dragon escaped to Heaven-Built River at the mouth of *Qiantang* River. The more he thought about it, the more irritated he was. He gnashed his teeth with hatred and vowed to take revenge.

During that time a senior monk, who was well-known for curing deadly diseases, was living at ***Qinglian* Temple**. When he learned about the monk, the dragon disguised himself as a strong, coarse man and visited the monk for some treatment for his eye injury. The senior monk looked at his deformed face and felt greatly confused. He exclaimed,

"It's so weird! How did you get your eye hurt like this?"

The dragon lied that his eye was hit by a tiny stone while he was drilling rocks on a hill.

The senior monk picked out something from the dragon's eye with a pair of tweezers, took a closer look and found it was a pellet. He dashed it on the ground and shouted,

"It's clearly a pellet. Why did you say it's a tiny stone? Who on earth are you? I won't treat you without knowing who you really are!"

Seeing that the senior monk had lost his temper and might refuse to do the surgery without being told the truth, the dragon had to tell the monk what had happened, and he added,

"After my eye is cured, I'll go and take my revenge!"

Hearing these words, the senior monk felt greatly surprised and thought,

"My temple was set up by the emperor's order, and I've enjoyed a happy life under the emperor's mercy. Now this man wants to hurt the emperor, I should not let him do so." He worked out a plan and put on an insincere smile,

"It's not difficult to cure your eye, but how would you thank me for the treatment?"

The dragon answered,

"I'll give you anything precious if only you can cure my eye."

The senior monk shook his head and said,

"I need no treasures but my temple lacks drinking water. How about digging a spring for me?"

Not realizing it was a trap, the dragon readily agreed to do as the monk asked. After the monk had decided on a spot, the dragon instantly somersaulted into the earth. Immediately, clean and clear spring water came out from the hole. The deeper the dragon got into the earth, the more spring water emerged. Soon a large pool formed. Then the senior monk hurriedly moved a small, refined, rock pagoda, for worshiping Buddha, from the shrine into the mouth of the spring. In this way, the dragon was completely imprisoned down in the earth.

The dragon was trapped by the senior monk and could no longer come out. The spring mouth, drilled by the dragon, gushed out cold water as clear as a pure jade; so people called it "Jade Spring". Near Jade Spring, there are other two pools. One is named "Pearl Spring", the other one "Showers on a Sunny Day Spring". It's said that the dragon's head lies under "Pearl Spring". When an earthquake occurs, the dragon wakes up with a start and takes a deep breath. Lots of small bubbles appear on the surface of the spring water. The tail of the dragon is set under "Showers on a Sunny Day Spring". That is thought to be the reason why there is always fog and mist there, even on sunny days.

【文化背景】【Cultural Notes】

▶ **御林军**:禁军,中国古时保卫京城或宫廷的军队。

Imperial Guards: Military forces that protected the capital city and the imperial palace in ancient China.

▶ **清涟寺**:玉泉旧有寺庙,名清涟寺,南齐年间(479—502),僧人昙超在此开山筑庵,五代(907—960)时改为净空寺,南宋(1127—1279)又称净空院,

1699年清朝康熙赐名“清涟寺”。因寺内有玉泉,人称玉泉寺。1964年整修玉泉风景时,拆去清涟寺和寺内的龙王庙,在原址上重新设计建造起来玉泉庭院。

***Qinglian* Temple**: There used to be a temple in the site of Jade Spring. During the Southern *Qi* Dynasty(479—502), a monk named *Tan Chao* cut through the mountain to build a Buddhist convent here. It turned into *Jingkong* Temple during the period of the Five Dynasties(907—960)and renamed as *Jingkong* Garden in the Southern *Song* Dynasty (1127—1279). In 1699 Emperor *Kangxi* named it “*Qinglian* Temple”. Since it has Jade Spring in it, the temple got another name as Jade Spring Temple. In 1964 when Jade Spring scenic site was renovated, *Qinglian* Temple and the Dragon King Temple in it were both pulled down. Instead a new Jade Spring Garden was erected there.

肆 ◎ 飞来峰
Feilai Peak

【简介】

飞来峰耸立在西湖西北面灵隐寺前,峰高209米。山中绿树掩映,怪石林立,富泉水,多溶洞。有冷泉、一线天等名胜。山上崖壁和溶洞中有五代、宋、元时石刻、佛像,神采奕奕如生。相传东晋时,印度僧慧理曾称此山很像天竺国的灵鹫山,“不知何时飞来”,因此得名“飞来峰”。

【Brief Introduction】

The peak stands directly facing the well-known *Lingyin* Temple to the northwest of West Lake. The 209-metre peak is covered with green woods, odd-shaped rocks, and has several springs, and many limestone caves. Cool Spring and A Thread of Sky are its most famous spots. On the cliffs and in the caverns, there are a number of rock inscriptions and statues of Buddha, which were carved during the Five Dynasties, the *Song* Dynasty and the *Yuan* Dynasty. These artistic works are brimming with energy and vitality. Legend has it that during the Eastern *Jin* Dynasty, an Indian monk by the name of *Huili*, upon his arrival in the valley, was surprised to see a mountain towering in the valley. He claimed, "It looked exactly like Mount Grahrakuta in India. When did it fly all the way from India to this place?" Hence the name, *Feilai* Peak, which literally means "peak flown from afar" was given to the peak.

【传说读本】

从前,四川**峨眉山**上有一座会飞的小山峰,它一会儿飞到东,一会儿飞西。它飞到哪里,就会压坍许多房子,压死很多人。

那时候,西湖灵隐寺里的和尚济癫,整天疯疯癫癫的,不守佛门清规,拿把芭蕉扇子东游西荡,到处打哈哈,但人们都喜欢他。

有一天,济癫算知中午辰光那座奇异的山峰将要飞到灵隐寺前的村庄上方。他担心山峰落下来会压死很多人,五更天时就爬起来,奔进村庄,挨家挨户地劝说:"今天中午有座山峰要落到庄上来,大家赶快搬家呀,迟了就来不及啦!"

老头儿听了直摇头,骂道:"你这疯和尚,你又来寻开心了。山是顶重的东西,谁见过会飞的山呀?"

当家人听了叹口气道:"我们穷**佃户**能往哪里搬呀!要是真的有山掉下来,压死也只好怨命苦!"

小伙子听了哼鼻子,气呼呼地道:"别编谎话吓人啦!山压下来就拿肩膀扛着,我们不怕!"

小伢儿(小孩子)们嘻嘻哈哈地跟在济癫后面,指手画脚地看热闹。

济癫这家进、那家出,全村百十户人家都关照过了。他说得嘴唇破、唾沫干,却没有一个人相信他的话,没有一户人家准备搬的。

太阳越升越高,中午眼看就要到了,济癫急得团团转。这时,他忽然听到"滴滴答、滴滴答"的吹唢呐的声音,赶紧顺着声音奔过去。一看,嗬哟,原来有户人家娶媳妇,新郎、新娘正磕头**拜天地**哩!屋子里人进人出,喜气洋洋,热闹极了。

济癫挠挠头皮想一想。啊，有了！赶忙推开众人，不管三七二十一，把新娘子往肩上一扛，出大门往村外飞跑。

新娘子头上的红方巾还没有揭掉呢，糊里糊涂地叫人扛着飞跑，也不知发生了什么事，吓得哇哇直叫。

济癫抢走新娘子了，这还了得！人们气得抓门闩的抓门闩，抡扁担的抡扁担，挥锄头的挥锄头，举钉耙的举钉耙，没命地追赶上来。一面追，一面大声叫喊："抓住济癫呀！抓住济癫呀！前面快快拦住呀，别放济癫跑啦！"

这一下，全村的人也不管是不是亲戚，是不是朋友，男的、女的、老的、少的，都追了出来。只有村东一家财主没有动，反倒站在门前看热闹，讲风凉话："哈，**活菩萨**去抢新媳妇，真是件新鲜事，嘻嘻！"

济癫背着新娘子，一个劲往前奔。他跑得真快哩！大家一直追出十几里路还没追上他。等到太阳当头，济癫站住脚不跑啦。他放下新娘子，自己往地上一坐，摇着扇子扇风凉。

人们赶到他跟前，刚要揪住打他，却没料霎时间天昏地暗，伸手不见五指，大风刮得呼呼地响。突然，"轰隆隆"一声，人们都被震得跌了跤，爬起来一看，哟，已经风停云散，太阳又照在头顶上了，却见一座山峰刚刚落在他们的村庄上。人们这才明白过来：济癫抢新娘子，原来是为了救大家的性命啊。

村庄被压在山底下，大家都无家可归了。有的人急得捶胸顿脚，哇哇大哭起来。济癫和尚说："哭什么！你们不知道，村里的财主已被压死在山下了，今后你们各人种自己的田，还怕盖不起房子！"

人们一想，对啊！这才高兴起来。欢欢喜喜地正想散去，济癫和尚又讲话了："别走、别走，大伙听我说。这座山峰既然能从别处飞来，也就会从这儿飞走。飞到别的地方，又会害死许多人。我们在山上凿它五百尊石罗汉，就能把山镇住，不让它再飞往别处害人啦，你们看好不好？"

大家听了，齐声说好，马上就动起手来。一时间锤的锤、凿的凿，叮叮当当忙了一夜，五百尊石罗汉就凿全了，山上山下布满佛像。只是凿了罗汉的身躯，却来不及凿出眉毛、眼睛。济癫说："我有办法，让我来！"他不用锤也不用凿，只用长长的手指甲到石罗汉脸上去划。半天工夫，五百尊石罗汉统统都被安上了眉眼。

从此，这座小山峰就再也不能飞到别处去，永远留在灵隐寺前面啦！因为它是从别处飞来的，所以人们就叫它"飞来峰"。

【English Version of the Original Story】

Long ago a peak on ***Emei* Mountain** in *Sichuan* was able to fly, sometimes to the east, and sometimes to the west. Wherever it went, a large number of houses collapsed and people were crushed to death.

At that time, a monk called *Ji Dian* lived at *Lingyin* Temple near West Lake. He idled all day long with a palm-leaf fan in his hand and never obeyed the Buddhist life style. He greeted all people he saw cheerfully and was very popular among them.

One day, *Ji Dian* learned that a bizarre mountain peak would fly over and fall onto the village in front of *Lingyin* Temple. He panicked and worried that the peak would kill many people, so he got up at dawn and rushed into the village. He went from house to house, breaking the information to the villagers and urging them to leave the village at once. He said,

"At noon a hill peak will be flying onto the village. Please move quickly or it'll be too late!"

Unfortunately, no one believed him. Old men shrugged their shoulders and cursed him,

"You're mad. You're joking. Hills are heavy, so who has ever seen a hill flying?"

Heads of families sighed in despair,

"We are poor **tenant farmers**, where could we go? If a hill peak falls and crushes us, that's our destiny."

Young men groaned in anger,

"Don't threaten us with lies. We'll prop up the hill with our shoulders, even if it falls on us. We are not afraid!"

Children followed *Ji Dian* and watched the commotion in such a happy mood that they couldn't help jumping for joy.

Ji Dian rushed in and out of each family, and urged more than a hundred families to evacuate. He was exhausted with persuasions. However, no family would believe him, or was ready to escape.

The sun rose higher. Close to noon, *Ji Dian* became more anxious and his despair grew deeper. Suddenly he heard some music of the *suona* horns, so he ran towards it. As it happened, a wedding ceremony was taking place in a corner of the village. A young bride and groom were **bowing to Heaven and Earth**. Villagers came in and out of the house. Everyone was in high spirits and enjoying a happy time.

Ji Dian scratched his head for a moment. An idea suddenly occurred to him. He sailed into the crowds. To everyone's great surprise, he suddenly put the bride over his shoulder, rushed out, and ran towards the outskirts of the village.

The bride, still with a piece of red, square head-covering over her head, was frightened because she had been kidnapped, so she cried loudly in fear.

How could the villagers tolerate the monk kidnapping the bride? They got so angry that they grabbed all sorts of farming tools such as door bars, carrying poles, hoes and spike-toothed rakes, in a desperate attempt to catch the monk! They shouted out,

"Stop him! Stop him! Don't let him run away!"

Regardless of age and gender, whether they were friends or relatives or not, all the villagers rushed out to catch the monk, except for one rich landlord's family. Instead, the rich family watched while making irresponsible and sarcastic remarks,

"Aha! **A Buddha incarnate** has kidnapped a bride! What great fun!"

The monk carried the bride and ran desperately out of the village. He ran so fast for about ten miles that the villagers could not catch him, and he didn't stop running until the sun was right overhead. Then he put down the bride on the ground, relaxed and fanned himself with his palm-leaf fan.

The villagers caught him and wanted to beat him. In a split second the bright day changed to complete darkness. Nothing could be seen. Strong winds blew. A thundering sound came from behind. All the villagers fell down quaking with fear. When they got up from the ground they were surprised to find the strong winds had stopped and the dark clouds had gone. The sun came out again. To their horror the villagers saw a hill peak had fallen right on their village. The villagers suddenly realized that the monk's dramatic kidnap was actually to save everyone's life.

With the village crushed and all the houses gone, some villagers were so worried and hopeless that they beat their chests and stamped in an agony of bitter crying. The monk said,

"Why are you crying? Don't you know the landlord has been killed under the hill? Therefore, you are all free to grow crops and rebuild your own houses."

Hearing these words, the villagers became relieved and excited. The monk said again, "Don't go away. Listen to me, everyone. The hill peak has flown here from afar, so it'll fly away again and kill more people. If we sculpture five hundred rock arhats on the hill and the arhats will control the hill, so the hill can no longer fly anywhere else. Do you agree?"

All agreed with him and started to work at once. Fully occupied with the work throughout the whole night, the villagers accomplished five hundred rock arhats standing all over the hill. However, they didn't have time to work on the eyes or brows on the sculptures' faces. The monk offered an idea,

"I have a solution. Let me do it!" With neither hammer nor hoe, the monk drew eyes and brows on the faces of all the rock sculptures with his long fingernails. In less than half a day all the five hundred arhats had vivid facial features.

Since then the peak has no longer flown anywhere, and has always stood in front of Lingyin Temple. Because the peak had flown from afar, people called it "*Feilai* Peak", which literally means "peak flown from afar".

【文化背景】【Cultural Notes】

▶ **峨眉山**:在四川省峨眉县西南。有山峰相对如峨眉,故名。中国佛教四大名山之一。

***Emei* Mountain**: It is in the southwest of *Emei* County of *Sichuan* Province. The two highest peaks of the mountain are located opposite to each other as if they are a pair of young lady's arched eyebrows. The mountain is one of the four famous mountains in Buddhism in China. So the mountain is named after *Emei*, which means arched eyebrows in Chinese.

▶ **佃户**:租种某地主土地的农民称为某地主的佃户。

Tenant farmers: It refers to farmers who pay rent for the use of a landlord's land.

▶ **拜天地**:旧时新郎、新娘结婚时对天、地和父母行敬礼,结成婚姻关系。

Bow to Heaven and Earth: In ancient wedding ceremonies a new bride and groom bowed to the heaven, to the earth, and to their parents for respects, which meant their marital relationship was tied.

▶ **活菩萨**:比喻心肠慈善、救苦救难的人。

A Buddha incarnate: A person who is full of compassion for the needy and the suffering.

伍 虎跑泉
Hupao Spring

【简介】

虎跑泉位于西湖西南面大慈山麓的虎跑寺内,三面被高山包围,形成马蹄形的汇水洼地。泉眼在这洼地中,即使数月无雨,泉水终年不断。泉水从山岩间流出,甘洌醇厚,为杭州三大名泉之首,被乾隆帝赞为"天下第三泉"。

【Brief Introduction】

Hupao Spring is located at the *Hupao* Temple at the foot of *Daci* Hill southwest of West Lake. Surrounded by hills on three sides, the spring is a U-shaped pool. Because the mouth of the spring is in the pool, it never dries up, even during long droughts. The spring water, filtered through the rocks, is clear and charming. It ranks first among the top three springs in *Hangzhou*, and was considered to be among the top three springs in China by Emperor *Qianlong*.

【传说读本】

从前有兄弟俩，哥叫大虎，弟叫二虎。他们打过多次仗，立下许多功，是两条力大无比的好汉。因他们爱打抱不平，奸臣看着不顺眼，就给他们找了条罪名，发配到远地去充军。此后，他俩就流落他乡了。

有一年，大虎和二虎流浪来到杭州一座山下的小山坳。山坳里住着七八户人家，山边还有一座破败的小寺院。他们走到小寺院门口，恰巧老和尚出来关寺门，兄弟俩请求老师父让他俩借宝寺住几天。老和尚看看是两个穷苦的出门人，合起手掌说："请呀，不过，小寺只有粗茶淡饭，要怠慢二位了。"当下进去安顿了住处。

第二天吃晚饭辰光，兄弟俩都称赞杭州这个地方好。老和尚听了叹口气告诉他俩，杭州是个好地方，但是这寺庙周围缺水。兄弟俩问道："老师父，听您讲，挑担水有这样难，那么水源又在什么地方呢？"

老和尚用筷儿指着远方，说："就在坡那面，远着呢！不瞒二位，这寺院过去和尚也勿缺，后来因为挑不动这担水，都走啦！我年轻时也和你们一样，啥都不在乎，可一晃就过去了二十多年！如今脚力不行啦。"

兄弟俩想这位老和尚孤孤单单，自己也需要有个落脚的地方，一心要留下来帮助他，于是齐声道："老师父呀，我们兄弟俩单身，有的是力气。您如果不嫌弃我们，就收下当徒弟吧！"老和尚看看哥弟俩，很实在，又长得像**金刚**，心里喜欢，便满口答应下来。

从此，大虎和二虎干活都抢在前头，对师父照顾备至。每天开门第一件事就是翻坡去挑水。半天挑下来，不光寺里有足够的水可以饮用，连全村十来户人家的水缸都装满了。小山坳里的人见大虎和二虎这样力大无比，又肯助人，都欢喜亲近他们。

转眼过去了许多年。有一年秋冬，天气奇旱，山外的那条小溪很快干涸了。兄弟俩想起以前流浪到南岳**衡山**时，见到过一股活水，叫"童子泉"，这泉水清冽香甜，真是稀世宝水！他们下决心要去取这股宝水。

第二天一早，兄弟俩把这个心愿向师父一说，就要辞行。老和尚舍不得他们离去，但看他们去意已决，只得含着眼泪说："徒儿呀，这一去路途千里，不知何年何月才能见面啊！不要忘记，师父在这里等着你们。菩萨保佑我徒弟一路平安！"两个徒儿就这样和师父告别了。

大虎和二虎认准了南岳的方位，朝西南走去。一路翻越了千山万水，衣裳、鞋底破了，还是不停地走。有一天，他们走到衡山脚下，已是精疲力竭，好不容易支撑到童子泉跟前，终于看见了晶亮的水波，听到叮咚的泉声。但是他们已经用完最后一丝力气，昏倒在地上。

朦胧中，他们只觉得狂风大作，暴雨劈头盖脸地落下来。过一会，又好像雨过天晴，百鸟在四周歌唱。兄弟俩忽然苏醒了过来，只见眼前站着一个头梳双髻的小孩，右手轻轻地挥动着一根柳枝，正朝着他们笑哩。兄弟俩想：童子泉……难道他就是管这泉水的小仙童么？正想着，又见那小孩柳枝向他们一拂，水滴儿一沾身，大虎和二虎一下子感到浑身长了力气，便从地上一跃而起，跑过去向小孩恳求："让我们把这泉水搬走吧！"

小孩跳到一块岩石上，轻轻地挥动着柳枝，大笑着说："行呀！你们倒试试看能不能搬动它！不过我阿公说过，只有世上最有毅力，最不计较荣辱的人，才能搬得了它！"二虎说："我们千里迢迢拼死到这里，难道不是最有毅力的人吗？"大虎也说："我们连死都不怕，还计较什么荣辱呀？"

小孩一下子被问住了，兄弟俩又跑过去拉住他恳求。小孩想了想，说道："好吧。既然你俩是豁出了性命的人，那就变成两只能拔得起山泉的老虎吧！"说着，又用柳枝一拂，把水滴儿洒在两人身上。这一洒不要紧，大虎和二虎顿时感到五脏六腑的变化，浑身皮肉膨胀，只一歇工夫就变成了两只斑斓猛虎，踞在童子泉两旁。小孩跃上虎背，老虎仰天长啸一声，就往东北方向飞跑。

这天夜里。老和尚在**打坐**时睡着了，梦见有双虎在**禅房**外面盘桓，好像在寻找着什么。老和尚觉得好奇怪，就开门去看，一眯眼老虎就没有了。但是老虎盘桓过的地方却有一潭晶亮的清水。老和尚高兴得大笑起来，梦也就醒了。

次日一早，老和尚把自己的梦讲给村里人听，大家都说也做了同样的梦。众人纷纷议论起来：大虎二虎就是双虎，一定是大家太想他们了。恰好，外面跑进来一个陌生的小孩。这小孩头梳双髻，手里拿了根柳枝，边跑边叫"大虎二虎来了！"，拉着老和尚就走。

老和尚被拉到寺院边的竹院前面，小孩一晃眼就不见了。老和尚抬头一看，哎呀，好大的两只黄毛老虎！这老虎一左一右伏着，呜呜地轻叫。老和尚一听这声音很熟悉，心想：难道他们真是大虎二虎变的么？于是大着胆子走过去，叫一声："大虎！二虎！"两只老虎也不答应，只向老和尚亲热地摆着尾巴。老和尚用双手拍它们的背脊，说："徒儿呀，自从分别之后，我把眼睛都望穿了，今天总算见到了你们。为什么变成这个样子了呢？唉，徒儿呀，起来吧！"

老和尚话说完，两只老虎果然站了起来。几个躲在屋上、树上偷看的乡邻,一见这样,胆子也就大了,都一个个爬了下来。就在这辰光,那两只老虎轻吼了一声,纵身一跃,跳到老和尚**禅房**外的空地里,一低头,四只前爪"啪、啪、啪"地刨起土来,只一袋烟工夫就刨成了一大坑。刨好坑,两只老虎绕着老和尚走了一圈,又看看众乡亲,突然一声长啸,腾空而起。这下可不得了,只见大风过处,整个小山坳树木摇晃,竹林呼啸。乡亲们都被惊呆了,像木鸡似的呆立不动。等到风平浪静,老虎早已无影无踪了。大家这才嘘了口气转过头来,却见虎爪刨出的大坑里已积起半潭清泉。

清泉亮晶晶,再看看潭底,像飞丝一样的一股泉脉还在不断地向上冒,一会儿便涨成满满的一潭。人们越看越喜爱,便用双手捧起来喝。泉水甘美,直透心里。于是村里人用木盆舀,用木桶挑。但不管怎么舀呀、挑呀,潭水始终不浅。因为挑水的人太多,常常把水搅浑。后来有几个勤劳的小后生就搬了一些青石板,砌出一口方方正正的泉井来。后来这儿又盖起大寺院,就是现在的虎跑寺。

【English Version of the Original Story】

Long long ago there lived two brothers, the older one named Elder Tiger and the younger one Younger Tiger. Both had taken part in a lot of battles and had won great honours. Furthermore, they never hesitated to defend people against any injustice. What they did offended disloyal ministers, who did not like the two brothers and fabricated a charge against them. The two brothers were deported to a distant place for penal servitude. Since then they lived a wretched life far from home.

One year the two brothers came to a small hamlet at the foot of a hill in *Hangzhou*. Only about half a dozen families lived in the hamlet and there was also a small, dilapidated cloister nearby. When the brothers arrived at the cloister, a senior monk was just about to close the gate. They begged the monk to let them stay for a few days. Seeing the two poor young men were homeless, the monk replied with his palms together,

"Please come in. This small cloister has only meager meals. I have not enough to give you proper care."

With this, he led them in and arranged for their beds.

During dinner the next day, the two brothers commented that *Hangzhou* was a nice place. The senior monk sighed and told them,

"Beautiful as *Hangzhou* is, it lacks drinking water around the cloister."

The two brothers asked,

"Respected master, you mentioned it is rather difficult to carry water here. Where on earth is the water source?"

The senior monk pointed to the distance with a chopstick in his hand and answered, "It's far away over the hill. To tell you the truth, the cloister used to have young monks, but they all left due to the unbearable burden of carrying water. When I was as young as you are, carrying water was nothing to me. But now, twenty years later, I am getting older and my physical energy has gone. Carrying water is quite beyond me."

The two brothers considered that the lonely, senior monk needed companionship; at the same time they wanted to find a place to settle down. So they decided to stay and help him. They said in unison,

"Dear respected master, please accept us as your disciples, if you don't mind. Both of us are single and energetic."

The senior monk looked at the brothers and thought:

"They are as strong as **Buddha's warrior attendants**, and loyal and down-to-earth."

He was quite satisfied with them, so he agreed at once.

After that the two brothers did all sorts of work and took good care of their master. The first thing they did every morning was to climb the hill to get water. With half a day's work, they filled all the water containers both at the cloister and at all the villagers' houses. Seeing the two brothers had enormous strength and were ready to help others, all the villagers liked them very much.

Many years passed. One late autumn, it was extremely dry. The small stream over the hill ran dry. The two brothers recalled that they had once seen a stream of water while they were roaming about **Mount *Heng*** in South China. The stream was named "Boy's Spring" and it was clean and sweet like precious water. They determined to go there to fetch the stream water.

In the early morning of the following day, the two brothers told their master about their wish, and said goodbye to him. The senior monk did not want to let them go, but he understood their intention. So he said, with tears in his eyes,

"Dear disciples, the destination is thousands of miles away. We had no idea when we will meet again. Don't forget that your master will always be waiting for your return. May **Buddha** bless my disciples for a pleasant journey."

The two brothers went in the direction of Mount *Heng*. They crossed numerous mountains and rivers. Their clothes and shoes all wore out, but they still continued their journey. On arriving at the foot of Mount *Heng* one day, they became extremely exhausted. They heard the bubbling sound of spring water and saw shining ripples. They managed to drag themselves to the water, but this sapped their last ounce of strength and they fell senseless to the ground.

Later, in the dimness, they felt a high wind was springing up, and heavy rain was pouring down. Soon, the rain stopped. When the sun shone again, all birds were happily singing. The two brothers came to life and saw a child who had twisted double-knots of hair on his head, and in his right hand he was waving a branch of weeping willow. He smiled at them. The two brothers thought to themselves,

"Is it Boy's Spring? Is he the little celestial in charge of the spring?" At that moment the child touched them with the willow branch and drops of water fell on them. The two brothers suddenly felt they had enormous energy. They jumped up towards the celestial and begged him,

"Let us carry the spring water away!"

The little celestial jumped to a big rock, lightly waved the branch of willow and laughed,

"Fine! Try it! As my grandfather said, only those who have strong willpower and don't take honour or disgrace into account can carry it away!"

The younger brother said,

"We risked our lives to come here all the way from a distant place. Don't we have the greatest willpower?"

The elder brother added,

"We are not afraid of death, let alone honour or disgrace."

The little celestial was surprised to hear that. The two brothers ran to him, grabbed him and begged again. The celestial thought for a moment, and said,

"Since both of you are prepared for risks, how about turning yourselves into two big tigers lifting up a mountain spring?"

With these words, he waved his willow branch lightly to touch them, and drops of water fell on them. Instantly, the two brothers felt a total change in their vital organs, though the water and willow branch looked no special at all. Their whole bodies grew much bigger. They turned into two, big, fierce, multi-coloured tigers crouching on either side of Boy's Spring. The little celestial jumped onto a tiger's back. The tigers uttered cries which shattered the air, and then they ran towards the northeast.

During that night the senior monk fell asleep whilst **meditating**. In a dream two tigers were lingering outside the **meditation abode** as if looking for something. Surprised, he got up from his bed, opened the door and had a look. In an instant the tigers disappeared. The spot where the tigers had lingered was now a pool of clean water. The senior monk laughed happily and wakened from the dream.

In the early morning the monk told the villagers about his dream. All of them responded that they had had the same dream too, and were excitedly speculating that the two tigers must have been the two brothers, for everyone had missed them so much. At that time a strange child, with double-knots of hair and a branch of weeping willow in one hand, ran into the crowds, and shouted,

"Elder Tiger and Younger Tiger have come!"

The child pulled the senior monk outside the cloister. As soon as the senior monk got outside, the strange child disappeared. The monk looked up and found two big, yellow-haired tigers, roaring gently from either side of the gate. Their voices sounded so familiar.

"Is it possible that they are the incarnation of the two brothers?" The monk thought. He then walked courageously towards them, calling,

"Elder Tiger! Younger Tiger!"

The two brothers made no reply but waved their tails intimately and warmly. The monk patted them on the backs with both hands and said,

"My dear disciples, since your departure I've been looking forward to seeing you. Fortunately we met again today! Why do you look like this? Oh, get up please, my dear disciples!"

At the senior monk's words, the two tigers stood up. Some villagers who had been hiding under the roof and in the trees became brave enough and climbed down to the ground. At that moment, the two tigers roared in low voices, jumped to the open space outside the senior monk's abode, lowered their heads, and clawed the earth with their four front claws. Soon a big pond in the ground was accomplished. The two tigers walked in a circle around the senior monk and looked at the whole village again. Suddenly with a loud sustained cry, the two tigers soared into the sky, and the whole area was overwhelmed by a huge storm. All the trees in the small hamlet were shaken violently. Bamboos and other trees uttered loud cries. All the villagers were stunned. When the wind stopped and the waves in the pond calmed down, the tigers vanished. The villagers felt relieved and found the big pond had become half-full of clean, clear water.

When they looked at the bottom of the pond, the villagers saw a spring-fed stream. The stream, like a flying line, was still emitting water upwards. Shortly after, the pond became full of water. The water was clean and fresh. People loved it so much that they held up water with their hands to drink. Then they fetched water with wooden basins and buckets. No matter how much water people carried away, the spring water never diminished. However, the pond became muddy because too many people came for water. Later on, several young men built a square-shaped spring well there with a few grey flagstones. Afterwards, a big temple was built there, which is what we can see today as *Hupao* Temple. The name literally means "tiger Running temple".

【文化背景】【Cultural Notes】

▶ **金刚**：梵文 Vajra 的意译，比喻牢固、锐利，能摧毁一切。也指佛的侍从力士，以强壮勇猛而著称。

Buddha's warrior attendants: It's a transliteration of *Vajra* From Sanskrit. *Vajir* is a guardian spirit of Buddhist monasteries and can be described as the firm, keen and unbeatable. It here refers to Buddha's warrior attendants who were strong and brave.

- **衡山**:山名。又名南岳,中国五大名山之一,位于湖南省西面,山势雄伟,俯瞰湘江。山体长达150公里,有七十二峰。

Mount *Heng*: Also known as *Nan Yue*, it is located in west *Hunan* Province and is one of the Five Great Mountains in China. It is grand and magnificent, overlooking the *Xiang* River. It is 150 kilometres long with 72 peaks.

- **打坐**:中国古代一种养生健身法,也是僧道修行的方法。闭目盘膝而坐,调整气息出入,不想任何事情。

Meditating: It was a way to keep spiritually fit in ancient China, Buddhism monks meditate sitting in a cross-leg posture, and breathing smoothly, with an empty mind.

- **禅房**:修禅者的房舍,泛指寺院。

Meditation abode: It refers to a Buddhist temple.

陆 ◎ 白公堤
Bai Causeway

【简介】

白堤在西湖断桥以西,约1公里长,3.3米宽,有断桥、锦带桥等景点。堤上景色秀美,堤内侧种植婀娜垂柳,外侧生长绚丽碧桃,远望如一彩色锦带。逢春日,暖风熏面,游人如醉。此堤是欣赏西湖全景和周边诸山的极佳观景点。

【Brief Introduction】

Bai Causeway stretches westward from the Broken Bridge for about 1 kilometre and is 3. 3 metres wide. Broken Bridge and Brocade Ribbon Bridge are the most famous spots there. The smooth embankment looks like a riot of colour with those pretty and charming willows along the pavement, and colourful peaches along the lakeside. During spring days visitors are enchanted by the breeze and feel drunk with the lake's beauty. It's a best spot for visitors to enjoy the full view of West Lake and the sceneries of the surrounding hills.

【传说读本】

有一年,杭州大旱。西湖边大批农田龟裂,稻禾晒得像火烧过一样。老百姓天天到衙门里请求放西湖水,可那些官儿都顾自寻欢作乐,理也不理。

有一天,百姓们又涌到衙门前,有的喊:"**青天大老爷**,赶快放西湖水,救救农田吧!"

有的喊:"再不放西湖水,我们百姓都活不下去啦!"

闹得衙门里的太爷头昏颠倒,只好匆匆走到衙门口,怒气冲冲地说:"谁说放西湖水?把西湖水放了,那湖里的鱼就没地方栖息啦!"

老百姓说:"那么请问大老爷,鱼龙性命要紧,还是百姓性命要紧?"

太爷一听,又气呼呼地说:"谁说放西湖水?把西湖水放了,荷藕菱芡还活得成么?"

老百姓说:"那么请问大老爷,荷藕菱芡为重,还是稻米为重?"太爷一时无话可答。

这辰光,人群中忽然有人高声说:"讲得对呀,讲得有理!"百姓们回过头去,只见那人五十开外,五绺长须,身穿青衫,笑眯眯地站在那里。

太爷一听更生气,冲着那人说:"啊,你说什么?嗯,原来是你在这里煽动!"

那人说:"对不起,我刚来。我说当官的,难道不应该听听父老乡亲们的呼声么?"

听那人这么一说,太爷皱起眉头想一想,便问:"你是谁?"

那人说:"我姓白,白居易就是我。"

太爷一听是白居易，赶忙三脚两步从台阶上滚下来，打躬作揖地说："哎呀，我当是谁，原来是白大人到啦，下官有失远迎，得罪得罪！请，快请到里面歇息。"

原来白居易新任命为杭州**刺史**，他为了察访民情，没穿官服就到衙门里来啦！

白居易一上任，第二天果然放了西湖水。百姓们望着碧绿碧绿的湖水哗哗地流进自己的农田，都说："白居易一来，我们农家有救了。"

白居易上任不久，就访问了附近农家。第二年，在钱塘门外，修了一条堤，造了一座石**涵闸**，把湖水蓄得满满的。他又怕后来的地方官不了解堤坝与农家的利害关系，还亲自写了篇《钱塘湖闸记》，刻在石碑上，详细地记载了堤坝的功用，以及蓄水、放水和保护堤坝的方法，其中甚至写明了一寸湖水能灌溉多少顷农田。

百姓们都围着来看这块石碑，大家都为白居易深知百姓痛苦而感动，为他精密设计的水利工程而赞叹，纷纷要为白居易向朝廷请功。

白居易在杭州做了三年刺史，对西湖水管理得很严。一次，白居易在湖上观赏风景，看到湖南岸的一处湖面上，有人在挑土填湖，建造亭台楼阁。白居易就查问是哪一家造的。当差的查明后回禀说："这是衙内二爷的老丈人在造一座花园哩！"

白居易就把二爷的老丈人传来，说："西湖是大家的，你一个人怎么好占用呢？现在罚你开葑田一百亩。"那位二爷的老丈人晓得刺史说一不二，只好雇了一批人，挖了一百亩湖泥。

又有一次，白居易从灵隐道上散步回来，看见有人砍了两株树，背回来当柴烧。白居易就对那人说："山上的树砍光了，泥沙就流到西湖里去了！罚你补种十株树！"那人只好到山上去补种了十株树。从此，再没有人敢占湖造屋、上山砍树了。

白居易爱杭州百姓，也爱西湖。处理政事之余，他常去白沙堤、孤山一带细细游玩。烟波浩渺、堤柳轻拂，大大助长了他的诗兴，因而杭州三年，他写下了许多著名的山水诗。西湖的景色，经他的笔墨一点染，在人们眼里，就显得更加美丽可爱了。

白居易在杭州三年，发动百姓兴筑湖堤，把西湖整治得水绿山青，湖水蓄放便利，大批农田受益，地方上渐渐富庶起来。皇帝知道了白居易的功绩，就把他调到京城里去。

白居易去后，杭州的百姓都怀念他，亲切地称他为“**白舍人**”。有人画了他的像，供在家里；有人把他的诗抄写了贴在墙上。

白居易在西湖修的这条堤，已经淹没了。但是千百年来，杭州人一直把那条连接断桥和孤山的“白沙堤”，叫成“白公堤”。后来改称为“白堤”，以纪念这位为杭州人民做了许多好事的大诗人。

【English Version of the Original Story】

One year there was a severe drought in *Hangzhou*. Near West Lake, a large amount of farmland cracked and the rice plants were parched as if burnt in a fire. Common people appealed every day for a water tunnel from West Lake but the local officials indulged in seeking pleasure and making merry, totally ignoring the people's appeals.

One day the common people gathered again in front of *yamen*. Some shouted,

"My **upright Lord**, please channel the lake water immediately into the farmland!"

Others said loudly,

"We common people can no longer suffer the drought because no water comes from the lake!"

The unrest made the lord feel so giddy that he hurried to the office gate and said with fury,

"Who said the lake water should be drained? If the lake water was drained away, fishes in the lake would have nowhere to live!"

The common people argued,

"My lord, which is more important, fish or the people?"

Hearing these words, the lord answered in a towering rage once more,

"Who said the lake water should be drained? If so, how could all the water plants such as lotus, lotus root, water caltrop and wild rice stem grow?"

The common people responded,

"Which one is vital, water plants or rice crops?"

This question struck the lord dumb for a moment. Then a man among the crowds said in a high voice,

"Well said! It did make sense!"

The common people turned their heads and found a man in his fifties, with a long beard and long hair, wearing an indigo robe. He was standing there with a smile on his face.

The lord was offended and raged,

"What did you say? It is you who have stirred up this unrest!"

The man responded,

"Excuse me. I've just arrived. As an official, why don't you listen to the voices of the fellow countrymen?"

Hearing these words, the lord frowned for a moment and asked,

"Who are you?"

The man answered,

"My family name is *Bai*, and *Bai Juyi* is me."

Hearing the name, the lord hurriedly rushed down the steps, made deep bows and offered humble apologies,

"Good Lord, Lord *Bai*, I didn't know you have arrived. Pardon me for not having welcomed you from afar. Please forgive me! Please come in and have a good rest!"

It turned out that *Bai Juyi* had just been appointed **Governor** of *Hangzhou*. He came to the government office, without wearing his ceremonial robe, in order to acquaint himself with the condition of the people.

The day after he took office, *Bai Juyi* channeled the lake water into the farmland. Watching the green lake water go into their cultivated fields, all the farmers said,

"Since *Bai Juyi* comes, we farmers have hopes!"

Soon after taking on his official post, *Bai Juyi* visited some nearby farmers. In the second year, one causeway and a rock culvert and sluice[3] were built outside *Qiantang* Gate. The lake was full of water. However, he worried that his followers wouldn't understand the functions of the causeway for agriculture, so he wrote an article entitled *About the Culvert and Sluice of Qiantang Lake*. These words were also carved on a rock with detailed descriptions of the causeway's functions, ways to store and draw off water to protect the causeway. It was even specified that water of a *cun* of lake surface can irritate how many hectares of farmland.

Reading what was written on the rock, people were all deeply moved by *Bai*'s deep concern of the people's sufferings and his well-designed irrigation project. They asked the Imperial Court to record his meritorious deeds.

Working as Governor of *Hangzhou* for three years, *Bai* achieved great success in managing West Lake. Once, while enjoying a beautiful view over the lake, he saw some people filling the lake with earth to build a pavilion in the south of West Lake. *Bai Juyi* inquired about what was happening there. A petty official reported back,

"It's the Second Lord's father-in-law that is building a pavilion."

Bai Juyi sent for the Second Lord's father-in-law and told him,

"West Lake is for all the people. How dared you occupy one part of the lake for yourself? Now you are fined to scoop up one hundred *mu* of lake sludge." Knowing *Bai* would mean what he said, the Second Lord's father-in-law had to hire several labourers to scoop up the required quantity of lake sludge.

On another occasion, returning from a relaxing walk on *Lingyin* Road, *Bai Juyi* saw a man carrying two trees which had been cut down for firewood from a hill. Bai told the man,

"If all the trees on the hill were cut down, the rich soil of the farmland would be washed away into the lake. So you are fined to plant ten trees!" The man had to go to the hill and plant ten trees there. Since then, no one dared to occupy the lake for a house or cut down trees in the hills.

Bai Juyi loved West Lake as well as local people. In his free time, he usually went to *Bai* Causeway and Solitary Hill to appreciate the beautiful sceneries; especially mist-covered water, peaches and willows along West Lake, greatly spurred his poetic writing. During his three years of work in *Hangzhou*, he composed a number of famous landscape poems which made West Lake more charming in the eyes of the world.

Meanwhile, he motivated local people to build causeways, and to clean the lake water. The lake got so improved that the hills around were green, and the lake water was clean and easy for farmland irrigation. Local people benefited from the water management and became rich. Hearing about *Bai's* achievements, the emperor promoted him to a post in the capital.

Since *Bai*'s departure, local people missed him so much that they named him "*Bai Sheren*." Some drew portraits of him and others copied his poems on walls.

The causeway built during *Bai*'s time in *Hangzhou* is now buried under water. For more than a thousand years local people, however, have named the White Sand Causeway between Broken Bridge and Solitary Hill as "*Bai* Causeway" to honour this great poet in the *Tang* Dynasty, who had done good for people in *Hangzhou*.

【文化背景】【Cultural Notes】

▶ **青天大老爷**:对法官或县官的称呼。比喻清官。

Upright lord: A term of address for an upright judge or magistrate.

▶ **刺史**:古代官名。

Governor: A provincial or prefectural governor in ancient China.

▶ **涵闸**:涵洞和水闸的总称。涵洞指公路或铁路与沟渠相交的地方使水从路下流过的通道,作用和桥类似,但一般孔径较小。水闸指修建在堤坝中用来控制河渠水流的水工建筑物,调节水闸开闭的大小或高低,可以改变通过的水量。

Culvert and sluice: A culvert is a ditch or channel for water that passes under a road, a railway line, bank of earth, etc. The culvert usually has a small diametre aperture, and functions as a bridge. A sluice is an engineering structure for water with an opening (a sluice gate or sluice valve) through which the flow can be controlled or stopped.

▶ **舍人**:古代官职名。最初见于《周礼·地官》。历代都设置,到清朝废除。各代舍人职权大小不一样。三国时期(220—280),魏国(220—265)的舍人,负责发布皇帝诏书以及将大臣的奏章呈给皇帝批阅。隋唐时期(581—

618)，中书舍人由文学水平较高的人担任，负责撰拟皇帝的诏书和主旨。宋朝(960—1279)时仍然设有此官，但不再有实权。

Sheren：A term for an official position in ancient China. The term was first recorded in the chapter of the Confucian work the *Local Officials*, *Zhouli*. The position was designed in different dynasties until it was abolished in the *Qing* Dynasty. People holding this position had different status and powers in different dynasties. During the Three Kingdom Period (220—280), a *Sheren* in *Wei* Kindom (220—265) was responsible for reading out the imperial's edicts and presenting memorials from ministers to the emperor. During the *Sui* and *Tang* Dynasties(581—618), *Zhongshu Sheren* (general secretary), acted by top literary scholars, bore the responsibility for drafting the imperial's edicts. In the *Song* Dynasty(960—1279), this position still existed but had no real power.

柒◎六和塔
Liuhe Pagoda

【简介】

六和塔位于西湖以南，钱塘江畔，月轮山上。塔呈平面八角形，外观十三层，色呈殷红，高近 60 米。是中国古代砖木结构的名塔之一，也是杭州必游之地。塔名源于佛教的“六和敬”思想，即身和同住，口和无争，意和同悦，戒和同修，见和同解，利和同均。

【Brief Introduction】

Located to the south of West Lake, *Liuhe* Pagoda, or literally Pagoda of Six Harmonies, stands majestic on Full Moon Hill overlooking the *Qiantang* River. The dark-red pagoda is made in plane octagonal form, has 13 stories on the surface, and is nearly 60 metres high. It's one of the most prominent wood-and-brick structures of ancient China. It's a must for tourists who come to *Hangzhou*. The name of "six harmonies" is related to the six codes of Buddhism. Six harmonies mean the harmonies of body, mind, speech, opinion, wealth and abstinence from temptation.

【传说读本】

原先,住在钱塘江里的那个龙王性情非常暴躁,把潮水弄得涨落没有个定时,因此沿江两岸的田地常常被淹掉,害得人们成天提心吊胆地过日子。

那时江边住着一户穷苦的渔民,夫妻俩带着儿子六和过日子。六和五岁那年,他爸在江上打鱼翻了船,淹死了。

没有船打不成鱼,从此六和一家更苦了。娘儿俩用两根竹竿,上面各拴上个小圆网,趁涨潮的时候,赤着脚跑在潮头前面捞潮头鱼。捞潮头鱼是很危险的,跑得稍慢一步就会被潮水卷去。娘儿俩为了生活,不得不冒这个险。

有一天,娘儿俩正在捞鱼的时候,不料这次潮水来得特别快,特别凶。六和看看势头不妙,想牵住娘的手拔腿飞跑,可是已经来不及了,一个浪头猛拍过来,把她娘卷进漩涡里去啦。六和人小机灵跑得快,三脚两步窜到岸边,一纵身抓住江岸悬崖上的倒挂藤,手拉脚蹬,终于攀上了江边的小山头。

六和没了娘,望着江水,又伤心又愤怒,就一面哭着,一面尽力把江边山上大大小小的石块儿搬下来,使劲扔进江里去。他发誓要用石块把钱塘江填满,不让潮水再横冲直撞,到处害人。他手里扔着石块,嘴里还不停地咒骂着:"可恶的潮水啊,该死的龙王!我要把山搬下来,填没你这钱塘江!"

水晶宫的屋顶和门窗,被六和丢下的石块砸了许多窟窿。石块在水晶宫前的台阶上堆成了一座小山,大门都快堵死啦。龙王听到咒骂声,走到水晶宫门口探探头,不料又被六和丢下的石块砸在头上。唉呦呦,把只龙角都砸歪了,后脑勺上肿起一个大疙瘩,痛得他嗷嗷直叫。

六和在江边一边哭,一边骂,一边往江心扔着石块。一天,两天,整整扔了七七四十九天。这天正好是八月十八,他忽然听到轰隆隆的声音自远而近,钱塘江潮水涌过来了。潮头上站着个横行霸道的蟹将军,领着一队弯腰屈背的虾小卒。后面**黄罗伞**下站着那个龙王。不一会,龙王来到六和面前,说道:"小孩,小孩,不要哭,不要骂,不要扔石块。你要金、要银、要珍宝,我都给你。"

六和听了,恨恨地说:"龙王,龙王,你听着,我不要你的金银,不要你的珠宝,你得依我两件事才行。如若不依,我就用石块压坍你的水晶宫,填没这条钱塘江！”

龙王听了慌忙问道：“哪两件事呀？你说，你说说看。”

六和说：“第一件，你马上把我娘送回来。第二件，从今以后不许乱涨大潮，潮水只许规规矩矩顺着河道走，涨到小山这里为止。”

龙王满心不愿意，但是又怕六和真的把钱塘江填没了，压坍他的水晶宫，只好都答应下来。龙王赶快叫人把六和娘送了上来，六和见了娘，这个快活啊！娘儿俩高高兴兴地回家去了。

从那个时候起，**钱塘江潮水**便小了许多，而且涨到那座小山边便稳定下来。只有每年八月十八那一天，潮水比平常要大些。那是因为龙王吃过六和的亏，怕他的部下再闯祸，亲自出来巡江的缘故。

人们摸到了潮水的脾气，就不再怕它，把沿江两岸的荒滩都开辟成良田，种上绿油油的庄稼。为了感谢六和制伏了龙王，后人就在六和搬石块的小山上修筑起一座宝塔，这就是如今的“六和塔”。

【English Version of the Original Story】

Long ago, the dragon king in *Qiantang* River was in a very ferocious mood and caused tides to flow in and ebb irregularly. So the farmland along both banks was often inundated and people were in constant fear every day.

A poor fisherman's family lived on one bank. The family was a couple with their son who was named *Liuhe*. The fisherman was drowned when his boat capsized on the river, while he was fishing. His son was only five years old.

They could not go fishing without a boat. Since then, life for the mother and her son was even worse. They tried to catch fish with two long bamboo poles with a small round fishing net attached to each of them. When the tides came in, they followed the water, running barefoot, in order to capture fish in the tidewater. It was very dangerous, for people could be swept away by the tides. The mother and her son, however, had no choice but to take risks in order to survive.

One day, while they were fishing, they were unaware that the tide was coming in very fast and overwhelmingly. When *Liuhe* perceived this he wanted to grab his mother's hand to escape. It was too late. A huge whirlpool struck violently and swept away his mother. Little *Liuhe* sensed the danger and he quickly ran to the bank, jumped onto a rock and grabbed a hanging rattan. He climbed up the hill beside the river by pulling himself up through the rattan.

His mother was wept away, *Liuhe* was sad and he raged while watching the river. In tears, he threw stones of all sizes from the hill into the river. He vowed to fill the river with the stones and curb the tidewater from drowning people. He uttered curses while throwing the stones,

"Damned tidewater! Bastard dragon king! I'll move the whole hill and fill your *Qiantang* River!"

The Dragon King's crystal palace, which was under the river, was badly damaged by *Liuhe*'s stones. All the roofs, windows and doors were holed. The stones accumulated into a small hill and even the gate was nearly blocked. Hearing the curses, the dragon king came to the palace gate and took a look. To his surprise, his head was struck by *Liuhe*'s stones; the dragon king's horn was tilted, and the back of his head had a big swelling. dragon king uttered a wounded yell.

For many days *Liuhe* kept throwing stones into the river, with tears on his face and curses in his mouth. On August the 18th according to Chinese lunar calendar, all of a sudden, *Liuhe* heard a roll of thunder coming from far away. A tidal wave rushed forward with a bullying general of the crab army standing on the high wave, followed by a group of humble shrimp soldiers. There stood the dragon king behind them under **a round, yellow, silk umbrella**. After a short while, the dragon king came up to *Liuhe* and said,

"Hello, little child, don't cry, don't curse, don't throw stones. I'll give you whatever you like, like gold, silver or any other treasures."

Hearing these words, *Liuhe* answered angrily,

"Listen, you dragon king, I don't want your gold or silver, or other treasures. What I want is that you should do two things, otherwise I'll crush your crystal palace and fill up the river with stones."

The dragon king asked eagerly,

"What are the two things? Tell me."

Liuhe said,

"First, set my mother free at once. Second, you cannot let big tides flow as you like. All tidal water should go along the river course and never go beyond this small hill."

The dragon king was very reluctant to do so but he was afraid that *Liuhe* would fill *Qiantang* River with stones and cause his crystal palace to collapse. So he had to accept *Liuhe*'s requirements. *Liuhe*'s mother was sent back to the river bank. *Liuhe* and his mother were overjoyed to meet each other again and went home together.

Ever since then, the ***Qiantang* river tidal bore** has become far smaller and comes only to the foot of the small hill except on August 18th of the Chinese lunar calendar. On that day the tidal water was bigger than usual because of the dragon king's inspection tour. Being afraid that his soldiers would make trouble, he wanted to come out to have a look and make sure everything is fine.

People came to know a lot about the regular tidal water and was not afraid of it any more. They turned the barren beaches into rich fields with green crops along both banks. To express their cordial thanks to *Liuhe*, who brought the river tide under control, his descendants set up a pagoda on the hill from where *Liuhe* once threw stones into the river. That is the present *Liuhe* Pagoda.

【文化背景】【Cultural Notes】

▶ **黄罗伞:**"黄"指皇帝,中国古代传说中的帝王,代指权力。"罗"指丝织品。"黄罗伞"指用丝织物制成的供皇帝使用的伞。

A round, yellow, silk umbrella: It's a large round-roof umbrella made of pure silk for the emperor. The Chinese pronunciation in *huang luo san*. The colour yellow that is, *huang*, implies the power of the emperors in legends of ancient Chinese folk stories. *luo* is one sort of silk. The shape of the umbrella indicates the emperor's power.

▶ **钱塘江潮水:**钱塘江潮被誉为"天下第一潮"。大量潮水拥挤入狭浅的河道,潮头受到阻碍,后面的潮水又急速推进,出现壮观场面,潮头高度可达 9

米,潮水推进速度每秒达 10 米。每年农历八月十八的潮水最为壮观,大量游客群集,争睹奇景。观赏钱塘秋潮有三个最佳位置:盐官镇、八堡、老盐仓。

The *Qiantang* river tidal bore: The *Qiantang* River is known for the world's largest tidal bore. The tide rushing into the river mouth from the bay causes a bore which can reach up to 9 metres in height, and travel at up to 10 metres per second. The most magnificent tidal bore falls on August 18th according to China's lunar calendar every year, which attracts a large number of tourists flocking here to watch this natural wonder. The best locations to watch the tidal bore is *Yanguan*, *Babao* and Old *Yancang*.

第二章
物产传说

Chapter II
Legends of Products

杭州是一块富饶的土地，深得上天宠爱的城市。杭州人勤劳聪慧，创造了许多宝物，吃的有美味油条，品的有上品龙井，穿的有婀娜丝绸，用的有曼妙彩伞，不一而足。每一样都是宝贝，总有一款让你爱不释手。

Hangzhou is a rich land, the city of God's favour. Local people are both smart and diligent, creating many cherished products, from delicious Fried Bread Stick to top-grade Longjing Tea, from soft silk to colourful umbrellas. There are many valuable treasures produced in *Hangzhou*, and there must be a suitable one for you.

壹◎伞
Umbrella

【简介】

鲁班(前 507—前 444)，春秋(前 770—前 746)末期鲁国人，是中国古代的一位出色的木匠、工程师和发明家。鲁班有很多发明，中国的土木工匠们都尊称他为祖师。鲁班有个妹妹，聪明俊俏，心灵手巧。“伞”就是鲁妹的发明。汉字“伞”是象形文字，形象地表达了“伞”的外形。中国伞博物馆位于杭州，是世界首创的伞主题博物馆，展示伞的起源、伞历史、伞文化，及伞工艺。

【Brief Introduction】

Lu Ban(507 BC—440 BC), born in the State of *Lu* at the end of the Spring and Autumn Period(770 BC—476 BC), was a well-known Chinese carpenter, engineer and inventor. He was responsible for many inventions, which thereafter led him to be acknowledged as a master craftsman. *Lu Ban* had a sister, who was smart and beautiful, clever in mind and skillful of hand. The invention of umbrellas was attributed to her. The Chinese character for umbrella, 伞(sǎn), is a pictograph resembling the modern umbrella in shape. China Umbrella Museum, located in *Hangzhou*, is the world's first umbrella themed museum, whose exhibitions cover the origin, history, culture, and craftwork relating to umbrellas.

【传说读本】

早先，巧匠鲁班听说西湖的景致好，就带了他妹妹从山东到杭州来。

一天，鲁班和鲁妹来湖边游赏。只见太阳光芒金闪闪，西湖湖水亮晶晶，**白堤**桃花红，**苏堤**杨柳绿，果然是好看。

他们走走看看，看看走走，不知不觉来到“**柳浪闻莺**”。忽然，一阵大风刮过，天色变了，湖中翻着白浪，“唰唰唰”的一场春雨，飘个不停。鲁班和鲁妹只好躲在一棵大树底下避雨。西湖雨景很好看的，可是雨落得鲁班兄妹两人一身稀湿，再也没心思看西湖景致啦。鲁妹看着淋得像落汤鸡一样的哥哥，笑笑说：“哥哥呀，你的手艺这样巧，今朝碰到落雨天游湖便一点办法也没有啦！我想同你来比一比，各人自己去造个东西，要使人在落雨天也同样能游湖，看谁办法好。”

鲁班一听妹妹要同自己来比赛，差点笑出来，漫不经心地说：“好吧，比就比吧！但要定个时间，我说三天为期，如何？”鲁妹听了直摇头。

鲁班说：“那你说要多少时间？不够再加吧。”鲁妹说：“今天一夜工夫，到鸡叫为止。”

鲁班听了哈哈大笑说："好，好，好，统统依你。"当夜，两人就分头干了起来。

鲁班找来些木头，刨得光光洁洁，又雕上各种花样，在西湖边立起四根红彤彤的柱子，盖上顶，顶边还有四只翘耸耸的角，挂上四只"叮当叮当"响的铜铃，造好了一座四角形的亭子。他在亭子里东看看，西望望，心里想：这下好了，千瓦盖顶，四面通光，哪怕雨落得再大，坐在亭子里也好看西湖景致啦！

鲁班造好亭子，回到屋里。看看他妹妹房里，还一点没有动静。又急急赶到西湖边，立起六根红彤彤的柱子，盖上顶，顶边还有六只翘耸耸的角，挂上六只"叮当叮当"响的铜铃，造了一座六角形的亭子。

鲁班再看看他妹妹的房里，还是一点动静没有。又在西湖边上立起八根红彤彤的柱，盖上顶，顶边还有八只翘耸耸的角，挂上八中"叮当叮当"响的铜铃，造了一座八角形的亭子。

鲁班再看看他妹妹的房间里，还是一点没有动静。又要西湖边造了第四座、第五座、第六座……一口气造了九座式样不同的亭子。

正当鲁班开始造第十座亭子的时候，鲁妹偷偷地跑了出来，看到鲁班已经在西湖边造起了九座亭子，正笑嘻嘻地在造第十座，忙得满头大汗。鲁妹就偷偷地学了一声鸡叫。鲁班刚把第十座亭子造好三只翘耸耸的角，一听鸡叫，以为天亮了，就停工不再造了。这就是西湖"**三潭印月**"九曲桥上留下的那座三角亭。

过一会，"喔喔喔！"鸡真的啼了，随后天就亮了。朝霞映着红色的亭子，显得格外美丽。

鲁班得意扬扬地坐在亭子里，看看自己一夜工夫造起来的十座亭子，心想：自己造得又快又好，妹妹今朝一定输啦！

忽然，他眼前一亮，好像迎面飞来了一只孔雀。定神一看，原来是妹妹从屋里走出来，把个东西向上一张，那东西立刻变得像亭子顶一样：四周有三十二只翘耸耸的角，每只角下面挂着黄澄澄的绸须须，上面遮着一块彩色绸子，绣着凤凰牡丹图。顶下只有一根"柱子"。

鲁班好奇地从妹妹手里拿过来，仔细一看，这东西是用山上的竹子做的，有三十二根长竹条，三十二根短竹条，长竹条与短竹条之间，装有灵活的插销，要用时一张就散开来，不用时一收就缩拢去，真是又轻巧，又美观。

鲁妹笑着对鲁班说："哥哥，你一夜工夫造了十座亭子，我一夜工夫就造这'半个亭子'，但这'半个亭子'，可以抵得上千千万万个亭子，落雨天，你只好坐在亭子里面看西湖景致。我撑着这'半个亭子',可以走来走去,在湖边到处耍子儿(游戏)。"

鲁班越看越有趣,笑着说:"好妹妹,你的心儿比我巧,你的手艺比我妙!"

鲁妹说:"不,哥哥,你的手艺当然比我高!你造的十座式样不同的亭子,不是把西湖景致打扮得更好看啦!我只不过受到你的启发,才造了这'半个亭子'哩。"

从此,鲁班更尊重他的妹妹,遇事都要与她商量。据说,鲁班造的那些亭子,就是后来**西湖十景**里面的十座亭子。

鲁妹造的这"半个亭子"因为在落雨天一张开可以散开来,所以刚开始大家叫它"雨散"。后来,有个欢喜造字的人,依着这"半个亭子"的样子,造出一个"伞"字,人们看看很像,就都用起"雨伞"两个字来。

【English Version of the Original Story】

Long, long ago, hearing that West Lake was amazingly beautiful, *Lu Ban*, who was a skillful craftsman, took his sister and left *Shandong* province for *Hangzhou*.

One day, *Lu Ban* and his sister came to West Lake to enjoy the wonderful view. The sun was shining, and the water in West Lake was sparkling; with pink peach flowers at ***Bai* Causeway** and green willows at ***Su* Causeway**.

Walking around the lake and enjoying the view, they arrived at the attraction of **Orioles Singing in the Willows** before they realized *Hangzhou* was indeed beautiful. Just at that time, a strong wind blew, the sky became dark, and torrents were swelled by the storm. It began to rain, endlessly. *Lu Ban* and his sister had to hide under a big tree to avoid being caught in the rain.

Though West Lake looked even more beautiful in the rain, they were wet through and were in no mood to appreciate the view any more. Looking at her brother, who was like a drowned rat, Sister *Lu* laughed and said,

"Brother, your craftsmanship is very skillful, but today, in such weather, you cannot do anything about it. I'd like to have a competition with you. Let's see who can make something to help people to enjoy the view even in rainy weather. The one who can solve this problem better will be the winner."

Hearing that his sister wanted to have a competition with him, *Lu Ban* couldn't help laughing. He said casually,

"All right. Why not? Let's fix a time, say three days, OK?"

Sister *Lu* shook her head. *Lu Ban* said,

"Then you set the time. If three days is not enough, you can set a longer time."

His sister replied,

"Just tonight, till the cock crows."

Lu Ban laughed,

"Fine, fine, fine, it's all up to you."

That night, the two got started separately. *Lu Ban* got some wood, planed it smooth, carved all kinds of designs on it, set up four red pillars at the lakeside, and then covered the top. The top had four upward angles, under which hung four, jingling, copper bells. This became the first pavilion, which was quadrangular. He looked around the pavilion, and said to himself,

"Now the problem is solved. With thousands of tiles on top and lights from all sides, one can enjoy the beautiful scenery of West Lake in this pavilion even when it rains cats and dogs."

After finishing making the pavilion, *Lu Ban* came back to his house. Seeing that all was still quiet in his sister's room, *Lu Ban* went back to West Lake and set up another six red pillars and covered the top. The top had six upward angles, under which hung six jingling copper bells. This became the second pavilion, which was hexagonal.

Seeing that it was still quiet in his sister's room, *Lu Ban* set up another eight red pillars, and covered the top. The top had eight upward angles, under which hung eight jingling copper bells. This became the third pavilion, which was octagonal.

Finding that still nothing was happening in from his sister's room, *Lu Ban* continued to make a fourth, a fifth, and a sixth pavilion. He made nine pavilions in a row, all in different styles.

Lu Ban was just about to make the tenth pavilion when his sister slipped out. Seeing that *Lu Ban* had finished the nine pavilions at West Lake, and was busy sweating with the tenth one, she furtively imitated a cock crow.

At that point, *Lu Ban* had just finished making three angles of the tenth pavilion. He assumed it was dawn and stopped working. That is what we can see now at the Zigzag Bridge at the place of *Three Pools Mirroring the Moon* along West Lake—the triangular pavilion.

After a while, the cock really crowed, and the day broke. The red pavilions in the morning glow looked exceptionally beautiful.

Sitting in his pavilion, jauntily looking at all the ten pavilions he had made, *Lu Ban* said to himself,

"Since I made all this happen so quickly and so skillfully, my sister will definitely be the loser!"

Suddenly, it seemed that a peacock was flying towards him, which made his eyes light up. He looked up carefully and found that it was his sister coming out of her room with something in her hand. She held it up and it became something like the top of a pavilion, with 32 upward angles. A yellow silk tassel hung from each angle. On top of the "pavilion" was a coloured silk fabric with an embroidered phoenix and peonies. There was only one "pillar" underneath.

Curiously, *Lu Ban* took the "pavilion" from his sister's hands and looked at it carefully. He found out that it was made from the mountain bamboo with 32 long bamboo sticks and 32 short ones. Between them there were flexible bolts, which can be unfolded or folded as you like. How useful and beautiful it was!

Lu Ban's sister smiled and said to her brother,

"Brother, you have made ten pavilions overnight, and I have only made this 'half pavilion' instead. However, the 'half pavilion' I made can match thousands of your pavilions. On rainy days, you can only sit in the pavilions to enjoy the view of West Lake. Instead, holding my 'half pavilion', I can walk around the lake and amuse myself anywhere I like."

Looking at his sister's works, *Lu Ban* smiled and said,

"My dear sister, you are smarter and you have better handicraft skills than me!"

Lu Ban's sister said,

"Not really, brother, you are definitely more skillful than me! You have made ten pavilions in different styles. Haven't they made West Lake more fascinating? It was only because I was inspired by you that I made this 'half pavilion'."

Since then, *Lu Ban* showed more respect to his sister and consulted with her in all kinds of issues. Legend has it that the ten pavilions made by *Lu Ban* were exactly the ten ones among the Ten Scenes of West Lake.

It was on a rainy day that *Lu Ban*'s sister made the 'half pavilion', and because it could be unfolded, it was called "雨散" (*yu san* in Chinese pronunciation; "*yu*" literally means rain, "*san*" unfolded). Later on, someone who liked to fabricate new Chinese characters made a new one, i.e. "伞", which looked like the shape of 'half pavilion'. Since this new character "伞" looked exactly like what *Lu Ban*'s sister invented, people accepted it and it has become popular among people.

【文化背景】【Cultural Notes】

▶ **白堤**:西湖被苏堤、白堤、杨公堤和孤山分为五部分。白堤是唐朝诗人白居易在杭州任职期间所建。白堤是用湖底淤泥搭建而成,穿湖而过。

***Bai* Causeway**: West Lake is divided by *Su*, *Bai*, and *Yanggong* Causeways and Solitary Hill into five areas. *Bai* Causeway was built by *Bai Juyi*, a *Tang* Dynasty poet, when he served as a Governor in *Hangzhou*. It was built out of mud dredged from the bottom of the lake and ran across it.

▶ **苏堤**:北宋年间,苏轼来杭州任知州时(1089)利用疏浚西湖时取出的湖泥和葑草堆筑成苏堤。苏堤是一条贯穿西湖南北风景区的林荫大堤,现长2797米,为白堤的三倍长左右。

***Su* Causeway**: During the Northern *Song* Dynasty, while serving as the magistrate of *Hangzhou* (1089), *Su Shi* ordered the dredging of West Lake and had the causeway built with the silt and marshy weeds excavated from the lake. *Su* causeway is currently 2,797 metres in length, nearly three times as long as *Bai* Causeway. It runs across West Lake and unites the southern and northern scenic spots of the lake.

▶ **柳浪闻莺**：西湖十景之一，位于西湖东南岸，前身为南宋时的皇家花园，现在为对外开放的公园。公园占地 21 公顷，蜿蜒的堤岸，百年的古树，久远的亭台楼榭，垂柳依依，黄莺啼鸣。人们喜欢来此晨练，也是大型休闲娱乐和节日庆典的好去处。

Orioles Singing in the Willows: One of the Ten Scenes of West Lake. Located off the southeast bank of West Lake, Orioles Singing in the Willows, which used to be an imperial park in the Southern *Song* Dynasty, has been turned into a public park. It covers an area of 21 hectares, with luxuriant trees, surviving from the past dynasties, along the winding bank. Pavilions reveal their ancient romantic style, with weeping willows and singing Orioles. People like to do morning exercises here. It is also an ideal place for large-scale recreation and ceremonies.

▶ **三潭印月**：西湖十景之一，是西湖中最大的岛屿，被誉为"西湖第一胜境"，湖中有岛，岛中有湖，独具特色。岛南湖面，三座中空小石塔鼎足而立，环塔身分布五个小圆孔，中秋月明之夜，塔内点上蜡烛，人们便可以尽享天上一个月亮，水中多个月亮的奇异景观。第五套人民币的一元纸币的背面采用了三潭印月的盛景。

Three Pools Mirroring the Moon: One of the Ten Scenes of West Lake. It is the largest island in West Lake and is considered as its No. 1 attraction. It has a unique style of "islands in the lake and a lake on the islands". On the south side of the largest of the three man-made islands in the lake, there are three hollow stone pagodas rising from water, each with five openings. On the night of the mid-autumn festival, with candle light inside the pagodas, people marvel at the wonderful scenery of one moon in the sky but many reflections in the lake. This magnificent landscape appears on the back of the one *yuan* bill of the fifth set of RMB.

▶ **西湖十景**：源自南宋时期的传统西湖十景，每一个景点用一个四字词语表示。十景各擅其胜，组合在一起又能代表古代西湖胜景精华。

Ten Scenes of West Lake: Traditionally, there are ten best-known scenic places on West Lake, each remembered by a four-character epithet.

Collectively, they have been known as the "Ten Scenes of West Lake" since Southern *Song* dynasty. Each scenic spot has its uniqueness and fascination, and together, they represent the essence of the charm of West Lake.

贰◎西湖醋鱼
West Lake Fish in Vinegar Gravy

【简介】

西湖醋鱼又叫"宋嫂鱼",是浙江杭州传统风味名菜,起源于南宋。此道菜宜选用鲜活西湖草鱼做原料,烹制前一般先要在干净的水中饿养一两天,使其排泄肠内杂物,除去泥土味。最好先在沸水中煮约3分钟,烧好装盘后,淋上糖醋芡汁,该汁由烧鱼的水加醋、糖、米酒、酱油等调制而成。

【Brief Introduction】

West Lake Fish in Vinegar Gravy, also named Sister *Song*'s Fish, is a traditional recipe from *Hangzhou*, *Zhejiang* Province. This dish's origin can be traced back to the Southern *Song* Dynasty. Live grass carp from West Lake is recommended for making it. Before the fish is cooked, it is given no food and has to stay hungry in clean water for one or two days to get rid of its smell of mud. The fish is simply cooked by putting it in boiling water for about 3 minutes. Then all that needs to be done is to pour the sauce onto the fish. The sauce is made up from the water used to cook the fish, vinegar, sugar, rice wine, soy sauce, etc.

【传说读本】

从前,在**西湖断桥**边,有一间孤单单的茅屋。男主人宋五哥早已去世,只留下他的妻子宋五嫂和一个十二三岁的小弟弟。

宋五嫂年纪轻轻,长得俊秀,丈夫死后,乡亲们常劝她改嫁,她生怕小叔无人照顾,都婉言回绝了。宋五嫂总是记住丈夫临死时的话,一定要把小叔抚养长大,待小叔像亲弟弟一样。

宋五嫂十分勤劳,每天天不亮,便带着小叔,划着渔船,到西湖里捕捕鱼,捉捉虾。捕来鱼虾,便换点米换点盐,过着苦日子。

有一次,小叔因为年纪小,经不起湖上风吃雨打,忽然病了,而且病得很厉害,这可把宋五嫂急坏了。多亏得宋五嫂精心护理,小叔的病终于慢慢地好了起来。但小叔病后身体很虚弱,胃口一点不开。

有一天,宋五嫂打来一网好鱼。她将一条鲜龙活跳的草鱼,养在水缸里。把剩下的鱼拿到市上去卖。一路走一路想,怎样变个法儿把家里的那条新鲜草鱼烧得好吃点,让小叔开开胃口。她想起小时候听老年人说过,糖醋可以开胃,便打起用糖醋烧鱼的主意来。宋五嫂卖了鱼,在街上买来配料,回到家里,一边烧水,一边对小叔子说:“今天嫂嫂要做碗好菜给你尝尝哩!”

小叔好像猜到了宋五嫂的心思,说:“嫂嫂,我这两天一闻腥气就恶心,鱼我是不要吃的!”

宋五嫂说:“今天我用个特别的烧法,等会你一吃就知道啦。”

宋五嫂等水一开,将养在水缸里的一条草鱼活杀活剖洗干净,在滚水里一汆,放在碗里。又取出自己做的藕粉,配上糖醋,烧成羹料,浇在熟鱼上。然后,将这热气腾腾的一碗鱼,送到小叔跟前。她拿筷子夹一块,蘸上糖醋羹,给小叔吃。小叔子一闻,今天的鱼不但没有一点腥气,而且还很香。一尝,有点甜,有点酸,特别鲜嫩。他抢过筷子,说:“嫂嫂,这鱼真好吃,这鱼真好吃!”开始还一筷一筷地吃,后来就大块大块地往嘴巴里送啦。

这样一连几天,宋五嫂每天都把打来的活草鱼留下一条,烧醋鱼给小叔吃。小叔胃口大开,身体也很快好了起来,又帮着宋五嫂去打西湖鱼了。

附近的渔家,听说宋五嫂的小叔吃了她烧的醋鱼,胃口马上好啦,身体也健旺啦,都来向宋五嫂讨教烧法。因为这个菜是宋五嫂因爱惜小叔第一个烧出来的,人们就称它为“宋嫂鱼”。

宋五嫂看到大家都喜欢吃醋鱼,就积了些钱,和小叔商量商量,在茅屋里开个小店铺,卖起醋鱼来了。果然,你来我往,生意很好。

这一年春天,皇帝乘龙船在西湖上游玩作乐。忽然,一阵暖风吹过,从断桥那边飘来一股似甜带酸的香味儿。皇帝从来没有闻到过这种香味，心里好生奇怪，忙问左右道："这是什么香味儿呀？"

许多人都回答不出，其中有一个本地的官儿说："皇上，这是断桥边赫赫有名的宋五嫂卖醋鱼的香味儿哩！"

皇帝一听动了心，忙说："好，既然这样有名，寡人倒要去结识结识。"

那皇帝一时高兴，脱下龙袍，换上便服，带着太监坐小船一路来到断桥边。一上岸，抬头见宋五嫂满面春风地在店堂里招待顾客。

皇帝一见连声赞"妙"，忙走上去说："听说醋鱼的味道很美，不料你宋五嫂的相貌更美。今日一见，果然名不虚传。"

宋五嫂见来者不善，便放下脸不搭理他。那皇帝本来不想露出身份，现在见宋五嫂这样，心里急了，便颠三倒四地说："美人儿呀，这又何必呢！何必呢……呃！何必在这里烧鱼呢！……不配，不配，嗯！还是跟**寡人**进宫去才配呵。"

"寡人"两字一脱口，宋五嫂便知道站在前面的人便是那个昏君了，心里更加生气，但又不好得罪他，只得转弯抹角地说："宫里是有福之人住的，我是个打鱼的人，没有这份福气，一离开茅屋必定生病。我老早就打定主意要在这儿住一世了。"

皇帝见宋五嫂口齿活络，不大好对付，便笑着改口说："也罢！现在就带你上龙船去烧碗醋鱼，让寡人尝尝鲜吧。今后你的美名恐怕都要把断桥压断啦！"

宋五嫂见皇帝竟这样死皮赖脸，禁不住两道柳眉竖了起来，说："龙船难载我卖鱼妇，你皇上也不要走这断桥路！岂不见金兵一来，河山已经破碎！你皇上还是多去想想中原的父老吧。"

皇帝顿时怒容满脸，骂道："好一个放肆的刁妇！"便气冲冲地和太监下了小船，回到龙船里去了。

宋五嫂见皇帝气呼呼地一走，知道凶多吉少，便赶紧收拾一些东西，带了小叔，从后门溜出，跨上小船，双桨一荡，远走高飞啦。等皇帝派兵赶来捉人时，宋五嫂早已无影无踪了。

从此，宋五嫂和她的小叔改姓换名，隐落在别的小村子里，再不露面。后来，**孤山**一带学过烧"宋嫂鱼"手艺的渔家，有的人也学宋五嫂的样，开小店铺卖醋鱼，但他们怕冲犯皇帝，不敢说是"宋嫂鱼"，只挂个"西湖醋鱼"的菜牌。

【English Version of the Original Story】

Once upon a time, there was a lonely cottage at **the Broken Bridge of West Lake**. The man of the house, Mr. *Song*, had passed away years ago, leaving his wife, Mrs. *Song*, and his 12-13 year-old young brother.

Mrs. *Song* was young and pretty. After her husband died, the villagers often tried to persuade her to remarry. She refused politely since she was afraid that no one else would look after her little brother-in-law if she remarried. She always bore in mind what her husband had told her before he died, and decided to raise up her brother-in-law and treated him as her own brother.

Mrs. *Song* was so industrious that she went fishing by boat every day before dawn. She took her brother-in-law with her to catch shrimps. She lived by trading fish and shrimps they caught for rice and salt.

Once, her brother-in-law, who was too young to go through the strong wind and heavy rain on the lake, fell seriously ill. She was extremely worried about him. Thanks to her careful nursing, he recovered. However, he was still very weak and had no appetite at all.

One day, Mrs. *Song* caught a lot of fish. She put one live grass carp in a tank, and carried all the other fish to the market to sell. On her way to the market, she was trying hard to think about how to cook that fresh grass carp to make it more delicious and whet his appetite. She remembered being told that sugar and vinegar could stimulate one's appetite and decided to cook the fish with sugar and vinegar. After selling all the fish, she bought the ingredients and went home. While heating some water, she said to her brother-in-law,

"I'll cook something special and delicious for you today."

Her brother-in-law knew what she wanted to cook and said to her,

"Sister-in-law, the fishy smells have made me feel sick these two days. No fish today!"

Mrs. *Song* said,

"I'll cook the fish in a special way, different from before. You'll taste the difference soon."

Mrs. *Song* took the fish from the tank, killed and washed it. When the water was boiling, she put it in the boiling water for a short time. Then she took it out and put it into a bowl. She made some sauce with home-made lotus root starch, sugar and vinegar and then poured the sauce onto the cooked fish. Then she took the bowl of steaming fish to her brother-in-law. She dipped a piece of fish in the sweet and sour sauce and fed him. It smelt good without any fishy smells. He tasted it and liked the sweet and sour flavour. He grabbed the chopsticks and said to her,

"Dear sister-in-law, the fish is so delicious, so tasty!"

He put large chunks into his mouth.

On the following days, Mrs. *Song* kept a live grass carp and cooked it for her brother-in-law in the same way. He had a good appetite and recovered quickly. Soon he could go fishing in West Lake with his sister-in-law again.

Hearing that Mrs. *Song*'s special way of cooking fish helped her brother-in-law to recover so quickly, the fishermen nearby all came to ask her to teach them how to cook fish. Since Mrs. *Song* was the first person who cooked fish in this special way out of love to her brother-in-law, people called it "Sister *Song*'s fish".

Seeing that so many people liked fish cooked in vinegar sauce, Mrs. *Song* saved some money and opened a small restaurant with her brother-in-law and sold this vinegar fish. As expected, it sold well and the business flourished.

One day in spring, the emperor went to West Lake in a dragon boat to do sightseeing. Suddenly, a warm breeze blew over the Broken Bridge and brought a delicious, sweet and sour scent. The emperor had never smelt that before. He was so curious that he asked people around him,

"What is that smell?"

Many people didn't have any clue and made no response to the emperor. Then, a local official replied,

"Your Majesty, this is the aroma of vinegar fish cooked by Mrs. *Song*, It's a well-known dish in this area."

The emperor was tempted and said,

"Good. Now that she is so well-known, I want to meet her."

Being in a good mood at that point, the emperor took off his imperial robe and took on street-clothes. He went with his eunuch by boat to the Broken Bridge. When they went ashore, the emperor saw the smiling Mrs. *Song* receiving customers in her restaurant.

Seeing that Mrs. *Song* was so pretty, the emperor remarked,

"Terrific! Terrific!"

He went up to her and said,

"I heard that the vinegar fish is wonderful. What a nice surprise to see that you are even more wonderful. As I see you with my own eyes, you really deserve your reputation."

Realizing that this man did not have friendly intentions, Mrs. *Song* pulled a long face and did not reply to him. The emperor had not intended to reveal his identity, but he could not bear to be ignored. He became impatient and talked incoherently, "Beauty, Oh no, why ... Oh, You don't have to cook fish here! You deserve something better! Yes, something better! Hmm, why don't you come with ***Gua Ren*** to the emperor's palace?"

On hearing ***Gua Ren***, she knew the person in front of him was the fatuous emperor. She was more annoyed, but did not want to offend him. She had to beat around the bush, telling him,

"Only those people who are blessed can live in the emperor's palace. I am only a fisher woman, without any blessing. I'll surely fall ill if I stay out of the cottage. I made up my mind, ages ago, to live here for all my life"

Seeing that Mrs. *Song* was sensible and hard to deal with, the emperor laughed and said,

"Well, fine, come with me now to the dragon boat to cook vinegar fish. Let me have a taste. In future I'm afraid your huge reputation will break this Broken Bridge."

Seeing the emperor so shameless, Mrs. *Song* became annoyed,

"As a fisher woman, I won't go to your dragon boat. You, as the emperor, stay away from this Broken Bridge. Haven't you seen that our country has been crushed since the attack by the army from the kingdom of *Jin*? You should think more about the fellow countrymen in the Central Plain."

The emperor looked very angry immediately, and shouted,

"You cursed, unbridled shrew!"

He left the small boat with the eunuch and angrily went back to the dragon boat.

Seeing the furious emperor leave, Mrs. *Song* realized that something bad would happen. She hurriedly packed up and slipped out through the back door with her brother-in-law. They boarded their small boat, pulled on the oars, and went away from that place. When the soldiers sent by the emperor arrived to catch Mrs. *Song* and her brother-in-law, not the least trace could be found.

From then on, Mrs. *Song* and her brother-in-law changed their names. They stayed in another small village secretly and never showed up any more. After that, the fishermen who had learned how to cook vinegar fish, opened small restaurants around **Solitary Hill** to sell vinegar fish as Mrs. *Song* had done before. Afraid of offending the emperor, they did not dare to name it Sister *Song*'s fish, instead, they named it West Lake Fish in Vinegar Gravy.

【文化背景】【Cultural Notes】

▶ **西湖断桥**：西湖十景之一。位于杭州里西湖和外西湖的分水点上，一端跨着北山路，另一端接通白堤。在西湖古今诸多大小桥梁中，她的名气最大。传说中白娘子与许仙断桥相会，为断桥景物增添了浪漫色彩。桥的东北有碑亭，内立"断桥残雪"碑。

The Broken Bridge on West Lake: One of the Ten Scenes of West Lake. It is located between Outer West Lake and Inner West Lake, connecting *Baishan* Road and *Bai* Causeway. It is the most famous among all bridges in West Lake. The legend of Lady White and *Xu Xian* meeting on this bridge has added romance to it. At the northeast of the bridge there stands a pavilion housing a plaque, which reads "Lingering Snow on the Broken Bridge".

▶ **寡人**:古代中国帝王的谦称。

Gua Ren: It is a polite way for the emperors in ancient China to call themselves.

▶ **孤山**:孤山位于西湖风景区,是西湖的一个著名景点和湖中最大天然岛屿,山高不过35米,却是观赏西湖景色最佳之地。孤山既是风景胜地,又是文物荟萃之处。

The Solitary Hill: Located in West Lake Scenic Spot, Solitary Hill, is the largest natural island in the lake. Though it is no more than 35 metres high, it is the best place to enjoy the scenery of West Lake. It is famous not only for the picturesque landscape but also for abundance an in many cultural and historical relics there.

叁◎东坡肉
Braised *Dongpo* Pork

【简介】

东坡肉是杭州传统菜肴,由红烧五花猪肉制成。将猪肉切成大约2英寸的方块,半肥半瘦,加调味和酒红烧,然后用文火煨制。此肉肥而不腻,酥香味美。该菜肴是以中国北宋时期著名诗人苏东坡的名字命名。

【Brief Introduction】

Braised *Dongpo* Pork is a traditional *Hangzhou* dish made by cooking pork belly in red wine. Cut the pork to around 2 inches squares, each consisting of half fat and half lean meat, braise it with the other ingredients and wine, then slowly stew it on a low heat. The cooked pork is fat but not greasy, crisp and delicious, with the fragrance of wine. It is named after the famed Northern *Song* Dynasty poet *Su Dongpo*.

【传说读本】

苏东坡在杭州做**通判**的辰光，疏浚了西湖，替老百姓做了一件大好事。

西湖疏浚后，四周的田地就不怕涝也不愁旱了。这一年又风调雨顺，杭州四乡的庄稼得了大丰收。老百姓感念苏东坡疏浚西湖的好处，到过年时，大家都抬猪担酒来给他**拜年**。

苏东坡无论如何推辞不掉，只好收下许多猪肉。他叫人把肉都切成方块，焖得酥酥的，然后再按照疏浚西湖的民工花名册，每家一块，将肉分送给大家过年。

太平的年头，家家户户过得好快活！这辰光又见苏东坡差人送肉来，大家更高兴啦。老的笑，小的跳，人人都夸苏东坡是个贤明的父母官，把他送来的猪肉亲热地称呼为“东坡肉”。

那时，杭州有家大菜馆，菜馆老板见人们都夸“东坡肉”，就和厨师商量，把猪肉也照样切成方块，焖得红酥酥的；挂出牌子，上面写着“东坡肉”三个字。

这只新菜一出，那家菜馆的生意马上兴隆起来。从早到晚顾客不断，每天杀十头大肥猪还不够卖的呢。别的菜馆老板看得眼红，也都学着做起来，一时间，不论大小菜馆，家家都有“东坡肉”了。后来，经过同行公议，就把“东坡肉”定为杭州的第一道名菜。

苏东坡为人正直，不畏权贵，朝廷中有一班人本来就很恨他；这时见他得到杭州老百姓的爱戴，心里更不舒服。其中有个御史，乔装改扮，到杭州来找岔子，存心要陷害苏东坡。

那御史到杭州的头一天，在一家菜馆里吃午饭。堂倌递上菜单，请他点菜。他接过来一看，哟，头一道菜就是“东坡肉”！他皱起眉头想了想，不觉高兴得拍着桌子大声叫道：“我就要这头一道菜！”

他吃过“东坡肉”，觉得味道倒真是不错，向堂倌一打听，知道“东坡肉”是同行公议的第一道名菜。于是，他就把杭州所有菜馆的菜单都收拢来，兴冲冲地赶回京去。

御史回到京城，马上就去见皇帝。他说：“皇上呀，苏东坡在杭州做通判，贪赃枉法，把恶事都做绝啦！老百姓恨不得要吃他的肉哩。”

皇帝听了吃一惊，就问道：“你怎么知道的呢？”

御史就把那一厚沓沾满油渍的菜单呈了上去。皇帝本来就是个糊涂蛋，他看看菜单，哟，对呀，“东坡肉”，“东坡肉”，……人人头一口就都想吃“东坡肉”，苏东坡是不好啊！于是皇帝不分青红皂白，立刻传下圣旨，将苏东坡革掉官职,远远地发配到**海南**去。

苏东坡走了以后,杭州的老百姓还是没忘掉他的好处,仍然像过去一样赞扬他。就这样,"东坡肉"也一代一代地传下来,直到今天,还是杭州的一道名菜哩。

【English Version of the Original Story】

When *Su Dongpo* worked as **Perfect** in *Hangzhou*, he ordered the dredging of West Lake. This was a great bonus for the ordinary people. After that, the farmers around West Lake were not afraid of any flood or drought. One year people enjoyed favourable weather and had a good harvest again. At the Spring Festival, people were so grateful to *Su Dongpo* for his contribution to having West Lake dredged that they **paid** him **New Year's visit** with a large amount of pork and wine.

Mr. *Su* could hardly refuse such kindness and had no choice but to accept some pork. He had the pork cut into squares and slowly stewed on a low heat. Then he had those red-braised pork pieces sent to all the people who, according to the roster of workers, had been involved in dredging West Lake, one piece for each family.

In such a peaceful year, people really enjoyed their life. The red-braised pork sent by *Su Dongpo* made them even happier. The elders laughed, and the young people jumped, all saying that Mr. *Su* was a good and wise local magistrate and fondly calling the pork *Dongpo* Pork.

At that time, the boss of a big restaurant in *Hangzhou*, seeing that people all liked *Dongpo Pork*, consulted with the cooks and tried to cook pork in the same way. They cut the pork into squares, braised it on a low fire for a long time, then put up a sign that read, "*Dongpo* Pork".

Once the new dish was offered, the restaurant's business flourished immediately. Customers came constantly from morning till night. The restaurant ran out of pork even though they killed ten big fat pigs every day. Other restaurant bosses were jealous and tried cooking pork in a similar way. For a while, all restaurants, big or small, all offered *Dongpo* Pork. Later on, after peer discussion, it became *Hangzhou*'s first local specialty.

Some people from the Imperial Court hated *Su* because he had high integrity and had no fear for the powerful. Local people's affection for *Su* made the court feel even more uncomfortable. One Censor disguised himself and came to *Hangzhou* to find fault with *Su*, intending to frame him.

The first day the Censor arrived in *Hangzhou*, he had lunch in a restaurant. A waiter handed him the menu and asked him to order. The Censor took the menu and had a look. He found that the first dish was *Dongpo* Pork. He frowned and thought for a while. Then he hit upon an idea. He slapped the table and shouted,

"I want this first dish!"

Censor found the dish of *Dongpo* Pork very tasty. He was told that *Dongpo* Pork was the first local specialty after peer discussion. He collected menus from all restaurants in *Hangzhou* and went back to *Beijing* excitedly.

Once back in *Beijing*, the Censor visited the emperor immediately. He told the emperor,

"His Majesty, as the Prefect in *Hangzhou*, *Su Dongpo* did all kinds of evil things such as taking bribes and bending the law! People couldn't wait to eat his flesh..."

The emperor was shocked, and asked,

"How did you know that?"

The Censor handed all the oily menus to the emperor, who was such a fool that he believed what the Censor said. The emperor thought,

"Now that people wanted to eat the flesh of *Dongpo*, surely he was not a good guy."

Unable to distinguish black from white, the emperor had a message dispatched, discharging *Su Dongpo* from his position and sent him to ***Hainan***.

After *Su Dongpo* left, people in *Hangzhou* still remembered his kindness and contribution and spoke as highly of him as before. Therefore, *Dongpo* Pork recipe was handed down from generation to generation. It is still a famous dish in *Hangzhou* today.

【文化背景】【Cultural Notes】

▶ **通判**:中国古代官职之一,始于宋朝,掌管粮运、家田、水利和诉讼等事项。

Prefect: One of the official positions in ancient China, starting from the Northern *Song* Dynasty. The job is to take charge of food transportation, farmland, water conservancy and lawsuits, etc.

▶ **拜年**：春节，即农历新年，是中国最重要的传统节日。在春节期间，人们会相互拜年，尤其是拜家中尊长。这是中国民间的传统习俗，是人们相互表达美好祝愿、辞旧迎新的一种方式。

Pay New Year's visit: The Spring Festival, i.e. the Chinese New Year according to the lunar calendar, is the most important traditional festival in China. On the Spring Festival, people pay a New Year call to each other, especially to the elders in the family. This traditional custom is a way people deliver their wishes, discard the old and bring in the new in the New Year.

▶ **海南**：是中国最小的省份，位于中国最南端，曾经属于广东省，1988年设立海南省。历史上，很多人由于政治原因被贬发配至此。

Hainan: It is the smallest and southernmost province in China. It used to be part of *Guangdong* Province; then, in 1988, the island became part of the newly established *Hainan* Province. Historically, a lot of people were banished to *Hainan* for political reasons.

肆 ◎ 油炸桧
Fried *Hui*

【简介】

"油炸桧"，现在被称为"油条"，一种金褐色的长条形油炸面食。人们早餐喜欢吃烧饼夹油条，简称"烧饼油条"，通常搭配豆浆或稀饭一起吃。现发展为杭州风味小吃——"葱包桧儿"，也就是将薄饼卷油条、葱，抹甜面酱或辣酱，烤后食用。

【Brief Introduction】

Fried *Hui*, or *you zha hui*, now called *you tiao* or deep-fried twisted stick, is a long golden-brown, deep-fried strip of dough. Usually people like to stuff it inside a Chinese style baked roll to make a sandwich known as *shaobing youtiao*. This kind of is normally eaten at breakfast with rice congee or soy milk. In *Hangzhou* it has grown into a local delicacy, *cong bao huier*, which means "wrapped fried bread stick with shallot". It is made by wrapping a Deep-fried Twisted Stick in a pancake which has been mixed with shallot, and sweet or hot sauce. Then it is all toasted.

【传说读本】

南宋年间,卖国宰相**秦桧**和他和老婆王氏,在东窗定下了毒计,把精忠报国的岳元帅活活害死在风波亭里。消息传开来,老百姓个个义愤难平,酒楼茶馆,街头巷尾,都在议论这件大冤案。

那时候,在众安桥河下,贴隔壁有两个吃食摊:一家卖芝麻葱烧饼,一家卖油炸糯米团。这一天,刚刚散了早市,做烧饼的王二通通火炉,整好灶上卖剩下的一叠葱烧饼,看看没有买主,就坐在条凳上休息。这时,做糯米团的李四,也已收拾好油锅,蹲在那里咂旱烟。彼此一招呼,李四便走过来,两个人对面坐起来谈天。一谈两谈,不觉又谈到秦桧害死岳飞的事情上来啦。李四讲到气头上来,不由得捏起拳头在条板上用劲一敲:"卖国贼秦桧!我恨不得把你……"

王二听了嘻嘻直笑,说道:"李四哥别性急,你看我来收拾他们!"说着,从面团上摘了两个面疙瘩,捏捏团团,团团捏捏,捏成两个面人:一个吊眉毛大汉,一个翘嘴巴女人。他抓起切面刀,往那吊眉毛大汉的颈项上打横一刀,又往那翘嘴巴女人的肚皮上竖着一刀,对李四说:"你看怎么样?"

李四点点头,说:"不过,这还便宜了他们!"说完,他跑回自己摊子去,把油锅端到王二烤烧饼的炉子上来,又将那两个斩断切开了的面人重新捏好,背对背地粘在一起,丢进滚油锅里去炸。一面炸面人,一面叫着:"大家来看'油炸桧'啰!大家来看'油炸桧'啰!"

过往行人听见"油炸桧",觉得新鲜,都围拢来。大家看着油锅里有这样男女两个人,被滚油炸得吱吱响,肚子里都明白这是怎么一回事了,他们心里很痛快，都跟着叫起来："看呀看呀，'油炸桧'啰！看呀看呀，'油炸桧'啰！"

就在这时候，只听"噹，噹"一阵锣声响，正巧，秦桧坐着八抬大轿，从皇宫里退朝回府，经过众安桥。秦桧在轿子里听见嘈杂的叫喊声，纳闷什么是油炸桧呀。觉得这叫法不对头，忙叫人停下轿子，立刻派出亲兵去抓人。亲兵挤进人群，把王二和李四抓来，连那油锅也端到轿前。秦桧看见油锅里炸得焦黑了的面人，气得一根根络腮胡子都翘起来，走出轿来大声吼道："好大的胆子！你们想要造反呀？"

王二装作没事人似的，笑嘻嘻地回答说："我们是做小生意的，哪里造得了反呢？"

秦桧说："既然如此，怎敢乱用本官名讳，来骂我？"

王二说："哎呀呀，宰相大人，您是木旁的'桧'，我们说的是火旁的'烩'哩！"

这时，大家都嚷起来，"对呀，对呀，这是音同字不同呵！"

秦桧听听也是，被弄得无话可说了。他看看油锅里浮起的那两个面人，喝道："不要啰唆！这炸成黑炭一样的东西，如何吃得了！分明是你们两个刁民，聚众生事，欺蒙官府！"

听秦桧这么一说，人群中马上站出两个人来，说道："就要这样炸，就要这样炸！"说着就把油锅里的面人捞起来，一家一半分开，往嘴里一塞，"咯吱咯吱"地吃起来，还连声说道："好吃，好吃！我越吃牙根越痒，恨不得一口把它吞下去哩！"

这一来，秦桧哭笑不得，他只好瞪瞪眼睛，就往大轿里一钻，灰溜溜地走啦。

堂堂的宰相当众吃瘪，这件事情一下轰动了整个**临安**城。人们纷纷赶到众安桥来，都想吃一吃"油炸桧"。

李四索性不做糯米团了，把油锅搬了过来，和王二并做一摊，合伙做"油炸桧"卖。

老百姓当初吃"油炸桧"是为了消消恨的，但一吃味道不错，价钱也便宜，所以吃的人越来越多。一时间临安城里城外所有的烧饼摊，都学着做起来。以后，"油炸桧"这道美食就传遍了全国各地。

【English Version of the Original Story】

During the Southern *Song* Dynasty, the traitorous Prime Minister, ***Qin***

Hui, and his wife Madame *Wang* made an evil plan under the east window of their bedroom. Through this plan, the well-respected General, *Yue Fei*, who had been known for his loyalty to serve the country, was cruelly executed in Storm Pavilion. The news spread and all the people got so angry that everyone was talking about this case of gross injustice in every corner of the the town—in restaurants and tea houses, on streets and lanes.

At that time, there were two food stands right next to each other under the *Zhong An* Bridge. One sold pancakes with shallot and sesame-seeds, while the other sold fried glutinous rice balls. One morning after the morning market, *Wang Er*, who made pancakes, cleaned out the stove and sorted out a pile of leftover pancakes. Seeing no more customers, he sat on a bench for a rest. In the meanwhile, *Li Si*, who made fried glutinous rice balls, had already tidied up his frying pan and was squatting there smoking a cigarette. As they greeted each other, *Li Si* came over and the two started to chat. Speaking of the unjust case of *Yue Fei* who was put to death by *Qin Hui*, *Li Si* got so angry that he knocked hard at the batter with his fist.

"Traitor *Qin Hui*! How I wish I could have him..."

Wang Er couldn't help laughing and said,

"Don't be so impatient, bro. See what I can do to them!"

He picked up two lumps from the batter, rolled and pinched them into two dough figurines: a hefty man with lifted eyebrows and a woman with pouted lips. He grabbed a flour-cutting knife and stabbed the neck of the man and the belly of the woman. He then said to *Li Si*,

"What do you think?"

"Still, that's not enough!" *Li Si* nodded, and went back to his own stand and brought his frying pan over to *Wang Er*'s stove. He then glued together the two dough figurines, back to back, and threw them into the boiling oil, while shouting loudly,

"Come on, everybody! Come and see 'Frying *Hui*'! Come and see 'Frying *Hui*'!"

Hearing that, people passing by were attracted, and gathered around the frying pan. Seeing the two dough figurines being fried in boiling oil, they all understood what this was about and felt very happy. They all shouted,

"Look! Look! It's 'Frying *Hui*'! Look! Look! It's 'Frying *Hui*'!"

Just at that moment, with a burst of sound from a gong, clang, clang, *Qin Hui* happened to pass by *Zhong An* Bridge. He was on his way from the palace back to his home. He was in a sedan chair carried by eight people. Hearing noises and puzzled by what "Frying *Hui*" was, he felt something was wrong and immediately gave orders to have his sedan chair stopped. He sent his soldiers to go into the crowd, and bring *Wang Er* and *Li Si*, as well as the frying pan in front of him. *Qin Hui* took a look at the burned black dough figurines in the frying pan and got so furious that every inch of his beard stood up. He got out of his sedan chair and roared,

"How dare you! Are you trying to rebel?"

Wang Er, pretending that nothing had happened, grinned and replied,

"We only run a small business. How can we rebel?"

Qin Hui remarked,

"How dare you abuse my name to curse me?"

Wang Er replied,

"No! No! No! Your Excellency! The '*Hui*'(烩) in 'Frying *Hui*' is different from the '*Hui*'(桧) in your name. The left part of the character '*Hui*' in your name has the structural part "木", while what we were talking about is the character with "火" as a component."

By now, everyone started shouting,

"That's right! That's right! They are two different characters with the same pronunciation!"

Qin Hui thought that it did make sense and was rendered speechless. He looked at the two dough figurines floating in the frying pan and thundered,

"Stop this nonsense! How can anyone possibly eat this thing that's fried like black wood charcoal! You two are definitely unruly people who gathered a crowd to make disturbances and lie to the government!"

Upon hearing this, two people stood out from the crowd and shouted,

"That's the way it is! That's the way it is!"

They then fished out the dough figurines from the frying pan, divided it in two, and stuffed into their mouths. They seemed to enjoy it very much, with the dough figurines creaking in their mouths, and shouted repeatedly,

"Tasty, tasty! The more I eat, the more I want! I cannot wait to finish it in one bite!"

Finding it both funny and annoying, *Qin Hui* glared at the crowd, wormed his way into his sedan chair and gloomily left.

The public insult to the dignified prime minister of the country soon caused a splash in the whole ***Lin'an*** city. People swarmed into *Zhong An* Bridge to buy and eat Fried *Hui*.

Instead of making fried glutinous rice balls, *Li Si* moved his frying pan to join *Wang Er*. They formed a partnership to sell Fried *Hui*.

It was to cool down their hatred that people first started to eat Fried *Hui*. Not long after that, more and more people came to like it since it was both delicious and cheap. As time went on all the stands which used to make pancakes in and around *Lin'an* city all started to make Fried *Hui*, which then spread throughout China.

【文化背景】【Cultural Notes】

▶ **秦桧**:秦桧(1090—1155)宋朝两任宰相,前后在位19年,为宋高宗赵构宠臣。其迫害岳飞,利用对朝廷监察权的控制及高宗的宠信,陷害忠臣、异己,压制主战派,力主议和,实行向金进贡纳币政策,为中国历史上罪行滔天、臭名昭著的一代奸相。

Qin Hui (1090—1155) was appointed twice as Chancellor of the *Song* Dynasties. He was in office for 19 years, being one of the minions of Emperor *Gaozong* of *Song* named *Zhao Gou*. *Qin Hui* is widely regarded as a traitor for his part in the persecution and execution of *Yue Fei*. Through using his control over imperial censorship and, with the favour and trust he gained from the emperor, he persecuted loyal officials and political opponents, suppressed war hawks, insisted on reconciliation talks, and carried out the policy of paying tribute to the *Jin* Dynasty. The vicious crimes *Qin* committed have caused him to be remembered as a notorious, evil minister in Chinese history.

▶ **临安**:南宋都城叫临安,其位置就是现在的杭州市。现在的临安是杭州的一个县级市,位于浙江省西北面,离杭州市不远。

Lin'an: *Hangzhou* was the capital of the Southern *Song* Dynasty, which was called *Lin'an* at that time. Today, *Lin'an* is a county-level city, located in the northwest of *Zhejiang* Province, not far from *Hangzhou*.

伍◎龙井茶
Longjing Tea

【简介】

西湖龙井,产于浙江杭州,中国十大名茶之一。杭州是中国主要茶叶产地之一;龙井为西湖附近一村庄名,是西湖龙井的主要产地。龙井茶外形扁平挺秀,色泽嫩绿光润,香气优雅清高,味道清新怡人,深受人们喜爱。清代乾隆皇帝曾在龙井封过十八棵御树,称为"十八棵御茶",并题"龙井八景",这使得龙井村成为杭州一大旅游景点。中国唯一以茶叶为主题的博物馆——中国茶叶博物馆,就坐落在龙井村。

【Brief Introduction】

Longjing tea, also called Dragon Well Tea, is a variety of green tea from *Hangzhou*, *Zhejiang* Province, China. It is ranked among China's top ten famous kinds of tea. *Hangzhou* is one of China's leading tea-producing areas, while *Longjing* is a local village where the finest green tea is produced. It is renowned for its high quality, with flat and smooth tea leaves, light green colour, a subtle fragrant scent, and a refreshing taste. The emperor *Qianlong* designated eighteen of *Longjing*'s trees as "Eighteen Producers of Imperial Tea", and inscribed the Eight Views of *Longing*, making the *Longjing* village a major tourist attraction in *Hangzhou*. The China National Tea Museum, the only tea museum in China with a tea theme, is located in the *Longjing* village.

【传说读本】

早先，龙井是个荒凉的小村庄。在山坳里，稀稀拉拉地住着十来户人家。人们在远山上栽竹木，在近山上种六谷，一年到头累死累活地还吃不上一顿饱饭。

在村边有间透风漏雨的破茅屋，里面住着一个老大妈。老大妈没儿没女，孤苦伶仃一个人。她年纪大了，上不了山，下不了地，只能照管照管屋子后面的十八株老茶树。这些茶树还是她老伴在世的时候栽的，算起来也有几十年啦。老茶树缺工少肥，新叶出的很少，每年只能采到几斤**老茶婆**。

老大妈是个好心肠的人，她宁愿自己日子过得苦点，每年总要留下一些茶叶，在门口凉棚下摆两条板凳，天天烧镬茶放着，给上山下岭的过往行人歇脚时解渴。

有一年除夕，天落大雪，左邻右舍多少都办了点年货，准备过年。老大妈家里实在穷，米缸也快空啦，除了瓮里剩的几把老茶婆，别的什么也没有了啦。但她仍旧照着老规矩，清早起来，抓把茶叶在镬里，发旺火，坐在灶前烧茶。这时，忽听“吱呀”一声，茅屋的门推开了。进来一个老头儿，身上落满雪花。老大妈忙站起身来招呼道：“老大伯呀，这山上风雪大，快进屋里坐！”

老头儿撣撣身上的雪花，走进屋里，一面就着**灶洞**烤火，一面跟老大妈搭话：“老大妈，你镬里烧的啥东西呀？”

老大妈说：“烧的是茶里哩！”

老头儿惊讶地问道：“今天除夕，明天就过年啦。人家都忙着氽三牲福礼，你家怎么烧茶呢？”

老大妈叹口气，说道：“暖，我是个孤老太婆，穷呀，办不起三牲福礼供神，只好每天烧镬茶给过路人行个方便。”

老头儿听了哈哈笑道：“不穷，不穷，你门口还放着宝贝哩。”

老大妈听了很奇怪，伸出头去向门外看看，仍旧是松毛搭的凉棚，底下两条旧板凳，还有墙角落头一只破**石臼**，破石臼里堆满了陈年垃圾——一切还是老样子。

老头儿走过来指指那只破石臼，说：“喏，这就是宝贝啊！”

老大妈只当老头儿跟她寻开心，就笑着说：“一只破石臼也算宝贝？你喜欢，就把它搬走好啦。”

“哟，我怎么好白拿你的宝贝呢！把它卖给我吧，我这就去叫人来抬。”老头儿说完，就乐呵呵地冒着大雪走了。

老大妈望望破石臼，心想，石臼这么脏，叫人家怎么搬呀！便把里面盛的陈年垃圾扒在畚箕里，倒在屋后那十八株老茶树的树根上。又到龙井拎来一桶清水，把破石臼洗刷得干干净净，洗下来的污水也泼在老茶树的根头上。

她刚把破石臼弄清爽，那老头儿就带着人走来了。他到门口一看，不禁大声叫起来："哎呀，宝贝呢？哎呀，宝贝呢？"

老大妈给弄糊涂了，指着破石臼说："这—这不是好好摆着嘛？"

老头儿顿着脚说道："唉！你把里面的东西弄到哪里去啦？"

老大妈说，"我把它倒在屋后的老茶树根头了。"

老头儿绕到屋后一看，果然如此，不禁连连顿脚道："可惜，可惜，这破石臼的宝气就在那陈年垃圾上。你既然把它倒在茶树根上了，就成全这十八株老茶树吧！"说完就领着人走了。

过了除夕过新年，很快，春天又到了。

这年，老大妈屋子后面那十八株老茶树，竟然吐出许许多多葱绿的嫩芽来。采下的茶叶真是又细又嫩又香。

邻居见老大妈的茶树长得这样好，就砍掉竹木，收了六谷，用这十八株茶树的籽，在远远近近的山头上发起茶树来。一年一年，越发越多，越发越旺。到后来，龙井这一带漫山遍野都栽上了茶树。

因为这一带地方出产的茶叶又细又嫩又香，喝起来味道特别美，所以龙井茶便出了名。

直到现在，茶农们还说，那老大妈屋后的十八株茶树，是龙井茶的祖宗哩。

【English Version of the Original Story】

Long, long ago, *Longjing* was a small, bleak village of nearly a dozen families. People planted bamboos and trees on the distant hills and different kinds of grains on the near ones. They worked extremely hard throughout the year but they still didn't have enough to eat.

At the edge of the village an old lady lived in a shabby hut, which was unable to shelter her from wind and rain. She had no child and lived all alone. Given her old age, she could neither climb mountains nor go to the fields, which left her with no choice but to look after the eighteen old tea trees behind the house. Those tea trees had been planted when her husband was still alive decades ago. As the plants lacked care and fertilizer, few new leaves came out every year, and she could only collect a few *jin* of **old tea** leaves of poor quality.

The old lady was such a kind person that, although she lived a hard life, she took some tea leaves, heated water and made tea in a wok every day. She put this on two benches under a pergola, for passers-by to drink to quench their thirst.

On the Spring Festival eve one year, it snowed heavily. All her neighbours had more or less prepared some food for the New Year. The old lady was so poor that her rice jar was nearly empty and there was nothing else other than a few handfuls of old tea leaves in the jar. As usual, she woke up in the early morning, put some tea leaves into the wok, sat in front of the kitchen range, made the fire big and heated some water to make tea. Just then, the door was pushed open and came in an old man, who was covered with snow. She quickly got up and said,

"Old man, come on in and take a seat, please! It's windy and snowy outside!"

After brushing away the snow from his body, the old man warmed himself near **the hollow inside the kitchen range** by the fire. He asked,

"Old lady, what are you making in the wok?"

She answered,

"I'm just making tea".

In surprise, he asked,

"Today is the eve of the Spring Festival, and tomorrow is the Spring Festival. All families are busy cooking meat to offer to the divinity. How come you are only making tea?"

With a sigh, the old lady replied,

"Well, being an old lady on my own, I am too poor to cook meat for the divinity. What I can do is to make tea every day to provide refreshment for passers-by."

He laughed,

"No, no, you are not poor at all. There stands a treasure in front of your house!"

In her surprise, she peered out, but nothing looked special: a pergola made of pine branches with two old benches underneath it, and an old stone mortar in the corner with garbage of many years' standing in it.

The old man came over and pointed at the old stone mortar and said,

"Look, this is what the treasure is!"

The old lady thought he was teasing her, and replied laughingly,

"You call a shabby stone mortar a treasure? You can have it if you like."

"Well! How can I take your treasure for free? Sell it to me and I'll have someone come and collect it."

The old man left, in the heavy snow, with a cheerful look on his face.

The old lady took a look at the old stone mortar and thought that it was too dirty for people to carry. So she removed the garbage from the mortar and put it into a dustpan. She then poured the garbage onto the roots of the eighteen old tea trees behind the house. Afterwards she brought a bucket of clean water from the *Longjing* village, washed the stone mortar to complete cleanliness, and poured the water used for washing the mortar onto the old tea tree roots as well.

As soon as she had cleaned the old stone mortar, the old man came back with his people. He couldn't help shouting when he came to the door,

"What! Where is my treasure? What! Where is my treasure?"

The old lady was confused and pointed at the old stone mortar,

"This... Isn't it standing right here?"

He stamped his feet,

"Well! Where on earth did you bring the things in the mortar? "

The old lady replied,

"I poured it onto the roots of the old tea trees behind the house."

The old man went out and walked around the house and understood what had happened. He couldn't help stamping his feet repeatedly,

"What a pity! What a pity! It was the aged garbage inside the old stone mortar that made it valuable! Since you've poured the garbage onto the roots of those trees, so be it!"

With this he left the house with his people.

Very soon, spring came again after the Spring Festival.

This year, a great many new, verdant buds burst out on the branches of the eighteen old tea trees behind the old lady's house. The tea leaves she picked from those trees were slender, delicate and fragrant.

When the neighbours saw how well the tea trees were growing, they cut down the bamboos, gathered in the crops, and grew new tea trees on the hills with cuttings from those eighteen tea trees. Over the years, tea trees near the *Longjing* village flourished. As time passed, tea trees grew all over the mountains and plains in the *Longjing* area.

Since the tea leaves produced in this area are slender, delicate, fragrant and extremely tasty, *Longjing* tea has become well-known.

Even today the tea farmers still regard those eighteen tea trees behind the old lady's house as the forefathers of *Longjing* tea.

【文化背景】【Cultural Notes】

▶ **老茶婆**：指从茶树上采下的老叶子制成的粗劣茶叶。

Old tea leaves of poor quality: It refers to poor-quality tea leaves, made of the grown-up leaves from tea trees.

▶ **灶洞**：中国古代的灶是在地上用泥土或砖石砌成的生火做饭的设备，中空，洞内放入草或木屑等燃料以烧火做饭。

The hollow inside kitchen range: Kitchen range in ancient China is made with earth or bricks on the ground to make a fire to cook meals. It is hollow so hay or bits of wood can be used as fuel to make a fire inside it.

▶ **石臼**：用石凿成的器具，从上部开一大孔，用于舂米、谷等物。

Stone mortar: A utensil made of stone with a big hole in the upper part. Rice or grains can be put in the hole and smashed into pieces with a pestle.

第三章
人物传说

Chapter III
Legends of People

西湖不可谓不美。可再美的山水,若没有历史和传说中的名人,也无异于失去灵魂的躯壳。杭州有别于其他城市之处,正在于众多历史人物纷纷走过这片土地,上至历朝皇帝,下到奸臣秦桧,还不乏诸多文人墨客。

West Lake boasts of natural sceneries. However, beautiful mountains and water without people in it, either historical or legendary, is like a body without a soul. *Hangzhou* is unique since so many people came and lived here, from emperors, the treacherous court official *Qin Hui*, to a large number of men of letters.

壹 ◎ 苏轼
Su Shi

【简介】

苏东坡(1037—1101)即苏轼,东坡居士为号,为北宋重要的文学家、诗人、画家、书法家、政治家,擅长诗、词、赋多种诗歌形式,迄今有2700多首诗歌以及800封书信流传下来。苏轼也曾是北宋朝政重要人物，曾联手司马光等人上书立言王安石新法之弊。从公元1060年至其后的二十年间，其在宦海沉浮，在多地担任地方要职。在杭州任职期间，苏轼率众筑起了跨西湖的人行长堤，该堤被命名为苏堤，含苏轼之姓，并沿用至今。

【Brief Introduction】

Su Dongpo (1037—1101) was also known as *Su Shi*; *Dongpo Jushi* was his pseudonym. *Su Shi* was a writer, poet, painter, calligrapher, and statesman in the Northern *Song* Dynasty. He excelled in different types of poetry, and around 2,700 of his poems have survived, along with 800 written letters. *Su Shi* was also an important figure in the Northern *Song* Dynasty politics. He aligned himself with *Sima Guang* and others against the New Policy advocated by *Wang Anshi*. Beginning in 1060 and throughout the following twenty years, *Su Shi* went through ups and downs in politics and held a variety of government positions throughout China. While working in *Hangzhou*, *Su Shi* was responsible for having a pedestrian causeway built across West Lake, which is named *Su* Causeway after him.

【传说读本】

北宋时候，苏东坡来杭州任**知州**时，发现西湖长久不治，湖泥淤塞，葑草芜蔓，于是就决定学唐朝诗人白居易，疏浚西湖，为杭州人做件好事。

疏浚西湖的告示张贴出来了，可苏东坡却被一件事难住了：疏浚出来的葑草湖泥堆放在何处呢？如果堆在西湖西岸，既妨碍交通，又污染环境；如果挑运到远处去，则费工费事。这事愁得苏东坡三天三夜饭也吃不香，觉也睡不稳。第四天，他决定到西湖四周走走，看看如何更好地处理这件事。

苏东坡带上随从，骑马先到北山栖霞岭。一看这里是通灵隐、天竺要道，堆放葑泥，显然不妥当。于是，想转到南屏山净慈寺去看看。他站在西泠渡口，正想上渡船，突然听到柳林深处传来一阵渔歌声："南山女，北山男，隔岸相望诉情难。天上**鹊桥**何时落？沿湖要走三十三。"

苏东坡一听，心中一阵高兴：这不是在向我献计献策吗？对，天上可架"鹊桥"，湖上难道不能修长堤？这样，既解决了湖上葑泥堆放场所，又方便了南北两岸交通，真是一举两得啊！

苏东坡高兴得喊了一声："好！再到湖对岸去看看。"这时，从柳林中飞出一条小船，船头站着一个青年渔民，身打躬，手作揖，对苏东坡说："小民在此等候大人多时，快请上船吧！"

苏东坡又惊又喜，问道："你何以知道我要来湖边？"那青年回答道："听说大人要疏浚西湖，自然要到湖边来亲自察看，因此特来恭候。"苏东坡说："好啊，那刚才的渔歌一定是你唱的了！"小青年笑笑说："是啊，这就是我们南北山小民的心愿啊！"

苏东坡乘上渔船，来到南山。柳林中又驶出一只小船，飞扬起一阵清脆的歌声："南山女，北山男，年龄大过二十三。两情相慕难诉说，牛郎织女把堤盼。"

苏东坡听了，哈哈大笑道："唱得好！南山女，北山男，让我在湖上筑一条长堤，成全你们的好姻缘吧！"

要在西湖上筑堤的消息不胫而走，南北山渔民、农民和城里市民都闻讯赶来，自愿出工出力。苏东坡说："谢谢乡亲们啦，连年旱涝成灾，你们生活困难。我已申报朝廷，其决定拨出一批大米，以工代赈。"

乡亲们听说有粮米可发，更加踊跃。人多力量大，从夏到秋，终于在北山南山间筑好了七段长堤，每两段之间留有一处水道，共六处水道。最初，由于银钱不足未能造桥。一个青年樵夫想出了个好主意，砍了一批树木，拼成木板，造了六顶吊桥。平时吊桥拉起，让里外湖的船只往来通行，早晚把吊桥放下，让两岸乡亲通行。又在长堤两边种上桃树和柳树，一来保护堤岸，二来春天桃红柳绿，为西湖添一美景。

人们为怀念苏东坡浚湖筑堤的政绩，就将这条南北长堤称为苏堤。

【English Version of the Original Story】

During the Northern *Song* Dynasty, when *Su Dongpo* came to work in *Hangzhou* as ***zhizhou*** (chief magistrate), he was astonished to find that West Lake was almost silted up and overgrown with rampant, marshy weeds. He then resolved to do a good deed for *Hangzhou* people—to have the lake dredged, as the *Tang* Dynasty poet *Bai Juyi* did before.

Soon the poster for dredging West Lake was put up. However one thing baffled *Su Dongpo*—where could the dredged silt and weeds be placed? If they were piled on the western bank of West Lake, it would not only hamper traffic, but also pollute the surrounding environment. If they were carried away to a distant place it would be time-consuming and need considerable manpower. Haunted by these thoughts, *Su Dongpo* could not eat or sleep well for three days. On the fourth day, he decided to take a walk around the lake to see if anything could be done to help tackle this problem.

Taking several of his entourage with him, *Su Dongpo* rode on horseback and arrived first at *Qixia* Hill in Mount North. This was soon found not suitable for placing the silt because it was a vital route leading to *Lingyin* Temple and *Tianzhu* Hill. Then, *Su* decided to take a look around *Jingci* Temple in *Nanping* Hill. As he was about to get on the boat at *Xiling* Ferry, he was distracted by the sweet sound of a folk song coming from the depths of the willow forest,

Girls in Mount South,
Boys in Mount North,
Separated by the lake.
Magpie Bridge, Magpie Bridge,
When do you cross over the lake?
Don't let us wait,
Thirty-three days is so long,
For one trip.

Hearing the melody, *Su Dongpo* felt a thrill of joy.

"Aha!" he thought. "It's passing on good advice to me? If Magpie Bridge could be built in the sky, why can't we build a causeway across the lake? If this idea could be put into action, it would not only solve the disposal of silt issue, but also facilitate traffic between the southern and northern banks. This will kill two birds with one stone!"

"Great! Let's check the opposite bank of the lake!" *Su Dongpo* shouted in delight. Just at that moment, a boat emerged from the willow forest with a young fisherman standing on it. He made a bow with his hands folded in front and said,

"My lord, I have been waiting here for you for a long time. Please get on the boat."

Both surprised and delighted, *Su* asked,

"How did you know that I would come here today?"

The young man replied,

"I heard that you are planning to have West Lake dredged, and I guessed that you would surely inspect the lake in person. That's why I'm here, waiting for you."

Su remarked,

"It must have been you who sang that lovely song!"

The young man smiled,

"Yes, the song just conveys the very wish of people living in Mount South and Mount North."

Su Dongpo boarded the boat and soon arrived at Mount South where another boat came out of the willow forest. Floating in the air was a cheerful singing voice,

> Girls in Mount South,
> Boys in Mount North,
> Older than twenty three.
> Two lovebirds, seldom meet;
> Building a causeway,
> Every day they plea.

Hearing the lyrics, *Su Dongpo* gave a hearty laugh and said,

"Fantastic! Girls in Mount South, boys in Mount North, let me build a long causeway and bring you a happy marriage."

News that a causeway would be constructed across West Lake spread like wildfire. The fishermen and farmers living in Mount South and Mount North, as well as the town residents, came from all directions to volunteer for the construction work. *Su Dongpo* then said,

"Thank you so much! You have been living a tough life due to years of devastating floods and droughts. I have reported it to the royal court which has decided to assign you a batch of rice as the reward for your hard work."

Learning that the government would distribute rice to them, people showed even more enthusiasm. Many hands make light work. From that summer and through the autumn, a causeway, made up of seven disconnected sections, was built between Mount South and Mount North. Each part was separated from the next by a water gap—six water gaps in total. At first, the construction of the bridges was delayed due to a shortage of funds. Luckily, a young woodman came up with a brilliant idea and solved the problem—some trees were cut down and sawn into suitable boards. Then six hanging bridges were made out of these boards. In the daytime, these wooden bridges were packed away so that boats could pass freely between the inner and outer lake. In the early morning and in the evening, the bridges were put up to enable residents living on both sides of the lake to have an easy passage across. Also peach trees and willows were planted on both sides of the causeway, which not only sheltered the causeway, but also made West Lake more beautiful, especially in spring, when the peach trees were in bloom and the willows were turning green.

To commemorate *Su Dongpo's* achievements in dredging West Lake and constructing the causeway, people named the long north-south causeway *Su* Causeway.

【文化背景】【Cultural Notes】

▶ **知州**:中国古代官名。两宋以朝臣充任各州长官,称"权知某军州事",简称知州。知州是明、清正式官名,为各州行政长官。知州根据其所管辖区域大小可相当于现在的市长或省长。

Zhizhou: *Zhizhou* was an official title in the *Ming* and *Qing* Dynasties. A *zhizhou* was usually in charge of executive affairs of a region, and it could correspond to the modern-day magistrate of a city or a province, depending on the size of the area the official governed.

▶ **鹊桥**:传说,牛郎和织女被银河隔开,只允许每年的农历七月初七相见。为了让牛郎和织女能顺利相会,各地的喜鹊就会飞过来用身体紧贴着搭成一座桥,此桥就叫作鹊桥。牛郎和织女便在这鹊桥上相会。

Magpie Bridge: According to legend, the Cowherd and the Weaving Maid are separated by the Milky Way, and they are only allowed to see each other on the 7th day of the 7th lunar month each year (Double Seventh). In order to help the couple get together on that day, magpies would fly over from far and wide and press their bodies against each other to build a bridge where the Cowherd and the Weaving Maid could meet. The bridge is thus called Magpie Bridge.

贰 ◎ 岳飞

Yue Fei

【简介】

岳飞(1103—1142)是南宋最杰出的将领。公元12世纪,他率领南宋军队奋起抗击女真族统领的金朝军队。在宋金议和过程中,岳飞为奸臣秦桧诬陷,被捕入狱,最终在1142年因捏造的罪名,与长子岳云和部将张宪一起被南宋政府所杀害。岳飞是中国人心目中忠诚刚烈的化身。

【Brief Introduction】

Yue Fei (1103—1142) was the most prominent military general in the Southern *Song* Dynasty. He is best known for leading Southern *Song* forces to fight bravely against the *Nuzhen*-ruled *Jin* army in the 12th century. During the peace negotiations between the *Song* and *Jin* Dynasties, *Yue Fei* was framed by the treacherous minister *Qin Hui* and imprisoned. In 1142, *Yue Fei*, together with his oldest son *Yue Yun* and his subordinate *Zhang Xian*, was executed by the Southern *Song* government on fabricated charges. He has been widely regarded as an epitome of loyalty by Chinese people.

【传说读本】

杭州西湖**岳庙**精忠园的**照壁**上，刻着四个朱红色斗大的字“精忠報國”。仔细一看，那“國”字还少了一点。说起来，这里面还有一个慷慨激昂的故事。

北宋末年，**完颜宗弼**，中国北方金朝著名将领，率领大兵大举入侵中原，占领了京城开封。金兵烧杀抢夺，京城十室九空，连徽宗、钦宗二帝也当了俘虏。中原百姓忍无可忍，纷纷从军，欲与金兵决一死战，以雪**靖康之耻**。

岳飞在国难当头时，立志从军杀敌。他母亲忠厚慈祥，能识大体，教育岳飞从小熟读经史。家贫无钱买读书用品，她不惜卖了首饰，替岳飞买书籍纸笔；无钱买烛，又叫岳飞砍柴烧火，夜里借火光照明苦读。这次，岳飞要去投军，她特地在中堂摆下香案，焚香点烛，拜过天地祖宗，叫岳飞跪下。

岳飞听从母命，跪下问道：“孩儿明日从军，娘亲有何吩咐？”

岳母回答道：“为娘愿你此去英勇杀敌，做个忠臣良将。今日要在你背上刺几个字，以表为娘教儿一片苦心。”

岳飞十分孝顺，忙将上衣脱下，露出背脊，说：“娘亲说得有理，就与孩儿刺字吧！”

岳母提起笔来，先在岳飞背上写上四字，然后，将绣花针拿在手中，在他背上一刺，只见岳飞背上肌肉一抖，忙停针问道：“我儿疼吗？”

岳飞回答道：“娘亲刺也不曾刺，孩儿怎么会疼？”

岳母禁不住流下泪水，道：“我儿！你怕为娘手软，所以说不疼。”说罢，咬紧牙关，一针一针刺上四个字。刺完之后，涂上墨醋，永不褪色。

岳母取过铜镜，问岳飞道：“我儿，你看，为娘给你刺下什么字？”

岳飞对铜镜一照，只见背上闪烁着乌黑精亮的四个字“精忠報國”。但是仔细一看，“國”字少了一点，不禁问道：“娘亲，你刺的“精忠報國”四字，孩儿至死不忘。但不知为何“國”字少了一点？”

岳母听了，拭泪回答道：“只因金兵入侵，京城陷落，二帝被掳，如今国家无主啊！我儿一定要永记靖康之耻，早日恢复中原。”

岳飞点头回答：“母亲教导，孩儿终身铭记在心。”

岳飞投军后，牢牢记住背上“精忠報國”四字，带领岳家军奋起抗击金兵，所向披靡，一直把敌军逼到朱仙镇，正准备直捣**黄龙府**，谁知奸臣秦桧在昏君**赵构**面前挑拨说：“岳飞如将二帝迎还中原，将置皇上于何地。”他得到昏君的默许，将岳飞召回杭州，打入死牢。

为对外有个说法,秦桧捏造岳飞有私通**南蛮**、欺挟天子、朋比结党、克扣军粮、虚冒战功等十大罪状,并责令**大理寺**正卿周三畏严刑逼供岳飞。

岳飞在大理寺脱下衣服,准备受刑,露出背上的"精忠報國"四字。周三畏一见,大为钦佩,只是对"國"字少一点不解。岳飞就将岳母刺字以及自己的一片报国忠心说与周三畏。周三畏叹道:"这一点少得好!"他不忍屈害忠良,但又惧怕秦桧权势,只得挂印出走。

奸贼秦桧又让他的一死党充任大理寺正卿,严刑威逼岳飞招认十大罪状。他们在用刑时,发现岳飞背上"精忠報國"四个大字。阴险毒辣的秦桧一见"國"字少了一点,嘿嘿冷笑两声,说道:"岳飞之罪足矣!"

秦桧偷偷地跑到宫里,对昏君赵构说:"陛下,岳飞身为主帅,目无皇上。他背上刺了'精忠報國'四个字,但'國'字少了一点,就是说当今国家无主,一心迎接二帝还朝!"

秦桧这一番话,可刺到昏君赵构的心病了。因为赵构生怕父兄还朝,令他失去皇帝宝座。但是他又不敢加罪岳飞,只好佯装有病,不理朝政,一切大事任凭秦桧代行。秦桧也了解昏君心意,趁机以"**莫须有**"罪名将岳飞缢死在大理寺风波亭。

直到现在,少一点的"精忠報國"四个字,还赫然刻在杭州岳飞精忠园照壁上,显示出英雄岳飞的一片丹心。

【English Version of the Original Story】

The **screen wall** of *Jingzhong* Residence of ***Yue Fei's*** **Mausoleum** is inscribed with four big scarlet Chinese characters "精忠報國" (*jing zhong bao guo*, means "repay the country with supreme loyalty"). It is noticeable that a dot stroke "、" is missing from the upper right part of the Chinese character "國" (*guo*, means country). As a matter of fact, there is a touching and inspiring story behind the lost dot stroke.

During the last years of the Northern *Song* Dynasty, ***Wanyan Zongbi***, a well-known general of the *Jin* Dynasty in northern China, led his grand army and launched a large-scale invasion into China's Central Plains. After the army took the capital city, *Kaifeng*, its soldiers conducted brutal burning, killing and looting, and soon most parts of the city were robbed of even the last pin. Worse still, Emperor *Huizong* and Emperor *Qinzong* were taken captive. Driven beyond forbearance, the indignant men in the Central Plains all volunteered to join the army. They determined to fight to the death to wipe out **the Humiliation of *Jingkang***.

Faced with the national crisis, *Yue Fei* resolved to join the army and fight the invading enemy. *Yue Fei*'s mother, Lady *Yue*, was an honest, kind and sensible lady. She encouraged *Yue Fei*, from his youth, to read as many classics and historical records as he could. She had no money to buy educational materials, so she sold her jewelry to buy her son books, writing brushes and paper. She had no money to buy candles, so she told *Yue Fei* to cut firewood to make a fire so that it could provide light for his evening reading. Learning that her beloved son had decided to join the army, she deliberately set the incense burner table in the central living room, lit incense sticks and candles, said prayers to the gods and late forefathers, and then asked her son to kneel down.

Yue Fei followed his mother's words; he fell to his knees and said,

"I will join the army tomorrow. Is there anything Mother wants to remind me of?"

"As your mother, I hope that you will fight bravely in the battle field and be a loyal and competent soldier. Today, I will tattoo several words on your back as a reminder of my high expectations of you."

Yue Fei was a filial son. He took off his coat right away and turned his back to his mother, saying,

"What Mother said does make sense, please do it."

Lady *Yue* picked up the writing brush and first wrote four Chinese characters on *Yue Fei*'s back. Then, with an embroidery needle in one hand, she gave her son's back a prick, and *Yue Fei*'s back muscles twitched slightly. Seeing that, Lady *Yue* put down the needle and asked,

"Son, does it hurt?"

"Mother hasn't really done anything; how can it hurt?" replied *Yue Fei*.

Tears welled up in Lady *Yue*'s eyes. She said,

"Son, you said it didn't hurt because you were afraid that if you said it did, I would not have the heart to tattoo your back."

With these words, she clenched her teeth, held the needle firmly, and one prick after another; she finished four characters on her son's back. Then, she carefully applied ink mixed with vinegar to the characters so that they would never fade.

Lady *Yue* took a copper mirror, showed it to *Yue Fei* and said,

"Son, take a look at the characters I have tattooed on your back."

Yue Fei looked into the mirror and saw four shiny black Chinese characters "精忠報國". Looking closer, he found that a dot stroke was missing from "國". Confused, he asked,

"Mother, the four characters you tattooed on my back will be kept in my heart for ever, but why is a dot missing from '國'?"

With tears in her eyes, Lady *Yue* replied,

"Due to the invasion of the *Jin* army, our capital city fell into their hands, and our two emperors are also held captive. Hence, the missing dot symbolizes the absence of our leaders. We should never ever forget the Humiliation of *Jingkang* and must do our utmost to recover the lost Central Plains."

Yue Fei nodded his head and replied,

"I will bear Mother's teachings in mind forever."

Yue Fei joined the army, with the four characters in his heart and on his back. He led the army of the *Yue* family and fought bravely against the *Jin* army. *Yue Fei* mowed down the enemy army and soon cornered them at *Zhuxian* Township. As he was about to press forward to ***Huanglongfu***, the capital city of the enemy, something unexpected happened. The treacherous court official, *Qin Hui*, sought to alienate *Yue Fei* from the fatuous and self-indulgent Emperor *Zhao Gou*[6]; *Qin Hui* told the emperor that if *Yue Fei* brought the two previous emperors back to the Central Plains, *Zhao Gou*'s power would surely be at risk. With the tacit permission of the emperor, *Qin Hui* then recalled *Yue Fei* to *Hangzhou* and put him in the death cell.

To justify the arrest, *Qin Hui* also trumped up ten charges including collaborating with **Southern Barbarians**, deceiving and threatening the emperor, forming a clique for evil purposes, embezzling military grain, and claiming credit for false military exploits. *Qin Hui* also ordered *Zhou Sanwei*, head of the ***Dali* Temple**, to torture a confession out of *Yue Fei*.

At the *Dali* Temple, *Yue Fei* took off his coat, showed his tattooed back, and was ready to endure the torture. Seeing the four characters, *Zhou Sanwei* expressed his great admiration, as well as his confusion as to why a dot was missing from the character "國". *Yue Fei* then told *Zhou Sanwei* how his mother had tattooed the four characters, and how he had resolved to devote himself to his country. *Zhou Sanwei* was deeply touched.

"What a wonderful missing dot!" he sighed.

Zhou Sanwei could not bear to put an honest man to torture, but intimidated by *Qin Hui*'s power and influence, he eventually chose to flee from his post.

Qin Hui then appointed one of his loyal followers as the head of *Dali* Temple, and instructed him to torture *Yue Fei* into confessing the ten crimes. As the two evil men were to going to torture *Yue Fei*, they found the four characters on *Yue Fei*'s back. Spotting the missing dot, the dark, crafty *Qin Hui* sneered,

"This is more than enough to charge *Yue Fei*!"

*Qin Hu*i sneaked into the royal court.

"Your Majesty," he said to the emperor, "although he is a general, *Yue Fei* acts with utter disregard for your supreme power, and he has four characters'精忠報國' tattooed on his back, with a dot missing from '國'. Clearly he wants to use the missing dot to suggest that our country now has no emperor, and, it is also obvious, that he is plotting to help the two former emperors come back to the imperial court and regain their thrones."

These very words touched *Zhao Gou*'s sore point, for the fatuous emperor had always feared that the previous two emperors, his father and his elder brother, would come back and this would make him lose his throne. He did not dare to convict *Yue Fei* without proper charges. Therefore, he began to pretend to be ill and left all the major national affairs entirely to the discretion of *Qin Hui*. Knowing exactly what the emperor was thinking, *Qin Hui* took advantage and hanged *Yue Fei* at *Fengbo* Pavilion of *Dali*

Temple on the charge of committing a crime of **maybe there is** (a fabricated charge).

Until now, the four characters minus one dot "精忠報國" are still distinctly inscribed on the screen wall of *Yue Fei*'s *Jingzhong* Residence in *Hangzhou*. It quietly reminds people of *Yue Fei*—a great hero with a loyal heart.

【文化背景】【Cultural Notes】

▶ **岳庙**:又称岳王庙、岳坟。位于西湖西北角、杭州北山路上,是历代纪念英雄岳飞的场所。始建于南宋嘉定十四年(1221),明景泰年间改称"忠烈庙"。岳庙经历了元、明、清、民国时期的时兴时废,代代相传保存至今。

***Yue Fei's* Mausoleum**: *Yue Fei's* Mausoleum (also known as *Yuewang* Temple or *Yue Fei*'s Tomb) is located on *Beishan* Road, northwest of West Lake in *Hangzhou*. It's a historical site where people, through the ages, commemorate the hero *Yue Fei*. The mausoleum was first built in 1221, the 14th year of *Jiading* era in the Southern *Song* Dynasty. During the *Jingtai* era in the *Ming* Dynasty, it was renamed *Zhonglie* Temple (*zhong lie miao*, literally "temple of a loyal martyr"). Throughout the *Yuan*, *Ming*, *Qing* Dynasties and the period of the Republic of China, *Yue Fei's* Mausoleum was damaged and restored for several times and has been preserved until the present day.

▶ **照壁**:照壁是中国传统建筑中特有的部分,常用来遮挡入口的大门,明朝时较常见。它可以设置在它所庇护的门的里面或外面。据说鬼只走直线不会转弯,修上照壁后就可以断鬼的来路。

Screen wall: A screen wall is a unique part of Chinese traditional architecture. It is generally used to shield an entrance gate and was common in the *Ming* Dynasty. It can be positioned either on the outside or the inside of the gate it is protecting. A screen wall is tied to the belief that evil spirits can only walk in straight lines and cannot move around corners. The wall blocks them from going through the gate which it shields.

▶ **完颜宗弼**:完颜宗弼又名金兀术,女真族,金太祖第四子,在中国北方辅佐建立金朝(1115—1234),为历史名将。

Wanyan Zongbi: *Wanyan Zongbi*, also known as *Jin Wushu*, the *nüzhen* nationality, was the fourth son of Emperor *Jin Taizu* and a well-known general in history who helped establish the *Jin* Dynasty (1115—1234) in northern China.

▶ **靖康之耻**:靖康之耻又称为靖康事件,发生于北宋年间的1127年。当时入侵的金军攻克了北宋都城汴京(今河南开封),俘虏了宋钦宗、宋徽宗,以及大量皇族成员。靖康事件结束了当时的北宋王朝,北宋的剩余皇室成员被迫逃离,在临安(今杭州)建都,设立了新政府,即南宋。这一事件发生在南宋的宋钦宗统治的靖康年间,故得名。

The Humiliation of *Jingkang*: The Humiliation of *Jingkang*, also called *Jingkang* Incident, took place in 1127 during the Northern *Song* Dynasty, when the invading soldiers of the *Jin* army besieged and sacked *Bianjing* (the present day *Kaifeng*, the capital of *Henan* Province), the capital of the Northern *Song* Dynasty. The *Jin* forces abducted Emperor *Qinzong* and his father Emperor *Huizong*, along with many members of the imperial court. This ended the era known as the Northern *Song* Dynasty. The rest of the imperial family was forced to flee and establish a new government, now known as the Southern *Song* Dynasty, at *Lin'an* (the present day *Hangzhou*), which became capital of the Southern *Song* Dynasty. This incident was so named because it happened during the reign of Emperor *Qinzong* of the Sourthern *Song* Dynasty, whose reign title was "*Jingkang*".

▶ **黄龙府**:黄龙府位于如今中国东北吉林省农安县县城内,曾为辽金两代军事重镇和政治经济中心,是中国历史名城之一。公元1127年,金兵俘虏宋朝徽、钦二帝,曾将他们一度囚禁于此。

Huanglongfu: *Huanglongfu* is a well-known historic city, nowadays located in northeast China's *Nong'an* County, *Jilin* Province. It was once a financial, political and military center in the *Liao* and *Jin* Dynasties. In

1127, the *Jin* forces captured the two emperors of the Northern *Song* Dynasty, *Huizong* and *Qinzong*, and imprisoned them there.

▶ **赵构:** 赵构也被称作宋高宗,宋朝第十位皇帝,从 1127 年至 1162 年共在位 35 年。赵构是宋徽宗第九子,宋钦宗之弟。在靖康事变中,金军占领北宋都城汴京,于是赵构南逃建都成为南宋第一任皇帝。赵构政治昏庸,但精于书法擅诗作,传世墨迹有《草书洛神赋》等。

***Zhao Gou*:** *Zhao Gou*, also known as Emperor *Gaozong* of *Song*, was the tenth emperor of the *Song* Dynasties. He reigned for 35 years from 1127 to 1162. *Zhao Gou* was also the 9th son of Emperor *Huizong* and the younger brother of Emperor *Qinzong*. During the *Jingkang* Incident, the *Jin* forces occupied *Bianjing*, the capital of the Northern *Song* Dynasty. *Zhao Gou* then fled south and established what is now known as the Southern *Song* Dynasty and became its first emperor. Although *Zhao Gou* was an incompetent emperor, he excelled at calligraphy and poetry. Among his surviving works is *Cursive Script of an Ode to The River Goddess*.

▶ **南蛮:** 南蛮源于中国最古老的原生民族。他们是世界稻作文明、海洋文明的创造者之一,也是陶器、漆器等传统手工艺品的发明者之一。现今南方的少数民族大多由南蛮民族演变而来。

Southern Barbarians: The Southern Barbarians descended from the most ancient aboriginal people in China. They were the creators of a rice civilization and a marine civilization, as well as the inventors of many traditional handicrafts such as pottery and lacquer products. Many southern minority groups of today have evolved from the Southern Barbarians.

▶ **大理寺:** 大理寺是封建中国的官署名。相当于现今的最高法院,掌刑狱案件,其长官名为大理寺卿,在中国封建王朝很长一段时间内位九卿之列。

***Dali* Temple:** *Dali* Temple was the name of a government department in feudal China. It was responsible for ruling on criminal cases, roughly corresponding to the supreme court of the present day. The person in charge of this department was called *qin* of *Dali* temple that is, the head of *Dali* Temple, which was one of the nine most important titles of high-ranking officials in the imperial court of feudal China for a long time.

▶ **莫须有**:据传,当被问及岳飞究竟犯了什么罪时,秦桧答道:"尽管不确定岳飞是否做过背叛朝廷的事,但莫须有。""莫须有"一词意为"也许有",已经进入中文词条,意为捏造出来的指控。与该词条意义相近,用以描述当权者滥用权力的另一中文词条表述为"欲加之罪,何患无辞"。

"**Maybe there is**": Legend has it that when asked what crime *Yue Fei* had committed, *Qin Hui* replied, "Though it isn't sure whether there is something that he did to betray the royal court, maybe there is." The term "maybe there is" (*mo xu you*) has entered the Chinese language as an expression to refer to fabricated charges. Another famous Chinese statement with similar connotations, which is used to describe the abuse of power by the authorities, is: "Crimes can always be found to fit the punishment" (*yu jia zhi zui, he huan wu ci*).

叁 ◎ 秦桧
Qin Hui

【简介】

秦桧(1090—1155),宋朝两任宰相,前后在位 19 年,为宋高宗赵构宠臣。其迫害英雄岳飞,利用对朝廷监察权的控制及高宗的宠信,陷害忠臣与异己,压制主战派,力主和议,实行向金进贡纳币政策,为中国历史上罪行滔天、臭名昭著的奸相。

【Brief Introduction】

Qin Hui (1090—1155) was appointed twice as Chancellor of the *Song* Dynasties. He was in office for 19 years, being one of the minions of Emperor

Gaozong, *Zhao Gou*. *Qin Hui* is widely regarded as a traitor for his part in the persecution and execution of the hero *Yue Fei*. Through using his control over imperial censorship and, with the favour and trust he gained from the emperor, he persecuted loyal officials and political opponents, suppressed war hawks, insisted on reconciliation talks, and carried out the policy of paying tribute to the *Jin* Dynasty. The vicious crimes *Qin* committed have caused him to be remembered as a notorious, evil minister in Chinese history.

【传说读本】

西湖边有座岳坟。岳坟前跪着四个铁铸的人像,其中两个就是害死岳飞的秦桧夫妇。

早先,杭州城里来了一个新上任的**抚台**,那人也姓秦,是秦桧的后代。抚台上任不久,便带着手下人去逛西湖。他来到岳坟,看见自己的老祖宗跪在坟前,忙用衣袖把脸遮住,倒退了出来。

抚台回到衙门,坐不安,立不宁,便叫**师爷**来商量,想把铁像搬掉。师爷捋捋胡须,想一想说:“如果明着搬吧,老百姓一定不肯,说不定还会闹出事来。我看,不如在黑夜里把这对铁像丢进西湖里去,这么大的西湖,铁像沉在湖底,便是把水抽干了也找不到的。”

抚台说,“妙!妙!”,当夜便派人把铁像丢进湖里去了。

哪知第二天天刚亮就出现了一件怪事——西湖里的水变臭啦,臭气冲天,熏得来往行人都捂住鼻子,个个想呕吐呢。

不知是谁,发觉岳坟前的铁像少掉两个,就大声嚷起来:“大家来看啊!两个铁像不见了,一定是有人把它们丢进西湖里了,要不然,湖水怎么会发臭呢?”

老百姓很快知道了两个铁像丢失的事,就涌到衙门,要求拿办丢掉铁像的坏蛋。抚台还睡在床上,只听门外人声混杂,便起来查问。手下人告诉了情由,抚台做贼心虚,便叫人传出话去,说是自己生病了。

老百姓哪里肯走,人越聚越多,把抚台衙门前的石狮子都快挤倒了。抚台恐怕这样下去要出事情,便硬着头皮出来见焦躁的人群。他说:“这,这都是谣言,大家千万不可轻信,铁像怎么可能弄臭湖水呢?”

老百姓都争着说:“是不是谣言,你到西湖边看看就知道了。”说着,便围拢起来,一定要拉他走。

抚台只得按着老百姓的要求,坐上他的八抬大轿向西湖边去。离湖边还有好多路呢,一股恶臭,就直向轿门冲来。

轿到岸边,抚台从轿帘缝里往外一张望,只见外面密密麻麻全是人,他的心突突直跳,于是就慢慢地走出轿门,干咳了几声,说道:"湖水一时发臭,也是常情,你们不必大惊小怪。依我看,这事与铁像无关。"

这时,人群里有人吼起来:"你是秦桧什么人?居然敢袒护坏蛋!"

抚台一时不知怎样回答。他定了定神,安慰自己道:"莫慌!铁像已沉在湖底,没人找得到的。"想到这里,便神气起来,硬着嘴说:"你们不要胡闹!如果有人真从湖里捞出铁像,本官甘愿辞职请罪!"

抚台的嘴巴刚闭拢,墨黑的湖水一下子变得清澈见底。从湖底竟然慢慢浮起一对铁像,好像有人托着似的,直向抚台飘来。

抚台吓得脸色像黄纸,一面发着抖,一面钻进轿子,赶快逃到衙门里躲起来,好久好久不敢露面。铁像漂到湖边,老百姓把它们打捞上来,重新搬到岳坟前让它们按原样跪着。

第二年春天,抚台偷偷地到岳坟来凭吊。想想去年发生的事情,真是懊悔死了,于是就写下了一副对联:"人从宋后少名桧;我到坟前愧姓秦"。

【English Version of the Original Story】

By West Lake lies a historic site called *Yue Fei*'s Tomb. In front of it are four iron human-shaped sculpture, all in a kneeling position, and two of the four sculptures are the notorious *Qin Hui* and his wife, who plotted the death of *Yue Fei*.

In the past, a man was appointed as ***futai*** (governor) of *Hangzhou*; he also had the surname *Qin*, since he was a decedent of *Qin Hui*. Shortly after he took office, he took some of his subordinates to visit West Lake. When he arrived at *Yue Fei*'s Tomb and saw the sculptures of his forefathers kneeling in front of the tomb, he felt so ashamed that he immediately covered his face with his sleeve and slipped away.

The governor returned to the *yamen*, quite restless and anxious. Then, he called his ***shiye*** (private advisor) over and consulted with him about how to remove the two sculptures. The *shiye* stroked his beard, thought for a while and said,

"If we remove them openly, the local people will surely object and even make trouble. In my view, we might as well throw the pair of sculptures into West Lake at night. In such a big lake, once the sculptures sink to the bottom of the lake, they could never be recovered; even if the lake were drained."

"Good idea! Good idea!" said the governor in approval.

That night, he sent someone to throw the two sculptures into the lake.

Just after daybreak the next morning, something strange happened. Suddenly all water in West Lake began to stink. The smell was so disgusting that passers-by covered their noses and felt like vomiting.

Someone then noticed that the two sculptures in front of *Yue Fei*'s Tomb were missing, and he cried out,

"Come here, come here! The two sculptures are gone. Someone must have thrown them into the lake; if not, how could the water in the lake give out such an awful smell?"

Soon all the people learned that the two sculptures were missing. They swarmed to the *yamen*, demanding that the culprit be punished. The governor was still in bed at that moment. Hearing the noise, he got up to check what was going on. His subordinates then told him what had happened. The governor felt so guilty and uneasy that he asked someone to tell the people outside that he was sick.

People were unwilling to leave. The crowd got bigger and bigger, and the stone lion in front of the *yamen* was nearly knocked over. Fearing that the situation might get out of control, the governor reluctantly came out to meet the restless crowd.

"It's—it's all rumor. Please, d—don't fall for it! How could iron sculptures make the water s—stink?" he stuttered.

"Just go and check West Lake for yourself, and you will find out whether it's a rumor or not!" the crowd shouted.

With these words, people gathered together and insisted that the governor go with them.

The governor had to do as the people asked; he got into his big sedan chair carried by eight people and headed for West Lake. While they were still a long way off from West Lake, a horrible stench wafted through the sedam chair's door.

As the sedan chair got to the bank, the governor peeped through its curtain and saw many people outside, and his heart began to pound fast. Slowly getting out of the sedan chair, he cleared his throat and said,

"It's quite common for the lake to stink occasionally. Don't make a fuss about it. As I see it, it has nothing to do with the missing sculptures."

"What on earth is the relationship between you and *Qin Hui*? How dare you defend such a bad guy?" yelled someone in the crowd.

The governor was speechless for a moment. He composed himself a little and tried to reassure himself,

"Don't panic. The iron sculptures have sunk to the bottom of the lake, and no one could recover them."

With these thoughts, he picked up his spirits and responded boldly,

"Don't make trouble! If any of you could recover the missing sculptures from the lake, I will resign and deserve to be punished!"

The moment the governor closed his mouth, the black water instantly became crystal clear. A pair of iron sculptures slowly rose up from the bottom of the lake and as if invisible hands held them, floated towards the governor.

The governor's face turned pale with fright. Shuddering, he crawled into the sedan chair and fled to his *yamen*, where he hid himself and had no courage to show himself for a long time. As for the two missing sculptures, they drifted to the edge of the lake. The people got them out of the water and moved them back to *Yue Fei*'s Tomb where they were replaced; kneeling in the same position as before.

The next spring, the governor paid a secret visit to *Yue Fei*'s Tomb. Thinking of what happened the previous year, he was full of regret. He wrote a couplet,

> After the *Song* Dynasties, few would like to be named *Hui*;
> In front of the tomb, I feel ashamed of bearing the surname *Qin*.

【文化背景】【Cultural Notes】

▶ **抚台**:官名,中国明清时地方军政大员之一,又称巡抚。清代巡抚主管一省军政、民政,其官职等级相当于现今的省委书记。

Futai: also known as *xunfu*, was the title of a high-ranking government official in the *Qing* and *Ming* Dynasties of China. A *xunfu* in the *Qing* Dynasty had the power to govern the military and civil affairs of a province; similar to a modern-day governor of a province.

▶ **师爷**:师爷是中国封建社会官员的私人幕僚,参与地方衙门的法律、财政、秘书职责。

Shiye: A *shiye* was a private advisor to a ranking official in feudal China, attending to legal, fiscal or secretarial duties in a local *yamen*.

肆 ◎ 康熙

Emperor Kangxi

【简介】

康熙(1654—1722)是清朝第四位皇帝,其六周岁登基,在位六十一年,为中国历史上在位时间最长的皇帝。康熙被视作一代明君,他的统治给饱受战乱的中国带来了长期的繁荣稳定,开创了康乾盛世的大局面,并奠定了其后几代兴盛的根基。在康熙在位的末年,清帝国疆域逾1200万平方千米。

【Brief Introduction】

Kangxi (1654—1722) was the fourth emperor of the *Qing* Dynasty. He ascended to his throne at the age of six and his reign of 61 years makes him the longest-reigning Chinese emperor in history. *Kangxi* is also considered one of China's greatest emperors. His reign brought about long-term stability and relative wealth after years of wars and chaos. *Kangxi* initiated the period known as the Prosperous Era of *Kangxi* and *Qianlong*, which lasted for generations after his own lifetime. By the end of his reign, the *Qing* Empire covered an area of more than 12 million square kilometres.

【传说读本】

康熙皇帝下江南,来到了杭州。他在西湖四周到处游山玩水,吟诗题字,自称是个风雅的皇帝。

一天,有传他要到**灵隐寺**来耍子儿了。灵隐寺里的老和尚得知消息,真是又惊又喜,连忙撞钟击鼓,把寺里三百多个和尚召集拢来。和尚们披起崭新的袈裟,手敲法器,嘴里念着"南无阿弥陀佛"。大家跟着老和尚,赶到一里路外的石莲亭把康熙皇帝接到灵隐寺来。

老和尚陪着康熙皇帝,在寺前寺后游玩一番。康熙皇帝见到灵隐有高高的山峰、清清的泉水,山上长满绿荫荫的树,地下开遍红艳艳的花,真是一个好地方呵!他心里一高兴,就吩咐人在寺里摆酒用膳,想多耍子儿一歇。皇帝摆酒席可热闹啦!吹的吹,弹的弹,唱的唱,一时间,这个佛门净地变成了帝王之家。康熙皇帝一手拈着山羊胡须,一手捧着酒盏,又灌**黄汤**又吟诗。

老和尚早听说过康熙皇帝喜欢吟诗题字。当他注意到皇帝心情不错,便悄悄地跑过去与跟随皇帝的杭州知府商量道:"大人老爷呀,我想求求皇上给我们山寺题一块匾额,你看能不能呀?"

杭州知府听了听,点点头说:"好哩,如果皇上给灵隐寺题了匾额,我杭州府也会很荣光啊!"

钱塘县官也接上来说:"瞧,皇上酒兴正浓呢,你这辰光去求他题匾,我看一定能答应。"

老和尚心里落了实,就壮壮胆子,走至康熙皇帝面前跪下去磕头,说道:"皇上呀,看在灵隐寺大菩萨的面上,替我们山寺题块匾额,也让我们风光风光吧!"

老和尚这一请求,正好挠着了康熙皇帝的痒处。他点了点头,忙吩咐手下人摆好纸笔,抓起笔"唰唰"几下,就写了一个歪歪斜斜的"雨"字。那辰光,他差不多快喝醉啦,手腕有点发颤,落笔又太快了些。这个"雨"字竟占了大半张纸!"靈隱寺"的"靈"字,按老写法,"雨"字在上,中间三个"口","巫"字在下,即“靈”。现在只剩下这一点点位置,随你怎样也摆不下一个整个“靈”字了。重新写一个吧,那多么丢脸呀！康熙皇帝一只手抓着笔,一只手不住地拈他那撮山羊胡须,可是一点办法也没有。围在旁边的官儿们,明知道康熙皇帝下不了台,但是谁也不敢明说,只有站在旁边干着急。

这时,有个名叫高江村的官员想出了一个办法,他在自己手掌心写了“雲林”两个字,然后装作去磨墨的样子,挨近康熙皇帝身边,偷偷地朝着康熙皇帝摊开手掌。康熙皇帝一看到这两字,欢喜得连酒也醒了一半！哎呀,这真是救命菩萨呢！于是就连忙在雨字下写上云字(雨和云构成“雲”字),并写完剩下的“林禅寺”三个大字。写完,把手一扬,将毛笔抛出老远。

老和尚过来张望,不对呀！“靈隱寺”怎么写成“雲林禅寺”呢？他也不看看风色,就结结巴巴地问:“我们这里叫作‘靈隱寺’,不叫‘雲林禅寺’呀！是不是皇上落笔错啦?”

康熙皇帝听了,脸一沉,喝道:“放屁!”

老和尚哪里还敢再开口,只好恭恭敬敬地立在旁边了。

康熙皇帝回过头来,问官儿们:“这地方天上有云(雲),地下有林,你们说说,把它叫作‘雲林禅寺’好不好?”

“好啊,皇上圣明!”

听官儿们七嘴八舌地奉承他,康熙皇帝乐得哈哈大笑,便吩咐快把匾额雕起来。

皇帝一句话,官儿们就忙开啦。他们一面叫人将灵隐寺原来的匾额换下来,一面找来雕花匠,把皇帝刚写的“雲林禅寺”四个大字雕在红木匾上,贴金底,漆黑字,边上镶了精美的二龙戏珠,当场挂到山门正中。

从此以后,灵隐寺就挂着稀奇古怪的“雲林禅寺”大匾额。但是,杭州的老百姓并没有把它当回事,尽管“雲林禅寺”这块匾额一直挂了三百年,大家却仍然称呼它为“灵隐寺”。

【English Version of the Original Story】

Emperor *Kangxi* went on his southern inspection tour and arrived in *Hangzhou*. During his stay, he visited many enchanting scenic spots around West Lake, composed poems and wrote inscriptions, calling himself an emperor of good taste.

One day, word came that Emperor *Kangxi* was going to visit ***Lingyin***

Temple. The old monk at the temple was very excited and delighted at the news. He struck chimes and beat drums, and soon assembled more than three hundred monks in the temple. Then, dressed in brand-new Buddhist robes, hands stroking the wooden clappers, mouths murmuring the Buddhist prayer "Namo Amita Buddha", all the monks followed the old monk. They walked nearly half a kilometre to *Shilian* Pavilion where they met Emperor *Kangxi* and took him to *Lingyin* Temple.

Guided by the old monk, Emperor *Kangxi* made a tour around *Lingyin* Temple. From the front of the temple to its back, from the foot of the mountain to its top, the Emperor was totally fascinated by the beautiful scenes—high peaks, crystal brooks, luxuriant green trees, brilliant red mountain flowers—what a wonderful place! The emperor was so delighted that he ordered a feast to be held in the temple, for he wanted to stay there longer. The feast for the emperor was surely a fancy one; with some monks playing wind instruments, some playing string instruments, and some singing. In no time, the quiet temple turned into a bustling royal palace. With one hand stroking his beard and the other hand holding the wine glass, the emperor drank "**yellow soup**" and recited poems.

The old monk had heard, long before, that Emperor *Kangxi* was fond of composing poems and writing inscriptions. Noticing that the emperor was in a good mood, he quietly came beside one in the emperor's entourage, the magistrate of *Hangzhou* Prefecture, and consulted him,

"My lord, I want to beg His Majesty to inscribe a plaque for our temple. What do you say?"

"Good idea! It will also be a great honour to my *Hangzhou* official residence if His Majesty agrees to inscribe the plaque at *Lingyin* Temple," said the magistrate, nodding his head in approval.

The magistrate of *Qiantan*g County then added,

"Look, the wine has put His Majesty in high spirits, and I'm sure he will consent if you ask him right now."

Hearing these words, the old monk felt some relief; he plucked up his courage, went over to the emperor, knelt down, kowtowed to the emperor and said,

"Your Majesty, for the Buddha's sake, would you do us the honour of inscribing a plaque for our temple so that we can have something to boast about?"

The old monk's request hit exactly what the emperor was itching to do. Emperor *Kangxi* nodded his head and immediately asked his subordinates to set the table with a writing brush and paper. With several strokes, a shaky Chinese character "雨" was finished. However, at that moment, the emperor was almost drunk—his wrist trembled slightly, and the strokes were done a little too fast. What he wrote on the paper was the character "雨" which occupied more than half of the paper! As a matter of fact, the first character "靈" of "靈隱寺"(*Lingyin* Temple), written in traditional Chinese, is made up of "雨" at the top, three "口" in the middle, and "巫" at the bottom—that is "靈". With "雨" taking too much space, the small space left on the paper was obviously not enough to accommodate the whole character "靈". Write a new one? No! Too embarrassing! With one hand holding the writing brush, and the other hand stroking his beard, Emperor *Kangxi* was at a complete loss as to what to do next. The nearby officials knew very well that the emperor was in a dilemma. They didn't dare to mention it directly and had no choice but to stand by, uneasy and anxious.

Just at the very moment, an official called *Gao Jiangcun* came up with an idea. He wrote the two characters "雲林" on his palm, and went near the emperor pretending to help with "rubbing the ink stone" (preparing ink for brush writing), and then he quietly spread his palm and showed the two characters to the emperor. Seeing the two characters, *Kangxi* was so thrilled and relieved that he almost sobered up, "Buddha has come to my rescue!"

He promptly put the writing brush to the paper and added the character "云" below the "雨" ("雨"and "云" make up the character "雲"), and then he finished the rest of the three characters "林禅寺". With everything done, he tossed the writing brush aside in joyful relief.

"Oh, no! Why is it that '靈隱寺' is written as '雲林禅寺'?" murmured the monk in confusion.

Without reading the emperor's face, the old monk stuttered to the emperor,

"Your Majesty, this place is called '靈隱寺', not '雲林禅寺'! Is it possible that you miswrote the words?"

"Nonsense!" said the emperor, an angry look on his face.

The old monk was not brave enough to say more. He stepped aside in a respectful manner. The emperor then turned around and said to his subordinates,

"It's a place with clouds (雲) in the sky and forests (林) on the ground. Isn't it a wonderful idea to name this place '雲林禅寺'?"

"Yes, Your Majesty is so amazing!"

Hearing the lively flattery, Emperor *Kangxi* burst into hearty laughter and ordered that the four characters be carved onto the plaque immediately.

One word from the emperor made every official on the scene very busy. Some asked servants to take down the previous plaque; some arranged a craftsman to carve the four big characters "雲林禅寺" onto a red wooden plaque. After that, the plague was lined with golden paper; the four carved Chinese characters were painted pitch black; and the wooden frame was decorated with delicate ornaments shaped like two dragons playing with a pearl. Everything went well, and then the new plaque was mounted at the center of the temple gate.

Ever since then, the big plaque with the odd inscription "雲林禅寺" (*Yunlin* Temple) has stayed there. However, people in *Hangzhou* have never taken it seriously. Three hundred years passed; people still call the temple *Lingyin* Temple.

【文化背景】【Cultural Notes】

▶ **灵隐寺**:灵隐寺位于杭州西北角，建于东晋咸和元年(326),至今约有一千七百年的历史,为杭州最早的名刹,也是中国佛教禅宗十大古刹之一。五代十国(907—978)为其鼎盛时刻,寺内共筑有九座多层建筑,十八个亭阁,七十二座大殿,以及供三千多僧人住的一千三百多间居室。新中国成立后,灵隐寺进行多次过大规模整修,于今矗立的是一片欣欣向荣的建筑群。

***Lingyin* Temple**: *Lingyin* Temple (or literally translated as "Temple of the Soul's Retreat") is located northwest of *Hangzhou*. The temple was established in the first year of *Xianhe* era in the Eastern *Jin* Dynasty (326). With a history of more than 1,700 years, it is one of the earliest renowned temples in *Hangzhou*, as well as one of the ten ancient Buddhist temples of the *Chan* sect in China. At its peak, during the Five Dynasties and Ten States periods (907—978), the temple boasted nine multi-storey buildings, 18 pavilions, 72 halls, and more than 1,300 dormitory rooms, which were inhabited by more than 3,000 monks. Since the establishment of the People's Republic of China, *Lingyin* Temple has been renovated repeatedly until it became the grand group of buildings which we can see today.

▶ **黄汤：**即黄酒，略带有贬义。

Yellow soup: It refers to yellow rice or millet wine. It is a term of abuse which is somewhat derogatory.

伍 ◎ 乾隆
Emperor *Qianlong*

【简介】

乾隆(1711—1799)是清朝的第六位皇帝，其 1735 年登基，1796 年退位。乾隆退位给其子嘉庆帝意在避免在位时间超过其祖父康熙大帝，为孝顺之举。尽管不在其位，至其 1799 年驾崩，乾隆还是最终的掌权者。乾隆执政早期国家昌隆兴盛，但在其执政末期清帝国也经历了内忧外患的困扰。

【Brief Introduction】

Qianlong (1711—1799) was the sixth emperor of the *Qing* Dynasty, officially reigning from 1735 to 1796. *Qianlong* abdicated in favour of his son, Emperor *Jiaqing*—a filial act in order not to reign longer than his grandfather, the great Emperor *Kangxi*. Despite his retirement, he retained ultimate power until his death in 1799. Although his early years witnessed the continuation of an era of prosperity in China, his final years saw troubles, both at home and abroad, converge on the *Qing* Empire.

【传说读本】

乾隆皇帝游江南,其实并不是真心游山玩水。他只怕江南百姓造反,特意借个游山玩水的名义,到江南来探听消息,察看虚实。

那时,杭州南屏山**净慈寺**有个和尚,叫"诋毁和尚"。这和尚不讲究诵经打坐,专喜欢议论天下大事,要讲便讲,要骂便骂,毫无顾忌。只因他讲得有理,骂得有趣,所以老百姓都喜欢亲近他。

乾隆皇帝到了杭州,听说有这么个和尚,心想:这老和尚取这么个怪名号,必定是个隐迹山林的明朝遗老,不守本分的人。我倒要去听听他到底"诋毁"些什么。于是,他便换上一身朴素蓝衫,拿一把描金纸扇,扮成秀才模样,前往净慈寺,一到,便指名要会会诋毁和尚。

诋毁和尚从寺里出来,乾隆皇帝见了他,便问道:"老师父就是诋毁和尚吗?"

诋毁和尚回答说:"不错,我就是诋毁和尚,诋毁和尚便是我。"

乾隆皇帝又问:"老师父是从小出家的呢,还是半路出家的呢?"

诋毁和尚说:"我么,是半路出家的。秀才你问我这些做啥?"

乾隆皇帝没的话讲了,眼光一转,看见和尚身上那件千补百衲的破袈裟,便说:"听说老师父是个有德行的高僧,为啥穿这丝瓜筋一般的破衣衫呀?"

诋毁和尚笑道:"我年轻的时候,也穿过锦绣的衣衫哩!后来那锦绣衣衫被野狗撕碎了,我就做了和尚,穿起这破麻皮的袈裟来啦!不过我穿的虽然破烂,心术可是正的。不比那些着官服的老爷,看起来仪表堂堂,暗地里却男盗女娼呢!"

乾隆皇帝当头挨了一闷棍,心里恨恨地想:"这诋毁和尚果然名不虚传!总得找个岔子好狠狠地办他的罪。"他肚皮里打着算盘,面孔上却堆起假笑,叫诋毁和尚领他进寺去耍子儿。

他们进了净慈寺山门,见旁边的人在劈毛竹做香篮。乾隆皇帝眼珠一转,随手拾起一块劈开的毛竹片,把青的一面朝着诋毁和尚,问道:"老师父,这个你们叫什么呀?”

诋毁和尚说:“这个叫竹皮。”

乾隆皇帝把毛竹片掉转个面,将黄的一面朝着诋毁和尚,又问:“那么,这个叫什么呢?”

诋毁和尚道:“这个么,我们叫它竹肉。”

乾隆皇帝讪笑一声:“好个新鲜的名称呢!”

诋毁和尚听了打了个哈哈说:“老客人呀,如今这世道变啦,名称也得跟着变哩!”

乾隆皇帝吃瘪了,只好闷声不响。原来当时乾隆皇帝正在大兴“**文字狱**”,那些被发现使用某些禁忌语的民众会被投入监牢甚至招来杀身之祸。如果诋毁和尚照着老称呼把毛竹片青的一面叫篾青,把黄的一面叫篾黄,就会被乾隆皇帝抓住小辫子,诬他要“灭清”“灭皇”,杀他的头。显然,乾隆皇帝拿毛竹片问诋毁和尚,就是想找他这个岔子的。

然后,乾隆皇帝进到**大雄宝殿**拜过菩萨,又到**罗汉**堂看了佛像。最后,他们来到**香积厨**。

寺院里的伙房。乾隆皇帝东张西望,见灶旁歇着一篮豆芽菜。偏巧这时窜过来一条小狗,扯起后腿在豆芽菜上撒了一泡尿。乾隆皇帝看在眼里,就问道:“老师父,这豆芽菜算不算干净的东西?”

诋毁和尚说:“豆芽菜水中生,水中长,当然是最干净的东西啦!”

乾隆皇帝鼻孔里哼了一声,说道:“有狗尿浇在上面,怎么还说它是干净的呢?”

诋毁和尚呵呵大笑:“俗话说,眼不见为净,耳不听为真。你看见只当不看见,岂不就干净了吗?这点小事,何必如此认真呢!譬如有的人,日日夜夜挨天下百姓骂,但他却装作没听见,还厚着脸皮自吹自擂,说自己是圣人哩!”

乾隆皇帝听了这话语,气得火冒三丈,但怕泄露身份,又不好发作。这时,猛听得厨房后门外有个小贩在高声叫卖:“茶叶蛋要喔!茶叶蛋啰!”他灵机一动,就改口问道:“老师父,你们吃荤还是吃素?”

诋毁和尚回答说:“净慈寺海内闻名,清规很严,当然吃净素,不沾荤腥。”

乾隆皇帝一面说着“好,好”,一面盘算着:“这鸡蛋要说荤就荤,要说素就素。如果你说是荤的不肯吃,它却是没有血的东西;倘若你说是素的吃了,它却是能孵出小鸡来。吃也罢,不吃也罢,怎么也得给你安个欺君之罪!”于是,他打开后门,把小贩叫过来,买下两只茶叶蛋,送给诋毁和尚吃。

哪知诋毁和尚不慌不忙地接过茶叶蛋，也不剥壳，咕噜，咕噜，一口一个囫囵吞进肚子里去了。乾隆皇帝正想发作，诋毁和尚却念出一首诗来："混沌乾坤一壳包，也无皮骨也无毛。贫僧渡尔西天去，免在人间受一刀。"

念毕，张开嘴巴，哇哇两声，吐出一对小鸡来，停歇在他手掌上。转眼工夫，这对小鸡就变成羽毛一双绚丽的大鸡，一只公一只母。它们喔喔喔地啼叫了几声，飞上一座山头不见了。

乾隆皇帝惊得目瞪口呆，看来这和尚非同一般，惹他不起，就灰溜溜地从后门溜走了。

【English Version of the Original Story】

Emperor *Qianlong* was afraid that the people in the south of the *Yangzi* River might rebel against him. He used the excuse of "sightseeing" as a cover, and planned a tour there to fish for information and find out what was going on.

Back then, at ***Jingci* Temple** of *Nanpin* Hill, *Hangzhou*, there lived a monk dubbed "Monk Slander". He didn't pay too much attention to chanting Buddhist scriptures or sitting in meditation, but preferred to discuss state affairs. The monk presented views, uttered curses whenever and wherever he wanted to, and had never thought of restraining himself. However, people still liked him, because what he said usually made sense, and what he cursed was generally funny.

Emperor *Qianlong* heard about the monk soon after he got to *Hangzhou*.

"An old monk with such an odd nick name must be a secluded diehard supporter of the *Ming* Dynasty, a man who leads an unrestrained life. All right, let me take a look at what on earth he wants to slander," thought Emperor *Qianlong*. Dressed in a plain blue coat and holding an exquisite paper fan, the emperor disguised himself as a scholar and headed for *Jingci* Temple. On his arrival, *Qianlong* showed his clear intention of meeting Monk Slander. Just then Monk Slander came out of the temple.

"Old master, are you Monk Slander?" asked the emperor.

"Yes, I'm Monk Slander; Monk Slander is me."

"Did you become a monk at an early age, or late in life?"

"I became a monk late in life. Why do you ask me that?"

Emperor *Qianlong* was left speechless. Then, when he noticed the patched Buddhist robe the monk was wearing, *Qianlong* hit upon an idea.

"I hear that you are an eminent monk with high morals. Why are you dressed in such tattered clothes?" asked the emperor.

Monk Slander smiled,

"When I was young, I also wore fine silk clothes; unfortunately, they were shredded into pieces by stray dogs. That's why I ended up as a monk, wearing such a shabby robe! Anyway, I'm still an honest man in spite of the ragged clothes. Look at those government officials in decent clothes! They may look noble and dignified on the outside, but they are actually rotten inside and behave like thieves and prostitutes in the dark."

Hearing these words, Emperor *Qianlong* was struck dumb.

"Monk Slander is a tough guy who really lives up to his name," he thought with bitterness. "I've got to find a fault in him and send him to jail." With these thoughts in mind, the emperor put on a fake smile and asked Monk Slander to show him around the temple.

As they went through the gate into the temple, they saw some people who were making bamboo baskets with split bamboo pieces. The emperor then had a flash of inspiration. He picked up one bamboo piece and showed its outer, green side to Monk Slander and asked,

"Old master, what is this called?"

"It's called 'bamboo skin'."

"All right then, what is this called?" The emperor turned the bamboo piece and showed its inner yellow side to the monk.

"We call it 'bamboo flesh'."

"What a fresh new name!" said the emperor, managing a smile.

Monk Slander smiled and said,

"My guest, you know names change as times change!"

Emperor *Qianlong* was reduced to silence. During that time, he was launching a large-scale **Literary Inquisition** Campaign. Those who were found using certain taboo words would be put in jail or even sentenced to death.

If Monk Slander had called the outer green side of the bamboo "bamboo green" and the inner yellow side "bamboo yellow" as they are traditionally called, the emperor would have been able to arrest him and sentence him to death. For in Mandarin, the pronunciation of "bamboo green"(篾青) is the same as that of "overthrowing the *Qing* Dynasty"(灭清), both pronounced "*miè qīng*"; and the pronunciation of "bamboo yellow" (篾黄) is identical with that of "killing the emperor"(灭皇), both pronounced "*miè huáng*". Obviously, Emperor *Qianlong* had intended to find fault with Monk Slander using the piece of bamboo.

Then, Emperor *Qianlong* worshiped the Buddha at **the Grand Hall of the Great Sage**, the main palace of a Buddhist temple, and he also visited Buddhist statues at **Luohan** Chamber, a typical Buddhist hall that usually houses a great variety of Arhat statues in different postures. Finally, they got to **the *Xiangji* kitchen**.

The emperor looked around and saw a basket of bean sprouts sitting by the kitchen range. Suddenly, a puppy ran out from nowhere, lifted one of its hind legs and urinated on the bean sprouts. Seeing this, Emperor *Qianlong* asked,

"Old master, do you think the bean sprouts clean?"

"Yes, they grow in water. Naturally they are the cleanest thing," said Monk Slander.

"With dog urine on it, how could it be clean?" sniffed Emperor *Qianlong*.

Monk Slander laughed,

"As the saying goes, 'what the eyes don't see is regarded as clean; what the ears don't hear is regarded as real.' If you just pretend not to have seen it, it's clean. There is really no need to make a fuss about it! You know, for instance, somebody is cursed day and night by all the people; he pretends not to hear it. And what's more unbelievable is, he always brags about himself shamelessly; calling himself a saint!"

Emperor *Qianlong* flew into a rage at the monk's words, but he had to contain his anger for fear of giving away his real identity. Just at that moment, he heard a vendor hawking his goods outside the backdoor of the kitchen, "Tea-flavoured boiled eggs! Tea-flavoured boiled eggs!" Hearing this, the emperor hit upon an idea and asked,

"Old master, do you eat meat or vegetables?

"*Jingci* Temple is world-famous for its austere, monastic discipline. Of course we eat vegetables and never touch meat or fish."

"Well, well," the emperor said. He was thinking hard,

"An egg can fall into the category of 'meat', and it can also fall into the category of 'vegetables'. You can say it is 'meat' and refuse to eat it; however, it is also stuff without blood. (The emperor's logic was: It has no blood, so it is not an animal, so it is not meat.) You can also claim it is a "vegetable" and eat it; nevertheless, it can hatch a chicken. (The emperor's logic was: It is able to change into an animal, so it is not a vegetable.) Whether you eat it or not, I can convict you of deceiving the emperor." With these thoughts in mind, the emperor pushed the back door open, called the vendor over, bought two tea-flavoured boiled eggs and gave them to Monk Slander.

Much to the Emperor's surprise, Monk Slander leisurely took the two eggs and, without removing the shell, he swallowed the two eggs, one at a time. As Emperor *Qianlong* was about to lose his temper, Monk Slander composed an impromptu poem,

One tiny egg shell,
Out of the vast chaotic world,
No skin, no hair and no bone.
From hell I release your soul,
To the Western Paradise you pursue your hope,
One bloody stab you forever escape.

With these words, Monk Slander opened his mouth, cleared his throat and spat out a pair of chickens which perched on the palm of his hand. In an instant, this pair of chickens changed into big ones with brilliant feathers; one male, the other female. They crowed, flew onto a hilltop and then disappeared.

The emperor was completely dumbfounded. Realizing that the monk was by no means an ordinary one, and that trying to give him a hard time was just asking for trouble, Emperor *Qianlong* slipped away from the back door, depressed and discouraged.

【文化背景】【Cultural Notes】

▶ **净慈寺**:净慈寺是杭州西湖历史上四大古刹之一。净慈寺在南屏山慧日峰下,是公元10世纪五代的钱弘俶为高僧永明禅师而建,原名永明禅院;南宋时改称净慈寺,并建造了五百罗汉堂。该寺屡毁屡建,现在大部分寺院建筑都是20世纪80年代重建的。寺内有一口重达一百多公斤的铜钟,上面书写的《妙法莲花经》,计六点八万字。因为寺内钟声洪亮,"南屏晚钟"成为"西湖十景"之一。

***Jingci* Temple**: *Jingci* Temple is one of the four prominent Buddhist temples in *Hangzhou*. It is located at the foot of *Huiri* Peak, *Nanping* Hill. The temple was first built in the 10th century by *Qian Hongchu* of the Five Dynasties for an eminent monk, Master *Yongming*. It was initially called *Yongming* Temple. In the Southern *Song* Dynasty, its name was changed to *Jingci* Temple, and the Five-Hundred-Arhat Hall was built. The temple was destroyed and rebuilt several times. The majority of the present temple was rebuilt in the 1980s. One special feature is a cast copper bell, weighing over 100 kilograms. On it is carved the Buddhist scripture called *The Lotus Sutra*, with 68,000 Chinese characters. The temple hosts one of the Ten Scenes of West Lake, "Evening Bell Ringing at *Nanping* Hill".

▶ **文字狱**:文字狱(字面意思:由于文字而入狱)指的是中国封建王朝统治者从作者的诗文中摘取字句,罗织成罪,迫害知识分子的一种冤狱。文字狱历朝皆有,但以清朝最甚。有些文字狱是因一个简单的字词被统治者认为有罪而起;而有些文字狱是因一些姓名禁忌而起,例如所写的某个汉字涉及了帝王姓名。在极端的文字狱例子当中,不仅当事人会因此招来杀身之祸,其直系及旁系亲属都会受到牵连诛杀。

Literary Inquisition: Literary Inquisition (literally "imprisonment due to writings") refers to the official persecution of intellectuals in imperial China. This kind of inquisition took place under each of the dynasties, although the *Qing* Dynasty was particularly notorious for the practice. Some persecutions could be caused by even a single phrase or word which the ruler considered offensive. Some of these were due to naming taboos, such as writing a Chinese character that was part of the emperor's personal name. In the most serious cases, not only the one directly involved, but also his immediate and extended family would be killed.

▶ **大雄宝殿**：在佛教寺院中，大雄宝殿就是正殿，是整座寺院的核心建筑，也是僧众朝暮集中修持的地方。大雄宝殿的像设可分为三部分：

一是大殿正中的主尊佛像，即释迦牟尼像；

二是大殿两侧的十八罗汉像；

三是正中佛坛背后的观音像或三大士像。

各地佛寺因地因事制宜，其格局摆设会略有差异。

The Grand Hall of the Great Sage: In Buddhist temples, the Grand Hall of the Great Sage is the principal hall, the most important piece of architecture in the whole temple complex. It is a place where monks practice Buddhism on a daily basis. The statues which the hall houses can be divided into three groups:

I. At the center front stands the statue of Shakyamuni, the most important Buddha.

II. Arranged along the sides of the hall are images of the 18 Principal Arhats.

III. At the back of the main statue is usually the statue of Avalokitesvara (*Guanyin*) or statues of three primary Buddhas.

The statues and the floor plan of a temple may vary slightly depending on the cultures and traditions of each place.

▶ **罗汉**：罗汉，是阿罗汉的简称，梵名，含三层意思：无明烦恼已断（杀贼）；已了脱生死，证入涅槃（无生）；堪受诸人天尊敬供养（应供）。罗汉是佛陀得道弟子修证圆满的最高的果位。罗汉堂,是供奉罗汉的殿堂。在一般的寺庙里,在大雄宝殿两侧塑十八罗汉,而在规模较大的寺院,则专门建有罗汉堂,内塑很多罗汉,可能是五百罗汉。

***Luohan* (Arhat)**: Arhat, short for Arahant, is a Buddhist term with threefold connotations—*shazei* (杀贼) means nothing can bring vexation to an Arhat; *wusheng* (无生) means an Arhat has attained nirvana and no longer suffers from reincarnation of the soul; *yinggong* (应供) means an Arhat is supported by celestial devotees. An Arhat is usually believed to have risen to a domain of perfection in which one has been released from the state of suffering and has achieved profound peace of mind. Arhat Hall is a place where Arhats are arranged and worshipped. At an ordinary temple, 18 Arhats are organized along the two sides of the Grand Hall of the Great Sage. At a large-sized temple, there might be a specially built Arhats Hall which houses a great variety of Arhats—maybe 500 Arhats.

▶ **香积厨:**香积厨是指历史比较久远的寺庙厨房。许多规模比较大,在中国各地都有。

***Xiangji* kitchen**: A *Xiangji* kitchen usually refers to a temple kitchen with a long history. Such a kitchen is usually large and can be found in many places in China.

第四章
爱情传说

Chapter IV
Legends of Love

西湖是浪漫的,西湖的桥和其他景致是多情的,因为有许仙与白娘子断桥相会,梁山伯与祝英台长桥十八里相送,西泠桥上苏小小与鲍仁一见倾心,柳浪与莺姑娘的终成眷属……

West Lake is romantic and the bridges and the other scenic sites there are full of love. *Xu Xian* and Lady White Snake met on the Broken Bridge, *Liang Shanbo* saw *Zhu Yingtai* off on the Long Bridge, *Su Xiaoxiao* and *Bao Ren* fell in love at first sight on *Xiling* Bridge, while *Liu Lang* was eventually together with the Oriole Girl.

壹◎白娘子与许仙
Lady White Snake and *Xu Xian*

【简介】

白娘子与许仙的故事,即白蛇传,是中国四大民间传说(其余三个为梁山伯与祝英台、孟姜女、牛郎织女)之一,被列入第一批国家级非物质文化遗产之列,成为许多中国戏剧、电影、电视剧的主题。

【Brief Introduction】

The romance between Lady White Snake and *Xu Xian*, i.e. *The Legend of Lady White Snake*, is one of the four well-known Chinese folk tales (the other three are: *The Butterfly Lovers*, *Lady Meng Jiang*, *The Cowherd and the Weaving Maid*). Lady White Snake has been included in the first batch of "State-level Intangible Cultural Heritage" and has been presented in a number of major Chinese operas, films and television series.

【传说读本】

这一天,正值阳春三月,西湖边柳枝儿嫩绿嫩绿,桃花儿艳红艳红的,四处来耍子儿的人很多。**八仙**之一的**吕洞宾**,变成个白头发白胡须的老头儿,来西湖边卖**汤团**。吕洞宾把担子歇在断桥旁边的一株大柳树底下。他拉开嗓门叫起来:"吃汤团罗,吃汤团罗!大汤团一个铜钿买三只,小汤团三个铜钿买一只!"

人们听了吕洞宾的叫卖声都笑开了,并朝他的汤团担子围拢来,买他的大汤团吃。一歇歇辰光(一点点时间),大汤团就卖光了。这时,来了个五十来岁的老年人,怀里抱个小伢儿。这伢儿名叫许仙,吵着要吃汤团,但大汤团卖光啦,那人只好摸出三个铜钿,向吕洞宾买只小汤团。

谁知道这小伢儿自从吃了汤团以后,三日三夜都不要吃东西。阿爸着急得要命,就抱到断桥旁边大柳树下来寻那个卖汤团的。

吕洞宾听了那人如此这般一讲,哈哈一笑,说:"我的小汤团不是寻常之物,看来,你儿子是没福消受的!"说着就猛不防抓住小伢儿的双脚倒拎起来,大喝一声:"出来!"那个小汤团,竟从他小嘴巴里吐出来,掉入了西湖里。

这时候,有一条白蛇和一只乌龟,在断桥底下修炼。小汤团从桥上落下来,白蛇头颈长,先接在嘴里,吞进肚子里。乌龟没吃着汤团,大失所望,就跟白蛇吵架,吵着吵着,竟打起来啦。

白蛇和乌龟一样修炼了五百年,本领原是差不多的。但白蛇吞下这只实为仙丸的小汤团后,就添了五百年功力,乌龟就不能跟它比了。乌龟打不过白蛇,吃了败仗,一溜烟往西方逃去。

十八年后的**清明节**，湖底钻出一个穿着白闪闪轻纱衣衫的姑娘儿。那姑娘真好看呀，就像一朵刚出水的白莲花！原来白蛇有了千年修功能变化成人啦。她给自己取了个名字叫作“白娘子”。

那天，白娘子顺着苏堤漫步，看到一个乞丐手中拿着一条青蛇，想挖蛇胆去卖钱。她觉得它怪可怜的，便从乞丐那里买下了青蛇，救了它一命。青蛇感激不尽，从此便认白娘子为姐姐，取名小青。

一天，她们都化身为年轻女子，来到杭州，在断桥遇到了许仙。白娘子和许仙认识以后，你喜欢我，我喜欢你，不久就结了亲。小夫妻带着小青搬到镇江，开了一爿“保和堂”药店。

端午节那一天，有个习俗：家家户户门前挂起菖蒲叶，家家酿**雄黄药酒**。小青害怕喝了雄黄酒后现形，便去山里避避，白娘子有孕在身不能爬山，没有去。小青刚刚走，许仙上了楼，挨近白娘子说：“我们搬到镇江来，今天是头一回看赛龙船，你就和我一道去耍子儿吧！”白娘子说：“我身上勿适意，还是你自己去吧！”

许仙听白娘子说身上勿适意，给白娘子来搭脉。许仙叫起来：“没有病，没有病！你哄我。”白娘子笑了笑，说道：“我也没说生病呀，我是怀了身孕呢！”许仙一听到自己快要做阿爸了，高兴得一蹦三尺高，连赛龙船也不想去看了，在家里陪白娘子过端午。

吃午饭时候，许仙热了一串粽子，烫了一壶老酒，酒里和了些雄黄，让白娘子喝。白娘子说：“酒里有雄黄，我怀着身孕怕吃不得呢！”许仙听了，哈哈大笑起来：“别担心，这雄黄酒都驱恶避邪，定胎安神，你还该多吃两盏哩！”

白娘子怕许仙起疑，就硬着头皮喝了一口雄黄酒。哪晓得酒刚落肚，便马上觉得头疼脑涨，浑身瘫软，勉强爬到了床上。许仙便赶到床前，撩起帐子一看，白娘子已经无影无踪，只见床上盘着一条大白蛇，吓得他一下昏死过去。

不久，小青回到家，看见许仙死在床前，白娘子还在床上困着没醒哩！小青急忙推醒白娘子。白娘子下床见许仙死了，就大哭起来。白娘子摸摸许仙心口，还有一丝儿热气，就说：“凡间的药草是救不活他的了，我飞到昆仑山盗仙草去！”说着，白娘子便驾起一朵白云，飘出窗户，向昆仑山飞去了。

飞呀，飞呀，只一刻工夫，就飞到昆仑山顶上。昆仑山是座仙山，满山都是仙树仙花。山顶上，有几棵紫郁郁的小草，就是能起死回生的灵芝仙草。白娘子弯下腰，悄悄地采了一株仙草衔在嘴里，正想驾起白云飞走，忽听空中“咯溜溜”一声叫，那只看守灵芝仙草的白鹤从天边飞了下来。它见白娘子盗了仙草，哪里肯放过，便展开大翅膀，伸出长喙，朝白娘子扑过来。好险哪，就在白鹤的长喙刚要啄着白娘子的时候，忽然从后面伸来一根弯头拐杖，把白鹤的颈项钩住啦。白娘子转过身来一看，见眼前站着一个胡须白花花的老人，原来是南极仙翁。她就哭着向南极仙翁央求道：“老仙翁，老仙翁，给我一株灵芝仙草，救救我的官人吧！”南极仙翁捋捋白花花的胡须，点点头答应了。

白娘子谢过南极仙翁，衔着灵芝仙草，急忙驾起白云，白娘子飞回家来。她把灵芝仙草熬成药汁，灌进许仙嘴里。过了一会儿，许仙就活转来啦。许仙朝白娘子看看又看看，心里好害怕，讲出了那天见到的情景。白娘子一听，皱皱眉头，对许仙说：“我是好好的一个人，怎么会变成蛇呢？必定是你眼花看错啦。”

小青也忙着插嘴道：“相公没有看错，我也见着一条白闪闪的东西，又像是蛇，又像是龙，从床上飞起来，飞出窗外就不见啦。”

白娘子听着笑道：“哦，原来是这样的呀！恐怕是苍龙现形了。这正好应着我家生意兴旺，添子加孙。可惜我那辰光困熟（睡着）了，要不然，一定点上香烛拜拜它哩！”

许仙听她们讲得这样认真，也信以为真，满心疑惑一下子就化掉了。

十八年前被白娘子打败的乌龟变身为法海和尚，寻白娘子报仇。法海和尚趁如来佛打瞌睡那一会儿便偷了他三样宝贝：金钵、袈裟和青龙禅杖。他把宝贝带在身边，到处云游。一天，法海扮作化缘的头陀，寻到保和堂药店来。

法海走到药店门前，朝里张望，见许仙夫妻正忙着配方撮药。他在店门口等呀，等呀，等到黄昏时分，保和堂药店要打烊了。法海和尚见白娘子已上楼去，大模大样地走进店里来，朝许仙合起手掌，说道：“施主，你店里的生意好兴隆呀，给我化上个缘吧。七月十五到金山寺来烧灶香，求菩萨保佑你。”

许仙看他讲得好，给了他一串铜钱。法海和尚走出门口，又回头关照道：“到了七月十五日，施主一定要来呵！”

日子过得好快，七月十五转眼就到了。许仙独个儿来到金山寺，他刚刚跨进山门，就被法海和尚一把拉到禅房里。法海和尚对许仙说：“施主呀，你来得正好，今天我从实告诉你，你的女人是个妖精哩！”

许仙一听生了气,说道:"我娘子是个好端端的人,怎么会是妖精?你不要乱说。"法海和尚笑笑说:"这也难怪施主,你已被妖气迷住啦。凭着功力,老僧看得出她是白蛇变化的!"

这一说,许仙倒记得端午节那天的事来了,不觉心里一怔。法海和尚见他在一旁发愣,就说:"你不要回家去了,在这里出家为僧吧,有我佛法保护,就不怕她害你啦!"

许仙回答说:"娘子对我的情义比海还深,即使她是白蛇,也不会害我的,如今还有了身孕,我怎能丢下她出家做和尚呢?我无论如何也不肯出家。"法海和尚见许仙不答应,就把他关了起来。

白娘子在家里等着许仙哩,左等等不来,右等等不来,四天过去了,毫无音讯。她焦急起来,再也耐不住了,便和小青划只小舢板,到金山寺去寻找。

小舢板停在金山下。白娘子和小青爬上金山,来到金山寺,法海和尚见了白娘子,冷笑地说道:"大胆妖蛇,你竟敢入世迷人!"

法海和尚举起手里的青龙禅杖,朝白娘子兜头就敲。然而,白娘子身怀六甲,渐渐支持不住了,她们退到金山下,跳上小舢板。白娘子从头上拔下一股金钗,迎风一晃,霎时间,滔天大水滚滚而来,虾兵蟹将成群结队,一齐向金山涌去。法海和尚着了慌,连忙脱下身上袈裟,往寺门外一遮,忽地一道金光闪过,袈裟变成一堵长堤,把滔天大水拦在外边。白娘子看看胜不了法海和尚,只得叫小青收了兵。她们又回到西湖去修炼,等待机会报仇。

许仙被关在金山寺里,死活也不肯做和尚,逃了出来。许仙回到保和堂药店,看看白娘子和小青都不在了,人去楼空,真叫他伤心!又怕法海和尚再来寻他生事,不敢住在镇江,只得收拾东西回到杭州来。

许仙来到西湖断桥边,不禁想起了他们夫妻被法海活活拆散,不觉泪珠扑簌簌地滚下来,顿着脚叫喊道:"娘子呀娘子,你到哪里去了呀!你到哪里去了呀!"

这时,白娘子和小青正在西湖底下练功夫,隐隐约约听到许仙的叫喊。她俩大喜,马上从湖底下钻上来,捞片树叶,吹口气,变成一只小船,于是打起双桨,慢慢划着,来寻许仙。

许仙抬头一看,船上正坐着白娘子和小青。小青轻轻靠了船,扶白娘子登上岸,夫妻俩又在断桥相会了,都不禁流下泪来。日子过得很快,转眼到了元宵节,白娘子生下了一个白白胖胖的娃娃。

伢儿满月的那一天,许仙在家里办"**满月酒**"。突然许仙听得大门外有个货郎在叫喊:“卖金凤冠啰!卖金凤冠啰!”许仙一听是卖金凤冠的,便三脚两步奔了出去,找到卖货郎。拿过来一看,哦!这顶金凤冠美丽极啦!许仙便把它买下来,让白娘子戴上去试试看合适不合适。白娘子看看那金光闪亮的金凤冠,心里也很喜欢,就让许仙帮着戴到头上。不料这金凤冠一戴到头上,就紧紧箍住啦,再也脱不下来。它越箍越紧,越箍越紧……白娘子这时只觉得头重脑疼,支撑不住,便一头倒在地上,晕过去了。

许仙慌忙奔出门去,要找货郎算账。货郎不在了,原来那个卖金凤冠的货郎就是法海和尚变化的。法海和尚朝白娘子头上吹口气,金凤冠就变成金钵。金钵射出万道金光,把白娘子团团罩住。白娘子的身体在金光下面已渐渐缩小,最后,变成了一条白蛇,被法海和尚收进金钵里去了。

法海和尚收了白蛇,在净慈寺前的雷峰顶上造了一座**雷峰塔**,把金钵砌进去,镇住白蛇,自己便在净慈寺里住下来看守着。

之后,小青在深山里练功多年,直到练到炉火纯青的地步,赶回杭州来寻法海和尚报仇。小青寻到净慈寺,就跟他大战起来。他们打了三天三夜,还分不出谁赢谁输。干戈声震得山摇地动,如来佛的瞌睡被吵醒了,睁开眼来看看,发觉自己的三件宝贝被偷了去,心里很气愤,就踏着莲花去寻找。见法海和尚和小青正打得热闹哩,如来佛在空中用手轻轻一招,那青龙禅杖和袈裟就向天上飞去啦。

小青挥起一剑,又听“轰隆隆”一声巨响,雷峰塔倒塌了,砌在塔里的金钵也飞上了天。白娘子从塔里面跳出来,就和小青一道围打法海和尚。法海和尚本来就没有什么本事,全靠如来佛的三件宝贝,如今宝贝都叫如来佛收回去了,哪里还打得过白娘子和小青呢!他哀求如来佛救命。如来佛恨他心术太歪,飞起一脚,踢得他连连打了几个跟头,跌进西湖里去了。

白娘子见法海和尚掉进西湖里,便从头上拔下一股金钗,迎风一晃,西湖里的水便一下干了。湖底朝了天,法海和尚东躲西藏,找不着一个稳当的地方。最后,他便一头钻进螃蟹的肚子里,被严严实实地关在里了,从此再也出不来啦。

【English Version of the Original Story】

One sunny day in March, there were tender green willows and red peach blossoms beside West Lake. Many people came from far and near to enjoy the lake scenery. ***Lü Dongbin***, one of **the Eight Immortals**, disguised himself as a grey-haired and grey-bearded old man selling ***tangtuan*** near the lake. He put his carrying pole under a big willow tree near the Broken Bridge and shouted,

"*Tangtuan*! *Tangtuan*! One copper coin for three big ones! Three copper coins for a small one!"

People were laughing at what *Lü Dongbin* said and began to gather round his carrying pole to buy his big *Tangtuan*. Soon the big ones were sold out. Then a fifty-year-old man came, with a child named *Xu Xian* in his arms. *Xu Xian* wanted to eat *tangtuan*. Since there were no big ones left, the man had to buy a small one with three copper coins.

Strangely enough, after eating the small *tangtuan*, the child did not feel hungry for the next three days. The man was extremely worried so that he took his son back to the Broken Bridge to look for the seller under the big willow tree.

Hearing what the man said, *Lü Dongbin* laughed and said,

"My small *tangtuan* is magical, but it seems that your son is not good enough for it."

Suddenly he took the child by the feet, flipped him upside down and shouted,

"Out!"

With that, the child vomited the small *tangtuan* into West Lake.

At that time a white snake spirit and a tortoise spirit were practicing Taoist magic arts under the Broken Bridge. When the *tangtuan* dropped into the lake, the white snake caught it with his long neck and quickly swallowed it. The tortoise felt so disappointed at not getting the *tangtuan* that he quarreled and even fought with the snake.

They had both practiced Taoist magic arts for 500 years and had nearly equal magical powers. However, the *tangtuan*, which actually was a magic pill, gave the white snake another 500 years' worth of magic power, so the tortoise was no match for the snake. The tortoise was defeated and fled westward.

18 years later, during ***the Qingming* Festival**, a girl dressed in sparkling

white came up from the bottom of the lake. She was as beautiful as a lotus flower just rising from the water! It turned out that the white snake, after a thousand years of training and cultivation, had changed into a woman who called herself Lady White.

That day, while walking along *Su* Causeway, Lady White saw a green snake in a beggar's hand. The poor man intended to dig out the snake's gall and sell it. She felt sorry for the poor green snake, so she bought the snake from the beggar, and saved its life. The green snake, which was called *Xiaoqing*, was grateful to Lady White and regarded her as her elder sister.

One day, both of them transformed themselves into two young women and came to *Hangzhou*, where they happened to meet *Xu Xian* at the Broken Bridge. After Lady White and *Xu Xian* got acquainted, they gradually fell in love and eventually got married. They moved to *Zhenjiang* with *Xiaoqing*, where they opened a pharmacy called *Baohe*.

At **the Dragon Boat Festival**, it was customary to hang calamus leaves on the front door of every house and to make **realgar wine** by every family. For fear of revealing her true form after drinking the wine, *Xiaoqing* went to the hills without Lady White, who was pregnant and could not climb the hills. The moment *Xiaoqing* left, *Xu Xian* went upstairs and approached Lady White, saying,

"This is the first chance for us to watch the dragon boat race since we moved here. Shall we go together?"

"I am feeling unwell. You may go without me." replied Lady White.

Xu Xian felt her pulse and said,

"There's nothing wrong with you. Everything's fine. You are teasing me."

Lady White said smilingly,

"I didn't mean I was sick. I am just pregnant."

Knowing that he was going to be a father, *Xu Xian* jumped for joy and stayed home with her instead of going to the race.

During lunch, *Xu Xian* heated some *zongzi* and a pot of old wine mixed with realgar. He asked Lady White to drink, but she said,

"There is realgar in the wine. I'm afraid I can't drink it."

Hearing that, *Xu Xian* laughed and urged her,

"Don't worry. The realgar wine is believed to ward off evil spirits, calm anxiety and help the baby during pregnancy. You'd better drink some cups."

Afraid of making him suspicious, she forced herself to drink a mouthful of the wine, which suddenly made her feel dizzy and feeble. She barely managed to climb into bed. When *Xu Xian* rushed to the bed, he drew aside the bed curtain but could not see his wife, but saw a huge white snake coiled on the bed, which made him collapse with shock immediatelly.

Before long, *Xiaoqing* came back. She saw *Xu Xian* lying, apparently dead, in front of the bed and Lady White still sleeping. She hastily woke up Lady White. When she saw *Xu Xian* was half dead, Lady White burst into tears. She laid her hand on his chest and could still feel his weak heartbeat. She declared,

"Only a celestial herb on Mount *Kunlun* can bring him back to life. I must fly there and steal it."

With that, she created a white cloud and flew on it out of the window towards Mount *Kunlun*.

She flew and flew. Soon she reached the top of Mount *Kunlun*, which was an enchanted mountain covered with magical trees and flowers. At the top of the mountain, there were a few blades of violet-coloured, magic grass which could restore life. Lady White stooped down, quietly picked a blade of grass and put it into her mouth. She tried to fly away on a cloud when she heard a shrieking cry.

A white crane, guardian of the magic herb, flew down from heaven. It had seen her steal the herb so it would not let her go. It spread its big wings, stretched its long beak and rushed at her. It was incredibly dangerous. Its long beak began to peck at her when, suddenly, a hooked cane reached over the crane's back and grabbed the bird by the neck. Lady White turned around to see a white-bearded old man standing behind her. He turned out to be the Immortal of the South. She pleaded with him in tears,

"Immortal, Immortal, please give me a blade of magic herb to save my husband!"

The Immortal stroked his white beard and nodded his agreement. Lady White thanked him and flew back home with the herb in her mouth. She prepared the herb and fed it to *Xu Xian*, who soon came back to life. Looking at Lady White with fright, he told her what he saw that day. Lady White frowned and said,

"You're kidding! You see, I was fine! How could I turn into a snake? You must be mistaken!"

Xiaoqing quickly interrupted,

"He was not mistaken. I also saw something white resembling either a snake or a dragon which flew from the bed to the window and disappeared."

Lady White listened and said with a smile,

"Oh, I see. Perhaps it was a dragon descending from heaven. That's a good prediction of our booming business and the birth of a baby. Unfortunately I was fast asleep, otherwise I would have burned joss sticks and candles to worship it."

Seeing both Lady White and *Xiaoqing* so serious and innocent, *Xu Xian* believed what they said and his doubts were cleared up.

The tortoise spirit who had been defeated by Lady White 18 years ago, transformed himself into a Buddhist monk called *Fahai* and planned to take revenge on the lady. He stole three treasures from the Tathagata Buddha when the latter was dozing off. These were a golden alms bowl, a cloak and a Buddhist monk's azure-dragon cane. He carried them with him wherever he went. One day, he came to the *Baohe* pharmacy disguised as a mendicant Buddhist monk, begging for alms.

He stopped by the door of the pharmacy and peered in. He saw *Xu Xian* and his wife writing prescriptions and dispensing the herbal medicine. He waited and waited at the door until evening came and the store was closing. When *Fahai* saw Lady White go upstairs, he strode into the shop. He folded his hands and spoke to *Xu Xian*,

"Benefactor, your business is booming. Please give some money to our temple. If you come to *Jinshan* Temple on the fifteenth day of lunar July and burn a joss stick, the Buddha will bless you."

Pleased by what he said, *Xu Xian* offered him a string of copper coins. *Fahai* walked out the door and looked back, saying,

"Do come on that day!"

Time passed quickly. On July 15th, *Xu Xian* went to *Jinshan* Temple alone. As soon as he set foot in the temple, he was taken to a meditation room by *Fahai*. The monk said to him,

"Benefactor, it's a good thing you've come. To tell you the truth, your wife is a snake demon."

"My wife is surely a woman. How can she be a demon? How dare you say that?" Xu Xian replied angrily.

Fahai laughed and said,

"No wonder! You've been enchanted by her. By my powers, I've discovered that she is a white snake who has changed into a woman."

At these words, *Xu Xian* suddenly remembered what had happened on the Dragon Boat Festival and became terrified. Seeing him so horrified, *Fahai* said,

"Don't go home. Stay here and become a monk. With my protection, she can't harm you."

Xu Xian replied,

"Her affection for me is as deep as the sea. Even if she is a snake, she won't destroy me. Now she is pregnant, how can I leave her? I don't want to become a monk at all."

Since *Xu Xian* refused to stay, *Fahai* could do nothing but shut him up in the temple.

Now Lady White was waiting for *Xu Xian* at home. She waited and waited, but four days passed without any news. She became worried and could not wait any longer. Finally, she and *Xiaoqing* rowed a sampan to *Jinshan* Temple in search of *Xu Xian*.

They pulled up the sampan at the foot of *Jinshan* Mountain and went up to the temple. At the sight of Lady White, *Fahai* sneered,

"You bold demon! How dare you come to the mortal world to enchant people!"

Then *Fahai* lifted his azure-dragon cane and hit her on the head. She could not bear it because she was pregnant. She and *Xiaoqing* backed away down the mountain and jumped into the sampan. Lady White took her hairpin and flashed it, which caused a surging flood of water, with waves of shrimps soldiers and crabs generals moving towards *Jinshan* Temple. The panic-stricken *Fahai* quickly flung his cloak over the temple gate and, with a flash of golden light, the cloak became a long dyke which stopped the flood before the temple gate.

When Lady White found that they could not defeat *Fahai*, she asked *Xiaoqing* to give up. They returned to West Lake to practice their skills, hoping for an opportunity to gain more power and take revenge on *Fahai*.

Xu Xian was still imprisoned in *Jinshan* Temple, refusing to be a monk. He succeeded in escaping from the temple and returned to his drugstore. He was beside himself with sadness when he found his wife and *Xiaoqing* gone. Afraid of *Fahai* making trouble again, he did not dare to live in *Zhenjiang*. Instead, he packed and left for *Hangzhou*.

He came to the Broken Bridge near West Lake, where he couldn't help thinking of *Fahai* who had separated him from his wife and tears were running down his cheeks. He cried with a stamp of his feet,

"My love! Where are you? Where are you?"

Meanwhile, Lady White and *Xiaoqing* were practicing magic powers in the lake when they vaguely heard *Xu Xian* yelling out. They were overjoyed and jumped out of the lake. They took a leaf and breathed into it, making it into a boat. They rowed the boat slowly, looking for *Xu Xian*.

He looked up and saw Lady White and *Xiao Qing* sitting in a boat. *Xiaoqing* anchored the boat carefully and helped Lady White ashore. The couple met again on the Broken Bridge and both shed tears of joy. Time flew by and soon the Lantern Festival came. At this time Lady White gave birth to a plump baby boy.

When the baby was a month old, *Xu Xian* planned to throw a party for his **Full Moon Celebration**. Suddenly *Xu Xian* heard a peddler crying his wares outside,

"Golden phoenix crown for sale. Who wants to buy it? Golden phoenix crown."

Xu Xian rushed out to hail in the peddler and found the crown extremely beautiful. He bought it for his wife and asked her to try it on. Lady White was happy about the golden crown and asked her husband to put it on her head. Little did she expect that as soon as the crown touched her head, it became tighter and tighter until she could not bear the pain any longer. She felt a headache coming on and fell to the ground, unconscious.

Xu Xian rushed out to find the crown peddler, who turned out to be *Fahai*. He blew on the phoenix crown on Lady White's head and it changed back into a golden bowl. The bowl trapped her in its golden rays and made her shrink. She became smaller and smaller until she changed into a white snake and was held captive in the golden bowl.

After capturing the white snake, *Fahai* built ***Leifeng Pagoda*** on *Leifeng* Peak south of West Lake, in front of *Jingci* Temple. He kept her imprisoned in the alm bowl under the pagoda, and lived in the temple to keep watching over her.

Xiaoqing spent many years training herself in the hills until her magic powers were at their height. She hurried back to *Hangzhou* in an attempt to get even with *Fahai*. *Xiaoqing* went to *Jingci* Temple to fight with *Fahai*. They fought for three days and nights but neither of them could win. Finally their shouts and fighting woke up the Buddha. He opened his eyes and found his three treasures had been stolen. He got very angry and then looked for them while flying with his feet on lotus flowers. He saw *Fahai* and *Xiaoqing* fighting and waved his hand gently. This caused his azure-dragon cane and cloak to fly back to heaven.

Xiaoqing waved her sword, and *Leifeng* Pagoda collapsed with the sound of thunder. This caused the golden bowl to fly back to heaven. Lady White was released from the pagoda and joined *Xiaoqing* in their fight against *Fahai*. He used to depend on the Buddha's three treasures for his powers. With the three treasures taken away, *Fahai* was not powerful enough to fight against them. He turned to the Buddha for help, but was refused because of his evil nature. The Buddha kicked *Fahai* so hard that *Fahai* turned somersaults in the air and fell into the lake.

Lady White saw him fall and with a flash of her hairpin in the wind, West Lake dried up. *Fahai* had no safe place to hide except in the underbelly of a crab. He was tightly shut in it, never able to come out of it again.

【文化背景】【Cultural Notes】

▶ **八仙**:中国神话传说中的八位神仙，即铁拐李、钟离权、蓝采和、张果老、何仙姑、吕洞宾、韩湘子、曹国舅。据说他们大都生活在唐宋时期。他们手持不同法器,除魔卫道，拯救苍生。这八种法器合称为“暗八仙”。据说他们生活在渤海的五个岛屿群，其中包括蓬莱山岛。

The Eight Immortals: A group of legendary immortals in Chinese mythology, that is, Iron-Crutch *Li* (*Li Ningyan*), *Zhongli Quan*, *Lan Caihe*, Elder *Zhang Guo* (*Zhang Guolao*), Immortal Woman *He* (*He Xiangu*), *Lü Dongbin*, Philosopher *Han Xiang* (*Han Xiangzi*), Royal Uncle *Cao* (*Cao Yi*). Most of them are said to have been born in the *Tang* or *Song* Dynasty. Each immortal has a powerful tool that can destroy evil or save lives. Together, these eight tools are called The Covert or Hidden Eight Immortals. They are said to live on a group of five islands in the *Bohai* Sea, which includes *Penglai* Mountain Island.

▶ **吕洞宾**:唐朝学者、诗人,后得道成仙,成为八仙之一,在八仙中最为有名,经常在人间济世度人。

Lü Dongbin: He was a *Tang* Dynasty Chinese scholar and poet who has been elevated to the status of an immortal, and is one of the most widely known of the Eight Immortals, always with a genuine desire to help people and guide them.

▶ **汤团**:汤团,即汤圆,代表团圆,中国传统小吃。元宵节合家共聚吃汤圆,是中国的传统习俗。用糯米粉加水做的球形食品,可大可小,一般水煮带汤吃,可以有馅儿,也可以不加馅儿。

Tangtuan: *Tangtuan* is the same as *tangyuan*, a frequent metaphor for family union. It is usually eaten during the Lantern Festival in China. It is made from glutinous rice flour. Glutinous rice flour is mixed with a small amount of water to form balls and is then cooked and served in boiling water. A *tangtuan* can be either small or large, either filled or unfilled.

▶ **清明节**:清明节是中国的传统节日,是冬至后的一百零八天。人们在这一天里外出踏青和扫墓。

The *Qingming* Festival: It is also known as Tomb-sweeping Day. It is a traditional Chinese festival on the 108th day ofter the winter solstice, on which people often go on outings to enjoy the spring greenery and sweep the tombs of the departed ones.

▶ **端午节**:端午节是中国的传统节日和法定假日,为每年农历五月初五(即大约阳历五月底至六月中旬)。几千年来,人们挂艾叶、菖蒲、吃粽子(由粽叶包裹糯米甜馅而成)、喝雄黄酒及赛龙舟来庆祝端午节,纪念战国时期楚国爱国诗人屈原。现在举行的龙舟赛部分地是出于娱乐或竞争的目的。

The Dragon Boat Festival: The Dragon Boat Festival, or *Duanwu* Festival, is a traditional and statutory holiday in China, which falls on the fifth day of the fifth month according to the Chinese lunar calendar (approximately late-May to mid-June). For thousands of years, the festival has been celebrated by hanging mugwort and calamus on the front door, eating *zongzi* (rice dumplings wrapped in bamboo leaves with various sweet fillings), drinking realgar wine and racing dragon boats in memory of *Qu Yuan*, a patriotic Chinese poet from the kingdom of *Chu* who lived during the Warring States period. Currently, dragon boat races are held partly for entertainment or competitive purposes.

▶ **雄黄酒**:雄黄酒是一种用研磨成粉末的雄黄(即硫化砷)制作的中国米酒, 雄黄可解毒、辟邪、杀虫。人们习惯在端午节饮用雄黄酒,已达到防病辟邪之效。

Realgar wine: It is a Chinese rice liquor mixed with ground realgar (arsenic sulfide), which is an antidote for many poisons, and therefore believed to be most effective to drive away evil spirits and kill insects. Traditionally people would drink some realgar wine during the Dragon Boat Festival for protection from disease and evil for the rest of the year.

▶ **满月酒**:满月酒是为庆贺婴儿出世满一个月而设的宴席。宝宝的亲戚(如祖父母、外祖父母、姑姑姨妈、叔叔舅舅及表兄弟表妹)和父母的朋友被邀请来参加宴席。他们为孩子祝福,并希望其快乐、健康、前途光明。宴席上还为客人准备了很多不同的食品和饮料,其中最常见的是红蛋。蛋象征着人生新的道路,而红色象征着喜庆和好运,鸡蛋的椭圆形代表和谐与团结。

Full Moon Celebration: It is a dinner party customarily held in celebration of a baby's Full Moon. The baby's relatives (grandparents, aunts, uncles and cousins) and the parents' friends are invited to the party. They bless the baby and expect it to be happy, healthy and promising. There will be lots of different types of food and drinks prepared for the guests. One kind of food that is commonly seen is called red-dyed egg. The eggs symbolize a new passage in life whereas the red colour symbolizes celebration and good luck and the egg's oval shape represents harmony and unity.

▶ **雷峰塔**:雷峰塔是一座八面五层楼阁式塔,位于杭州西湖南岸,为西湖的标志性景点。雷峰夕照为西湖十景之一。原名黄妃塔,由吴越王钱弘俶于975年间庆黄妃得子而建。1924年雷峰塔倒塌,2000年重建。

***Leifeng* Pagoda**: *Leifeng* Pagoda, located south of West Lake, is an eight-sided, five-story pavilion-style tower, and a landmark attraction. *Leifeng* Pagoda in the Sunset is one of the Ten Scenes of West Lake. Tradition has it that the pagoda was built in 975 at the order of *Qian Hongchu*, the King of *Wu-Yue* Kingdom, to celebrate the birth of a son by one of his favourite concubines, Lady *Huang*. The pagoda collapsed in 1924 and was rebuilt in 2000.

贰 梁山伯与祝英台

Liang Shanbo and Zhu Yingtai

【简介】

梁山伯与祝英台的故事家喻户晓，是中国四大民间传说之一，是许多中国戏剧、电影、电视剧的主题。相传梁山伯和祝英台曾在坐落于西湖边凤凰山脚下的万松书院同窗读书。万松书院，建于1498年，是明清时期杭州最大最著名的书院，明代理学家王明阳曾在此讲学。现今的万松书院于2002年重建。

【Brief Introduction】

The romance between *Liang Shanbo* and *Zhu Yingtai*, also known as *The Butterfly Lovers*, a popular story in China, is one of the four well-known Chinese folk tales. It has been presented in a number of major Chinese operas, films and television series. Legend has it that *Liang Shanbo* and *Zhu Yingtai* once studied together in *Wansong* Academy, which is located at the foot of the Phoenix Mountain near West Lake. It was established in 1498. It was the largest and most prestigious college in *Hangzhou* during the *Ming* and *Qing* Dynasties. *Wang Yangming*, a famous philosopher in the *Ming* Dynasty, once gave lectures here. The present-day academy was rebuilt in 2002.

【传说读本】

从前，浙江绍兴府上虞县祝家庄里，有一个名字叫祝英台的姑娘儿。她不但人生得美丽，心灵手巧，还特别喜欢写字读书。等她长到十五六岁的辰光，便是一心想到杭州最上品的书院——万松书院里去读书。可是，那辰光的风气，女子是不允许外出读书的。

英台的贴身丫鬟银心最晓得小姐的心思了，她帮着英台想出一个主意：假扮成男伢儿，不就可以离开家里，远走高飞了吗？这一日，祝英台和银心各自打扮一番，英台变成一个公子，银心扮成书童，两人像模像样地来到客厅里。

祝英台的老爸祝**员外**此刻正在客厅里喝茶，忽然看见一个书童领着一个风度翩翩的相公进来向自己恭敬行礼，慌忙起身答礼，让座，请教公子尊姓大名。

英台见父亲大人也被瞒过，于是一边卸装一边向老爸说出了真相，请求他允许自己前往杭州读书。他开始时不肯答应，后来拗不过爱女的恳求，才勉强答应下来。

这一日，天气晴朗，她俩离了祝家庄，北上杭城，一路奔波来到杭州城东草桥门外草桥亭小憩，正好遇上一个书生和他的书童，也到亭子里来歇脚。同是读书人，双方互相招呼问候，英台得知这位书生名叫梁山伯，是从绍兴府会稽县到杭州万松书院来求学的，正好和自己同路。

英台和梁山伯一阵交谈，觉得十分投机，两人便在亭子里结拜为兄弟。随后，大家兴冲冲一同上路，直奔杭州城南最有名的万松书院。

在万松书院，山伯与英台开始了同窗读书的日子。他们背**四书五经**，写诗作文，交情也与日俱增。只是有一桩事山伯却被蒙在鼓里，他一点都不知英台原是个女儿身。

日月如梭，飞逝而去，转眼已经过去三年。这一日，英台接到家书，说他父亲病倒在床，思念爱女心切，要她快快返乡见面。祝英台向书院的先生请假后，又找到师娘，诉说她已经爱上了这位梁兄，恳请师娘等她回上虞后，替她向梁山伯提亲，还把一个玉扇坠儿郑重交给师娘，既做凭证又当信物。

英台即将启程回家，梁山伯闻讯来送她。谁晓得这一送，不知不觉就送了十八里。在相送途中，英台向他暗示自己是女儿身，可梁山伯就是不明白，甚至连同伴女扮男装丝毫都没有怀疑过。他们一直走啊走啊，来到了杭州城东钱塘江边，祝英台就从这里搭船回上虞去了。

祝英台回到家里，见父亲的病情并不严重，方知是老爸思女心切，故意称病，好让她回来团聚的。英台的老爸呢，看见女儿这么快就回乡省亲，心中很是快慰。他让女儿重着红装，再也不愿意她远离家乡外出读书了。这时，恰巧有邻村马家庄的大财主来提亲，英台的爸爸就一口应承，将英台许配给马家的儿子马文才。

英台得知后不禁大惊，她哪里肯答应这门亲事，于是实话实说禀报老爸，说她早已爱上了同窗学兄梁山伯。离开杭城前，还托过万松书院先生家的师娘**做媒**。可是,从来都是样样依着爱女的祝员外,这一回却不肯答应英台的请求,执意要祝英台嫁给马文才。

再说那天送别英台十几天后,师娘拿着祝英台临行前交给她的玉扇坠儿,来告诉梁山伯说:“祝英台啊,原来是个女儿身,还托我向你提亲哩!”梁山伯这才恍然大悟,原来祝英台那日在临行前的一番话是在向自己做表白啊!又惊又喜的梁山伯,立刻向老师请了假,赶往上虞祝家庄去,要快快和祝英台会面。

梁山伯赶到祝家庄,见到一副红装的祝英台,兴奋地说师娘已经为他俩提亲。哪知英台一听这话失声痛哭,她说道:“梁兄啊,你这么晚才来,我父亲已经硬将我许配给马家了!”

梁山伯一听此言,又是惊愕,又是难过,又是懊悔,只觉得自己如坠无底深渊,痛苦万分。晚了,晚了!他们两人抱头痛哭,发誓无论是谁也不能拆散他们。

伤透心的梁山伯回到家中,他想念祝英台,吃不下饭,睡不着觉,一场突然降临的大喜大悲,将这个忠厚老实的书生击倒了。他的病情越来越重,不久就含恨而死。临终前他告诉家里人,死后要把他埋在从祝家通往马家庄的路边,他的灵魂要去陪伴祝英台。

迎亲那一天,马家的花轿抬到祝家庄英台家门口,一边是吹吹打打的热闹,一边却是哭哭啼啼的英台。英台说什么也不愿意上轿,但在父亲的厉声呵斥之下,在家人的推搡扯拉之下,被硬生生逼近轿子,抬往马家庄去了。

花轿走到半路上,一阵狂风骤起,抬轿人被刮得再也走不动了。这时,丫鬟银心含泪告诉英台,前面路旁就是梁山伯的坟。

祝英台突然挣脱家人的拦挡,冲出花轿,一定要到梁山伯的墓前去祭拜。来到梁山伯墓前,英台扑在坟上放声大哭。霎时,忽然电闪雷鸣,风雨大作。梁山伯的坟墓哗啦一声裂开了一条大口子。祝英台纵身跳进坟里去了。

说也奇怪,英台跳进坟墓,雨就停了,云也开了,空中红日重现。一对美丽的蝴蝶,从梁祝生离死合的坟头上翩翩飞起,犹如在空中跳着舞蹈,越舞越远,一直向北飞去,再也不分离。

【English Version of the Original Story】

Once upon a time, there was a girl named *Zhu Yingtai* who lived in *Zhu* Village in *Shangyu* County, *Shaoxing*, *Zhejiang* Province. She was not only beautiful, but also brilliant and above all, she loved learning. When she was fifteen, she longed to study in the best academy in *Hangzhou*—*Wansong* Academy. Unfortunately the traditions of ancient China discouraged girls from going to school.

Yingtai's maid *Yin Xin* knew what was on *Yingtai's* mind and came up with an idea: If they dressed like men, they could leave home and go to a faraway place. One day, *Yingtai* and *Yin Xin* disguised themselves as a gentleman and a page and walked into the sitting room.

Yingtai's father, *Zhu Yuanwai*, was drinking tea when he saw a page walk in, followed by a handsome young man who bowed to him. Mr. *Zhu* got up and bowed too. Then he invited the young man to be seated and asked him what his name was.

Seeing her father was unable to recognize her, *Yingtai* took off her men's clothes and told him the truth, begging him to allow her to study in *Hangzhou*. Though he did not like the idea, he had no choice but to let her go since she was so determined.

One fine day, they left *Zhu* Village for *Hangzhou*. When they arrived, they rested at *Caoqiao* Pavilion outside the *Caoqiao* Gate east of *Hangzhou*. Here, they happened to meet a student and his page boy, who served him in his study. His name was *Liang Shanbo* who came from *Kuaiji* County, *Shaoxing*, and was on his way to the same academy.

Zhu Yingtai and *Liang Shanbo* talked for a while and felt like old friends. Soon they became sworn brothers. Then they traveled happily together and finally arrived at famous *Wansong* Academy, south of *Hangzhou*.

Since that day they studied together at *Wansong* Academy, where they recited ***the Four Books and Five Classics*** and composed poems and articles. Their friendship increased day by day, but *Liang Shanbo* was still kept in the dark about one thing: He did not have the slightest idea that *Yingtai* was actually a girl.

Three school years flew by. One day, *Yingtai* received a letter from her father, saying that he was seriously ill and missing her very much. He urged her to get back home as soon as possible. She asked her teacher for leave of absence. Then she revealed her true identity to the teacher's wife, saying that she had fallen in love with *Liang*. She requested her teacher's wife to do the matching-making after she returned to *Shangyu* and left her a jade pendant as a proof and as a love token.

Hearing that *Yingtai* was leaving for home, *Liang* came to see her off. They covered 18 *lis* before they realized it. During the journey, she hinted to him that she was actually a girl, but *Liang* did not catch her hints, and never realized that his companion was a woman in disguise. They walked and walked until they came to the *Qiantang* River on the east side of *Hangzhou*, from where *Yingtai* took the ferry across the river to *Shangyu*.

Yingtai arrived back home only to find that her father was not very sick and that he was only missing her and hoped for her return. Mr. *Zhu* was happy and relieved at the sight of his daughter coming back so soon. He asked his daughter to wear girl's clothes and did not let her go to school any more. It happened that a rich landlord in the neighbouring *Majia* village came to propose a marriage, and Mr. *Zhu* agreed to engage *Yingtai* to the son of the *Ma* family, whose name was *Ma Wencai*.

On hearing this news, *Yingtai* was greatly dismayed and wouldn't accept the proposal. She told her father that she had fallen in love with *Liang Shanbo* and that she had, before she left *Wansong* Academy, asked the teacher's wife to **the matchmaker**. However, Mr. *Zhu*, who used to let her do whatever she liked, rejected her request and insisted on marrying her to *Ma Wencai*.

More than ten days after *Liang Shanbo* saw *Yingtai* off, the teacher's wife gave him the jade pendant and said,

"*Yingtai* is a girl! She has asked me to be your matchmaker."

Liang Shanbo suddenly realized that what she said before her departure was to hint at her love for him. Both surprised and excited, *Liang Shanbo* immediately asked for leave and hurried to *Zhu* Village in *Shangyu*. He could not wait to see her.

When he finally arrived, *Liang Shanbo* saw *Yingtai* in girl's clothes and he excitedly mentioned the marriage proposal made through the teacher's wife. Upon hearing this, *Yingtai* burst into tears and said,

"*Shanbo*, why did you come here so late? My father has already engaged me to Mr. *Ma* without my consent!"

Liang was shocked, sad and regretful. He felt as if he was plunging into an abyss of great misery. Too late! Too late! They were hugging each other and crying bitterly, vowing that no one could separate them. Heartbroken, *Liang* returned home. He missed *Yingtai* so much that he could not eat or sleep. The mixed feelings of sudden happiness and sadness threw the honest young man into a deep depression. He became seriously ill and, not long after, died of a broken heart. Before dying, he told his family that he wanted to be buried at the side of the road between *Zhu* Village and *Ma* Village and that he wished to accompany *Yingtai* with his soul.

On the day of **bridal escorting ritual**, the bridal sedan stopped at the door of *Zhu Yingtai's* house, with drums beating and *Yingtai* crying. She refused to get into the sedan, but in vain. Rebuked by her father and pushed by her family, she was at last forced into the sedan and carried away towards *Ma* Village.

As the wedding procession moved off, there was a sudden, mysterious whirlwind which prevented the sedan chair carriers from moving forward. *Yin Xin* told *Yingtai* tearfully that *Liang Shanbo*'s grave was beyond the road. *Yingtai* broke free from her parents, rushed out of the sedan and left the procession so she could pay her last respects to *Liang*. She approached the grave, knelt down and wept bitterly. Suddenly, a storm broke with a clap of thunder and a flash of lightning. *Liang*'s grave opened. Without any hesitation, *Yingtai* jumped into the grave to join *Shanbo*.

Strangely enough, as soon as *Yingtai* had jumped in, the storm passed. The clouds parted and the sun shone in the sky. Then, from the grave, emerged a pair of beautiful butterflies which were fluttering as if they were dancing in the air. They danced and then flew away together to the north never to be separated again.

【文化背景】【Cultural Notes】

▶ **员外：**员外是中国古代的一个官名。根据其官职的相对声望和职责的重要性，在不同的朝代，其品级地位各有不同。在明朝之后常有商贾士绅花钱获得此官职，至此，员外成为对乡绅的一种尊称。

Yuanwai: *Yuanwai* was an official title in ancient China. It was ranked differently according to its relative prestige and importance of its duties in different dynasties. After the *Ming* Dynasty, this official title could often be bought by businessmen and squires. Thus the title came to be used as a polite form of address for squires.

▶ **四书五经**：四书五经是中国儒家的经典权威书籍。四书指的是《论语》《孟子》《大学》和《中庸》；而五经指的是《诗经》《尚书》《礼记》《周易》和《春秋》。四书五经是中国传统文化的重要组成部分，它对中国人的心理已经产生并将继续产生深远的影响。

The Four Books and Five Classics: The Four Books and Five Classics are the authoritative books of Confucianism in China. The Four Books refer to *The Analects of Confucius*, *The Mencius*, *The Great Learning* and *The Doctrine of the Golden Mean*. The Five Classics refer to *The Classic of Poetry*, *The Book of Documents*, *The Book of Rites*, *The Book of Changes*, and *The Spring and Autumn Annals*. The Four Books and Five Classics are an important part of Chinese traditional culture and have exerted and still continue to exert a profound influence on the mentalities of Chinese people.

▶ **做媒**：在旧中国，妇女不允许选择与她们结婚的人。相反，是由新娘的家人或媒人选择未来的丈夫。婚姻是根据生育能力、名声以及父亲和丈夫的需要来包办的。

Be a matchmaker: In ancient China, women were not allowed to choose the persons they married. Instead, the family of the bride or a matchmaker picked the prospective husband. Marriages were arranged based upon the needs of reproduction and honour, as well as the needs of the father and the husband.

▶ **迎亲**：迎亲是中国传统的结婚仪式之一，是由新郎把新娘迎娶到家。迎亲队伍是由一个传统的乐队、新娘的轿子、伴娘的轿子（如果有伴娘的话）及新娘的嫁妆组成的。

Bride escorting ritual: It is one of the Chinese traditional marriage rituals. The wedding procession from the bride's home to the groom's home consists of a traditional band, the bride's sedan, the maids of honour's sedans (if there are maids of honour), and the bride's dowry.

叁 ◎ 苏小小与鲍仁
Su Xiaoxiao and *Bao Ren*

【简介】

苏小小是南朝齐(479—502)时的钱塘名伎,样貌出众,诗才横溢。苏小小与鲍仁的爱情故事感人至深。苏小小死后葬于西泠桥畔,后人仰慕她的文采,在此建墓,墓上覆六角亭,叫作"慕才亭","文革"期间被毁,又于2004年重建。亭柱上刻有国内十二名著名书法家手写的十二副楹联。如今苏小小墓已经成为杭州的主要旅游景点之一。

【Brief Introduction】

Su Xiaoxiao was the most famous, beautiful and talented songstress in *Qiantang* in the Southern *Qi* Dynasty (479—502). The love story of *Su Xiaoxiao* and *Bao Ren* is touching. She was buried by the *Xiling* Bridge and out of admiration for her talent, people built a tomb here. On the tomb stood a hexagonal pavilion called the *Mucai* Pavilion (*mucai* in Chinese means admiring talents). The tomb and the pavilion were both destroyed during the Great Cultural Revolution, but rebuilt in 2004. The pillars of the pavilion are decorated with 12 poetry posters, handwritten by 12 famous calligraphers. *Su Xiaoxiao's* tomb has become one of the major tourist sites in *Hangzhou*.

【传说读本】

苏小小出身娼妓人家，自小也不知道父亲是哪一个。母亲死了以后，门户变得冷冷清清，生活贫苦。好在她的家庭就住在**西泠桥**旁边，天天受到西湖山水的滋润培养，再加上她生性聪明，容貌如画，好比九天仙女下凡。到十二三岁时，她长得更加出众，而且看过的书，过目不忘，讲的话语，句句成章在理。她自小见识不凡，经常坐着一辆小小的油壁香车，漫游**三竺两峰**，招引得一班年轻的公子像一群蜜蜂一样拥着她飞转。但苏小小十分自重，丝毫也没有流露出一点轻浮的模样，使得一班豪门子弟无法可想。

那些豪门公子，自以为有的是金银，都情愿出千金请人说媒，但一个个都碰了鼻头。苏小小一不爱金银，二不要金屋，生性只爱西湖山水，只喜遨游三竺两峰，把富贵荣华看作粪土。

有一天，苏小小到石屋洞游玩。那时正是深秋季节，天气有点冷了。她被满山红叶的景色吸引住，久久不想离去。正看得出神时，忽见对面寺前有一个青年书生，落落寞寞，在那里闲踱，见了苏小小的油壁香车，有点进退两难的样子。苏小小一点不嫌弃他寒素，落落大方地走上去同他交谈，言谈中知他有满腹文章，十分钦佩，约他到西泠桥旁家中细谈。

那个贫寒书生叫鲍仁，对苏小小能这样看重自己十分感动，便选了个日子来到苏小小家里。那一日，苏小小家里正好坐满了豪门公子，可苏小小一听到鲍仁来到，竟然像接待知心好友一样，把那些贵公子冷落在一边。一番谈话十分知己，苏小小拿出私房银钱两封赠给鲍仁，慷慨资助他**上京赶考**。

鲍仁走了，那些豪门公子都争着来邀请她去吃酒席，游西湖。她为了应付这些贵公子，只得硬着头皮去。她从来是卖艺不卖身，招得那些贵公子争风吃醋，打闹拼斗。这样一来，给苏小小带来无限的烦恼，终日闷闷不乐，久而久之，染病在身。可是那些贵公子一点也不体谅她，照样要苏小小去赴约。苏小小因病在身，只得回绝。这样，今天回绝这个，明天回绝那个，招得那些人恼怒不已，天天在客堂里闹事，弄得苏小小卧病也不安耽(安生)，毛病愈来愈重，无法医治。临死时，苏小小对身边的姐妹们说："我苏小小生于西泠，死于西泠，但愿能埋骨西泠，不负我爱西湖山水之癖。"说完，溘然而逝。众姐妹痛哭一场，将她入棺收殓了。因不是体面人家，不敢举行丧仪。

没过几天，两个差人飞马来报："滑州鲍刺史来拜。"原来鲍刺史就是苏小小赠银的贫寒书生鲍仁。大比之年，他金榜题名，放滑州刺史。今路过杭州，特地来拜谢苏小小。现在见苏小小去世,痛哭流涕。众姐妹见他心地纯正,就把苏小小临死前的愿望告诉了他。鲍仁刺史说:“苏姐姐待我如知己,我当仁不让,为她在西泠桥畔择地建坟。”下葬那天,鲍刺史白衣白冠,亲送苏小小灵柩。临别又哭祭一场,依依难舍。

从此,西泠桥畔多了一座坟墓,坟墓前立着一个大石碑,上面写着“钱塘苏小小之墓”。

【English Version of the Original Story】

Su Xiaoxiao was born in a brothel. She never knew who her father was. After her mother died, she lived a poor life in a lonely house. Luckily she lived beside the **Xiling Bridge** with a view of the beautiful West Lake. She was endowed with such intelligence and great beauty that she was just like a celestial maiden coming down to the human world. When she was twelve or thirteen, she looked more beautiful than ever before. She remembered what she had read and was an eloquent speaker. She often went sightseeing by riding in a small decorated carriage. She loved climbing the double mountains named **the Northern and Southern Peak** and visiting **Three Temples of *Tianzhu***. With a lot of wonderful experiences and a wide range of knowledge, she attracted a group of young men who followed her like a swarm of bees. Nevertheless her self-respect and lack of frivolity kept those young rich men at bay.

Those wealthy young men were proud of having a lot of gold and silver. They offered a large amount of money to hire matchmakers to propose a marriage to *Su Xiaoxiao*. She rejected them all, for she neither loved money nor a golden house. Instead, she only loved the natural beauty of West Lake, along with the mountains and the temples around there. She treated money and power as if they were dirt.

One cold day in late autumn, *Su Xiaoxiao* visited a stone cave. She was so fascinated by the beautiful view of the mountains, covered with red maple leaves, that she could not tear herself away from it. At this moment, she saw a desolate, young scholar walking up and down in front of the dilapidated old temple opposite the cave. He felt embarrassed as he saw her in her decorated carriage, and didn't know where to put himself. But *Su Xiaoxiao* did not care about his shabbiness. Instead, she walked gracefully up to him and began to talk to him. During the conversation she found he was talented and knowledgeable. Full of admiration, she invited him to come to her house, near the *Xiling* Bridge, for a long conversation another time.

That poor scholar was called *Bao Ren*. He was so deeply moved by *Su Xiaoxiao*'s admiration that he paid a visit to her one day. That day there was a roomful of rich young men sitting in her house. Seeing *Bao Ren* come, *Su Xiaoxiao* treated him as an intimate good friend, and gave those rich men the cold shoulder. After a pleasant conversation, she gave *Bao Ren* several nuggets of silver from her purse and urged him to go to the capital to take the **Imperial Examination**.

After *Bao Ren* left, those rich men competed in inviting her to attend dinners and visit West Lake. She had no choice but to force herself to go with them. However, she made a living only as a performer and never as a courtesan. This made those men jealous of each other and they even fought each other. This brought endless trouble to *Su Xiaoxiao*, causing her to be in a bad mood all day long. She came down with an illness, but those rich men did not care about her health. Instead, they made appointments with her as usual. *Su Xiaoxiao* was so sick that she had to turn down their invitations.

Her frequent rejections made them so angry that they came and made trouble in her house every day, which gave her no peace. She became so seriously ill that she could not be cured. On her deathbed, she said to her female friends,

"I was born and will die in *Xiling*. I hope to be buried here too, because I have always loved the landscape of West Lake."

With that, she died and her female friends cried bitterly. They placed her in a coffin without any funeral service, because what she did was not a decent job.

A few days later, two guards on horseback came to her house. They announced,

"*Bao Ren*, governor of *Huazhou* has come for a visit."

It turned out that *Bao Ren* was none other than the poor scholar to whom *Su Xiaoxiao* had offered a lot of money. He had achieved great success in Imperial Examination and was nominated Governor of *Huazhou*.

He made a special trip to *Hangzhou* to express his thanks to *Su Xiaoxiao*. He burst into tears on being told that she had passed away. *Su*'s friends thought he was amiable and told him about her last wish. *Bao Ren* said, "Lady *Su* treated me as a close friend and I must fulfill her wish. I will have her tomb built in a spot beside the *Xiling* Bridge." On the day when she was buried, he went into mourning and accompanied her coffin all the way. He wept bitterly in front of her tomb before he left.

Since then, a large memorial plaque has stood in front of her tomb beside the *Xiling* Bridge, which reads "*Qiantang Su Xiao Xiao*'s Tomb".

【文化背景】【Cultural Notes】

▶ **西泠桥**：西泠桥长桥、与断桥并称为西湖三大情人桥。它位于栖霞岭麓到孤山之间，是一座古色古香的环洞石拱桥。古时，原为一处风景如画的渡口。2004 年 6 月重修后，恢复并保持了它的原貌和特色。

***The Xiling* Bridge**: The *Xiling* Bridge, the Long Bridge and the Broken Bridge are seen as three bridges for lovers in West Lake. The *Xiling* Bridge is a bridge connecting *Qixia* Ridge and *Gu* Hill. It is an old, single-hole, stone-vaulted bridge. In earlier times, there had be a ferry landing here commanding a beautiful view. After a major repair in June 2004, the bridge has been restored and kept its original features.

▶ **三竺**：也称天竺三寺，坐落于杭州灵隐寺以南的天竺山，依山而建，依次称为上天竺寺、中天竺寺和下天竺寺。三寺均以观音为本尊。三寺彼此相似，历史相近，教观相同，历史上被誉为"天竺佛国"。天竺三寺香火极盛。

Three Tempes of Tianzhu: There are three old temples of *Tianzhu* located on the *Tianzhu* Hill south of *Lingyin* Temple in *Hangzhou*. Since they were built along the *Tianzhu* Hill, they were formerly known as Upper

Tianzhu Temple, Middle *Tianzhu* Temple and Lower *Tianzhu* Temple. The image of Avalokitesvara is consecrated in each main hall. The three temples resemble one another, just as they also have nearly the same history and share the same significance in Buddhism. The three temples make up what is believed to be the "Buddhist Heaven of *Tianzhu*". Every year a great number of Buddhist pilgrims flock here.

▶ **两峰**:两峰是指北高峰和南高峰。北高峰位于西湖以北,海拔高度为 300 多米,被称为第一财神庙的灵顺寺建于山顶,每逢阳春时节,前来拜求的生意人络绎不绝,香火极盛。南高峰高 250 多米,位于西湖的西南面,与北高峰遥遥对峙,山上的书画碑廊使其成为一方文化名胜。

The Northern and Southern Peaks: The Northern Peak lies north of West Lake at an altitude of over 300 metres above sea level, with *Lingshun* Temple, the No. 1 Mammon Temple, on its top. When spring comes, many businessmen flock here and pray for good fortune. The Southern Peak, which has a height of over 250 metres, lies southwest of the lake, opposite to the Northern Peak. The Chinese calligraphy stone tablets gallery there makes it a cultural tourist attraction.

▶ **上京赶考**:科举是历代封建王朝通过考试选拔官吏的一种制度。科举始于隋朝大业元年(605),成型于唐朝,一直延续到清朝末年,在 1905 年被废除,持续了 1300 年。现代社会公务员的选拔制度亦是从科举制间接演变而来。

Go to the capital to take the Imperial Examination: The Imperial Examination is an examination system in imperial China designed to select the best potential candidates to serve as administrative officials. It was established in 605 during the *Sui* Dynasty, and became systematized during the *Tang* Dynasty. The system continued until it was abolished under the *Qing* Dynasty in 1905. The system had a history of 1,300 years. The modern examination system for selecting civil service staff has indirectly evolved from the imperial one.

肆 柳浪与莺姑娘

Liu Lang and the Oriole Girl

【简介】

柳浪与莺姑娘的爱情故事发生在西湖著名景点柳浪闻莺。柳浪闻莺是西湖十景之一,位于西湖东南岸,其前身为南宋(1127—1279)时皇帝御花园,称聚景园。20 世纪 50 年代,经过一系列改造项目,公园又恢复了原貌。全园分友谊、闻莺、聚景、南园四个景区。今天,公园占地 21 公顷,柳树摇曳,黄莺鸣啭。它是休闲、娱乐的理想场所,也是不同的仪式和节日庆典的最佳选择。

【Brief Introduction】

The love story between *Liu Lang* and the Oriole Girl happened in a well-known scenic spot of West Lake, i.e. Orioles Singing in the Willows. It is off the southeast bank of West Lake and among the Top Ten Scenes of West Lake. It used to be an imperial park named *Jujing* Garden in the Southern *Song* Dynasty (1127—1279). The park came back to life again in the 1950s through a series of refurbishment projects. Today, the park includes four parts: Friendship Garden, Listening-to-Orioles Garden, Garden of Composite Views and South Garden. It covers 21 hectares, with willow trees swaying and orioles singing among the branches. It is an ideal place for recreation and entertainment, and also the best choice for various ceremonies and holiday celebrations.

【传说读本】

早先,这一带地方叫柳浦,满村是密层层的杨柳。住在这里的三百来户人家,都是郡王府的织锦户。他们家家织得上好的**杭州丝绸**,有一手好手艺;但家家都很穷困,过的是苦日子。有一户人家母子两个,儿子名叫柳浪,是个好后生,手艺很高,但因为穷苦,年纪不小了,还没有娶媳妇。柳浪的心事,也从来不向人透露,只向那柳林里游转的黄莺倾诉。这黄莺也真懂事,天天飞来为柳浪唱歌做伴,陪他织锦。日子一久,竟成了知心的朋友。

有一天,柳林里走出一个十八九岁的姑娘,圆眼睛,瓜子脸,一身金黄衣衫,显得十分俊秀。她就是黄莺姑娘。

她偷偷地在窗口看柳浪织锦,想进屋里去,又有点怕羞。这时,正好来了张二嫂。她是个热心人,喜欢管闲事,看到有姑娘偷偷看柳浪,暗暗地好笑。不料这姑娘一见二嫂,就迎上去叫声姐姐,还说自已是她的表妹金衣。二嫂想,我哪来的表妹呀!莺姑娘又编了一些家事,最后说是投奔姐姐来的。二嫂听她这么说,又仔细瞧瞧她模样,心里有了盘算。就过去高声地朝屋里喊道:"柳浪,你出来见见我的表妹!"柳浪在屋里织锦,他今天听不到黄莺鸣叫,正在纳闷哩!听到喊声,出门一看莺姑娘,竟觉得十分面熟,就笑吟吟地望着她。莺姑娘红着脸,也不说一句话。二嫂见了,拍着手说,"真是天生的一对!",就进屋去找柳婆婆了。

这桩婚事,经二嫂一撮合,大家都愿意,就定下来了。柳婆婆更是高兴得合不拢嘴,准备为儿子办喜事。

这一天,刚逢是缴锦的日子。柳浪定了这门亲事,心里乐滋滋的,就背起锦,兴冲冲地跟着乡邻到郡王府去了。

那郡王是皇帝的侄儿。这一年正是皇帝六十岁,郡王准备选一匹最精美的锦绸奉献上去,就将缴来的彩锦挑选起来。可是挑来挑去都不满意,后来看到柳浪织的那匹绵,才连连说好。但一听说这锦名叫西湖九景缎,连忙摇头说,"九字不到头,不能庆万寿",立刻唤进柳浪,要他在一夜之间赶织西湖十景缎,还规定这新添的一景,要有声有色。

柳浪高高兴兴去缴锦,却带着这灾难回家来了。

莺姑娘在村口等柳浪,见他回来,喊他不应,问他不响,只听他自言自语地说着:"有声……有色,色彩……一夜之间"。后来,他把事情告诉了莺姑娘。于是她说:"有色容易,一夜间织成也不难,只是有声怎么织呢?"过了会儿,她笑了起来说:"有了,有了,你不要急,今晚我夫妻俩同织就是了。"柳浪听莺姑娘能织,忧愁丢了一半。

当晚,柳浪就开手织起来。这有声有色的一景到底该怎样织,莺姑娘也心中无数,想找众姐姐去商量,就趁这月上柳梢的时候,走到堤边,轻轻地叫了三声姐姐。

一会儿，画眉鸟、八哥鸟、百灵鸟都飞来了。她们听说要织有声有色的美锦，也想不出好办法。最后还是画眉鸟有主意，拉着杨柳条，叫道："好姐姐，你替我们想想办法吧。"杨柳笑笑说："小黄莺，这有什么难！织上杨柳就有色，织上黄莺便有声。"

莺姑娘送别了姐姐们，急忙回到房间。这时已经三更天了，柳浪心灵手巧，也已织到第五景了。莺姑娘就接过鱼梭，继续织下去。柳浪在一边，看她织好一景又一景，看到开始织第十景，先是一条堤，再是一个旧祠堂，以后是一片成行的杨柳。柳浪看得着急起来，说："这倒像是我的家，怎么称得上风景？"

莺姑娘笑了笑："你的家为啥称不上风景呢？"她还是一梭接一梭地织下去，趁柳浪一转眼，她拔下根羽毛，铺到锦上又织了几只小黄莺。

柳浪越看越急。莺姑娘却故意慢吞吞地织好最后一只黄莺，剪下锦缎卷成了一筒。

"我明朝怎么讲呢？这算是什么风景？"

"就叫柳浪闻莺。"

"这越发不对了。"

"有什么不对？这不是柳浪闻莺是什么？"

"……有声有色……这声在哪里？郡王规定要有声音的啊！"

莺姑娘再把锦展开，指着杨柳问柳浪，有没有色，柳浪点点头；再指着黄莺叫柳浪细听，果然一只只黄莺，一齐鸣唱起来。这一下，柳浪可高兴了。从此，西湖九景缎也就改为西湖十景缎。

郡王验过这匹西湖十景缎，更是如得珍宝，赶快装上锦盒，派人押送进京，还赏赐柳浪一锭元宝。柳浪有了钱，就开始张罗喜事了。乡邻们晓得这件事，大家也高高兴兴来帮忙。不料成亲的那一天，郡王府的总管和旗牌上门来了。他们当众宣读郡王的旨令，要柳浪的妻子进府去。原来，郡王怀疑不一定是柳浪织的，就派旗牌去打听。去的人回来报告，柳家有一个天仙般的美女。郡王是个色鬼，一听说有美女，立刻下令，快快派**花轿**把她抬来，准备将莺姑娘娶作第十位夫人。

柳浪死也不肯让莺姑娘进府去，旗牌把他绑在树上。

莺姑娘这时也真着急，展翅飞吧，怕暴露了自己的秘密；不飞吧，一时又想不出好办法。正犹豫不决，几个旗牌上前把她绑进彩轿，抬走了。

就这样,旗牌抬着莺姑娘进殿来。郡王欢欢喜喜地打开轿帘,哪有什么美女,明明是一顶空轿。郡王大怒,旗牌们也都慌了。正在这时,府门外传来一阵急促的鼓声。门上人来报,说是柳浪镶门击鼓。

郡王哼了一声,说:“我正要找他算账呢!”他说着便要旗牌将柳浪带进来。柳浪一见郡王,据理指责他不该强抢民妻。郡王却指着空轿破口大骂,说他抗旨欺王。柳浪听说是空轿,以为莺姑娘被他们害死了,一面哭喊,一面大骂。郡王就下令把他绑起来。这时,柳浦的人纷纷赶到,大家哄闹起来。郡王大怒,连声说:“斩,斩,斩,把柳浪斩了!”

郡王刚说完,莺姑娘忽地站在他面前。他一见这俊俏的姑娘,立刻变了一个模样,呵呵笑着,连声说:“美人到了,赶快成亲。”

莺姑娘说:“慢! 先放了人,再来说话。”郡王放了柳浦的乡亲,却不肯释放柳浪。莺姑娘责问他:“为什么不放柳浪?”郡王说:“要放柳浪不难,只要你我先进**洞房**。”莺姑娘咬了咬牙,答应了。一些宫女立即把她拥进新房去了。

当天夜里,郡王府里闹盈盈,郡王喜洋洋地进了新房。柳浪却孤零零地绑在花园里的大槐树下。他忽然听见黄莺的啼声,又好像有人替自己解绳子,定睛一看,莺姑娘在他身边。莺姑娘替他解了绑,就拉着他,翻出墙去,只见两个人影子一闪不见了。

旗牌们没有追上他俩, 赶快去报告郡王。可是在房门口一连报了几十声,都听不见回应。撬进去一看,郡王竟被几株枯杨柳压住了,眨着白眼,嘴里塞满了泥巴发不出一点声音来。

莺姑娘和柳浪回到家里。柳婆婆正在哭泣,见到他们回来了,又是喜,又是愁,说:“逃是逃出来了,郡王追来还不是……”话未说完,又伤心地哭起来。莺姑娘说:“婆婆不要哭,我有办法。”她要柳浪将草鞋脱下来,就带了它奔出村去。大家正在奇怪,只见天上出现了几百只莺衔着一只大草鞋,慢慢地向郡王府飞去。飞到郡王府,“砰”的一声巨响,草鞋变成了山岭。郡王府从此就不见了。

柳浪和莺姑娘欢欢喜喜成了亲。他们织的柳浪闻莺一景,后来出了名。西湖边这一带,杨柳长青,黄莺常啼,春光也越发好了。

【English Version of the Original Story】

Long ago, there was a village called *Liu Pu*, which was surrounded by rows of closely planted willow trees. 300 families, who were all silk weavers, lived there and worked for the Duke. They were skillful at weaving beautiful silk, yet all of them were poor and led miserable lives. In one house lived a mother and her son who was named *Liu Lang*. He was a pleasant young man who could weave very good silk. He was so poor that he could not afford to take a wife although he was of marriageable age. He never told anyone about what was on his mind. The exception was the oriole that flew here and there in the forest of willows. This oriole was so considerate that she came to *Liu*'s window every day to sing and keep him company as he worked. As time went by, they became close friends.

One day, a beautiful girl of eighteen came from the willow forest. She had round eyes, an oval face and was wearing a golden blouse. She was the Oriole Girl.

She came to *Liu Lang*'s window to watch him weave. She didn't want to be seen but she also wanted to go inside, but was a little shy. It happened that Mrs. *Zhang* came by. She was warm-hearted and nosy. When she saw a girl stealthily watching *Liu Lang*, she was secretly happy. The girl was surprised to see Mrs. *Zhang*, and she addressed her as "Sister", saying she was her cousin called *Jin Yi*. Mrs. *Zhang* did not think that she had such a cousin, but the girl told her a story which convinced her that the girl really was her cousin. Mrs. *Zhang* looked at the girl's beautiful face and started thinking about matchmaking. She shouted to *Liu Lang* in the house,

"*Liu Lang*, come on here and meet my cousin."

At that point *Liu Lang* was weaving in the house and wondering why he could not hear the oriole singing that day. He went outside only to find the Oriole Girl standing in front of him, who looked familiar to him. He watched her smilingly. She flushed and was at a loss, not knowing what to say. Having seen what happened, Mrs. *Zhang* clapped her hands and said,

"You are made for each other!"

She then went into the house to see *Liu Lang*'s mother.

With the help of Mrs. *Zhang*, the matchmaker, *Liu Lang* and the girl both agreed to their marriage. *Liu*'s mother was beside herself with joy and started to prepare for the wedding ceremony.

The wedding day happened to be the day for offering silk to the Duke. Feeling happy about his marriage, *Liu Lang* and the other villagers cheerfully carried the silk to the Duke's palace.

The Duke was the emperor's nephew. That year the emperor turned 60 and the Duke wanted to offer the emperor the most beautiful silk as a gift. He went over all the embroidered silk but was unable to find any to satisfy him. Then he found *Liu Lang*'s silk very beautiful. When he was told that there were only nine beautiful views of West Lake woven into the silk, he shook his head and said,

"The number nine is not good enough to celebrate the emperor's birthday." He sent for *Liu Lang* at once and asked him to weave ten views into the silk overnight and required that the tenth view should be full of sound and colour.

Liu Lang had left home happily but he returned sadly. The Oriole Girl was waiting for him outside the village. When he came back, he was upset and refused to answer any questions. He kept saying to himself,

"Sound... sound, colour... colour, weave... overnight."

Later on, *Liu Lang* told the Oriole Girl about what had happened. After hearing that, she said,

"Colour is not a problem and finishing it overnight is not, either, but how can we put sound into the silk?"

After a while, she smiled and said,

"Don't worry! Let's weave it together this evening!"

Hearing that she could weave, he felt much relieved.

That evening, *Liu Lang* began to weave. The girl really did not have any idea about how to do it. She sneaked out of the house to turn to her sister birds for advice just as the moon was rising over the willow trees. She approached the dyke and said gently,

"Sisters, sisters, sisters!"

Then thrushes, starlings and larks all flew to her. Hearing about her trouble, they were all puzzled and could not work out a good solution. At last a thrush turned to the willow tree for help. She held the willow twig and exclaimed,

"Good sister, please figure out a solution for us."

The willow twig said smilingly,

"Little oriole, that's easy! If you embroider willow in the silk, you'll get colour. With orioles in it, you'll have sound."

Then the Oriole Girl said goodbye to her friends and hurried back. It was now around midnight. *Liu Lang* was skillful and began to weave the fifth view. She took over the shuttle and continued *Liu Lang*'s work. She wove and wove while *Liu Lang* watched. Seeing her working on the tenth view with a causeway, an old ancestral temple and lines of willow trees, he became worried and said,

"This is our village, not a view!"

"Isn't your village a view?"

she asked with a smile. She continued weaving and in a twinkling, without being noticed by *Liu Lang*, she plucked one of her own feathers, put it onto the silk and wove some orioles into it.

Liu Lang became more and more worried while the girl slowly wove the last oriole and rolled up the silk.

"How can I explain it tomorrow? What view is it?" *Liu Lang* asked.

"This is called 'Orioles Singing in the Willows'." she replied.

"This is not right."

"Why is it wrong? Isn't it a view of Orioles Singing in the Willows?"

"... With colour and sound... Where is the sound? The Duke asked for sound and colour!"

The girl unrolled the silk and pointed at the willows.

"Is this colour?" she asked.

"Yes!" *Liu* nodded.

She pointed to the orioles and asked him to listen. Sure enough, the orioles began to sing together. This made him very happy. Since then, the silk weaving with nine views of West Lake has given way to the silk with ten views.

The Duke treated the ten-view silk as if he had found a treasure. He packed it into a brocade box and had it sent to the capital. To show his satisfaction, he gave *Liu Lang* a shoe-shaped ingot as a reward. With the money, *Liu Lang* began to prepare for his wedding. The neighbours heard the news and all came to offer help.

As for the Duke, he suspected that *Liu Lang* himself could not have completed the silk weaving by working alone all night. He sent his soldiers to inquire about it. He was then told that there was a girl, as beautiful as a fairy, in *Liu Lang*'s home, who had helped with the weaving. The Duke was lecherous and wanted to take this pretty girl as his tenth wife. He gave orders at once that the girl should be brought to his palace in a **bridal sedan chair**. It was on *Liu Lang*'s wedding day that the Duke's house steward and soldiers came. They read the Duke's order that *Liu*'s wife be sent to the palace.

Liu Lang would rather die than let his wife leave, but the soldiers tied him to a tree. The Oriole Girl was worried. She could fly away but she was afraid of giving away her secret; she could not figure out what to do. While she was hesitating, a few soldiers tied her up and carried her away in the bridal sedan chair.

The soldiers brought her sedan chair into the palace. Expectantly, the Duke drew the curtain of the sedan chair. To his great surprise, he found it empty. He was so outraged that the soldiers were all thrown into a panic. Just then there came the sound of urgent drumming from outside the palace.

"It is *Liu Lang* who is beating the drum outside." announced a guard.

"Just in time! I was about to have my revenge on him" groaned the Duke. He ordered his soldiers to bring *Liu Lang* in. Seeing the Duke, *Liu Lang* accused him of taking away his wife by force. Pointing to the empty sedan chair, the Duke cursed *Liu Lang*, and said he had cheated him. When *Liu Lang* was told that the sedan chair was empty, he assumed that the Duke had had his wife to be killed. He cried and showered abuse on the Duke. The duke ordered him to be tied up. Just then people from the *Liu* village arrived and protested. The Duke flew into a rage and shouted,

"Kill him! Kill him! Kill him! Kill *Liu Lang*!"

No sooner had the Duke finished giving orders when the Oriole Girl stood in front of him. When he saw this pretty girl, he was overjoyed and said smilingly,

"Now you are mine, beauty. Marry me now."

"Wait! Let other people go free first." she said.

The Duke set the villagers free except *Liu Lang*.

"Why not let him go?" scolded the Oriole Girl.

"I'll let him go if you come to my **bridal chamber** with me first." said the Duke.

The Oriole Girl clenched her teeth and agreed unwillingly. She walked into the bridal chamber, followed by the palace maids.

That night, the palace was bustling with noise and excitement. The Duke joyfully walked into the bridal chamber while *Liu Lang* was still bound to a big locust tree in the palace garden. All of a sudden, *Liu Lang* seemed to hear the oriole singing and the rope that tied him up to the tree being unfastened. He took a close look and saw the Oriole Girl standing in front of him. She freed him and they both climbed over the palace wall and disappeared.

The soldiers failed to catch them and hurried to report to the Duke. They called outside his house, dozens of times, but without getting any response. Eventually they had to break into the house only to find the Duke buried under some dead willows, with mud in his mouth and unable to utter any sound.

When the Oriole Girl and *Liu Lang* returned home, *Liu*'s mother was crying. Seeing them back, she was both happy and upset at the same time. She said,

"Although you have escaped, the Duke will come again anyway..."

She cried before she finished.

"Don't cry, Mother. I have come up with a solution." said the girl.

She asked *Liu Lang* to take off one of his straw sandals and rushed out of the village with it. Everyone was confused when they saw hundreds of orioles slowly flying towards the Duke's palace with a big straw sandal in their beaks. When the orioles reached the Duke's palace, the straw sandal created a loud bang and became a big mountain. The mountain was right on top of the Duke's palace, and no one has ever seen the palace any more.

Liu Lang and the Oriole Girl got married happily. The view Orioles Singing in the Willows, which they wove into the silk, has become well-known. With evergreen willows swaying and orioles singing around West Lake, the spring here is more beautiful than ever.

【文化背景】【Cultural Notes】

▶ **杭州丝绸:**杭州被称为“丝绸之城”,其丝绸业享有近 4700 年的历史,早在唐宋时期,丝绸业兴旺发达,丝绸产品出口西方。目前杭州有超过六百家丝绸企业,经营各种真丝面料、丝绸服装、丝绸工艺品、围巾、领带及丝绸原料。著名的杭州丝绸品牌有都锦生、喜得宝、万事利、凯喜雅等。位于杭州西湖南岸的中国丝绸博物馆,是第一座全国性的丝绸专业博物馆,也是世界上最大的丝绸博物馆。它于 1992 年正式对外开放,2004 年以来,游客可免费参观,残疾人可免费使用轮椅。博物馆共有 5 个展厅,分别为序厅、文物厅、蚕桑厅、染织厅和现代成就厅。

***Hangzhou* silk:** *Hangzhou* is called "Silk City". Its silk industry enjoys a long history of about 4700 years. During the *Tang* and *Song* Dynasties, the silk industry became prosperous and then its silk products started to be exported to the West. Now *Hangzhou* has more than six hundred silk enterprises, and deals in a wide variety of pure silk fabric, silk garments, silk handicraft articles, scarves, ties and silk materials. The most famous *Hangzhou* silk brands include *Du Jingsheng*, *Xidebao*, Master Lee, and Kay. China National Silk Museum, located at the southern bank of West Lake, is the first state-level professional silk museum in China as well as the biggest of its kind throughout the world. It opened to the public in 1992 and since 2004 it has offered free admission for all visitors and even free wheelchairs for the disabled. The museum owns five exhibition halls such as the Preface Hall, the Relics Hall, the Silkworm and Mulberry Hall, the Dyeing and Weaving Hall and the Modern Achievements Hall.

▶ **花轿:**花轿主要用于接新娘到新郎家举行传统婚礼。花轿之幔通常选择红绸，其刺绣图案具有吉祥寓意。轿子装饰得明亮、华丽，以创造婚礼的欢乐气氛。花轿多为 4 人抬，在盛大的婚礼里，还有 2 人走在乐队前面，一个打伞，一个放鞭。去娘家的路上，花轿一般不可以空着，而是坐一名男孩，作为新郎未来得子的预兆。

Bridal sedan chair: The bridal sedan chair was mainly used to carry the bride from the bride's house to the groom's home for traditional Chinese wedding ceremony. Red silk was usually chosen for the curtain of the sedan chair, on which there are embroidered patterns with auspicious meanings. The sedan chair was brightly and richly decorated so as to create a happy atmosphere in a wedding ceremony. It took four people to carry this type of sedan. During a grand ceremony, two more people walked ahead of the band—one holding a ritualistic umbrella and the other in charge of the fireworks. The sedan chair could not be empty on the way to the bride's house; instead, a boy would sit there as an omen of the groom's future sons.

▶ **洞房**：旧时指新人完婚的新房。结婚仪式后，新婚夫妇被领进洞房，坐在床上，然后给他们斟酒，新娘新郎喝完交杯酒后，婚礼客人们便开始闹洞房，直至深夜离开。

Bridal chamber: The room prepared for the newly-married couple was formerly called a bridal chamber. Immediately after the wedding ceremony, the couple were led to the bridal chamber, where both sat on the bed. Wine was offered to them. The bride and groom took a few sips and then exchanged cups and drank it down. Then, wedding guests would play bridal chamber pranks and wouldn't leave till late night.

附　录
APPENDICES

壹 西湖十景（南宋时期，1127—1279）
Ten Scenes of West Lake in the Southern Song Dynasty（1127—1279 AD）

（每一景点名的拼音附在括号里。）

（For each scene, *Pinyin is given in the brackets*.）

1)苏堤春晓(sū dī chūn xiǎo)	Spring Dawn at *Su* Causeway
2)曲苑风荷(qū yuàn fēng hé)	Breeze-ruffled Lotus at *Quyuan* Garden
3)平湖秋月(pīng hú qiū yuè)	Autumn Moon over the Calm Lake
4)断桥残雪(duàn qiáo cán xuě)	Lingering Snow on Broken Bridge
5)柳浪闻莺(liǔ làng wén yíng)	Orioles Singing in the Willows
6)花港观鱼(huā guǎng guān yú)	Viewing Fish at Flower Harbour
7)三潭印月(sān tán yìng yuè)	Three Pools Mirroring the Moon
8)双峰插云(shuāng fēng chā yún)	Twin Peaks Piercing the Clouds
9)南屏晚钟(nán píng wǎng zhōng)	Evening Bell Ringing at *Nanping* Hill
10)雷峰夕照(leí fēng xī zhào)	*Leifeng* Pagoda in Evening Glow

西湖十景形成于南宋时期，基本围绕西湖分布，有的就位于湖上，是西湖旅游必去之处。十景各擅其胜，组合在一起又能代表古代西湖胜景精华。每一个景点用一个四字词语表示，统称为西湖十景。西湖十景的每一景边上，都曾有一个御碑，正面是康熙题的景点名，背面是乾隆为景点题的一首诗。可惜的是，后来因为种种变故，七块御碑不见踪影。虽然西湖新景不断推出，传统意义上的这十景依然是百年不衰。

A collection of ten scenic spots formed during the Southern *Song* Dynasty, they are distributed around and on the lake, and serve to show the charms of West Lake. Each scene is unique, and when taken together, are said to present the essence of West Lake scenery, and form the core of any West Lake tour. Each of the ten scenic spots is remembered by a four-character epithet. Collectively, they have been known as the "Ten Scenes of West Lake". There used to be a stele with each epithet in the front written in the calligraphy of Emperor *Kangxi*, on the back of which was a poem composed by Emperor *Qianlong*. Unfortunately, for various reasons, only three of them can still be seen, while seven of them were missing. Though people constantly explore new amazing views around West Lake, the classical Ten Scenes recognized for hundreds of years still enjoys the best reputation exclusively.

1）苏堤春晓 Spring Dawn at *Su* Causeway

自南宋(1127—1279)以来，苏堤春晓被列为西湖十景第一位。苏堤是北宋大文学家、书法家苏东坡任杭州知州时，疏浚西湖，利用挖出的葑泥构筑而成，后人为了纪念苏东坡治理西湖的功绩将该堤命名为苏堤。苏堤南起南屏山麓，北到栖霞岭下，全长2.8公里，长堤卧波，连接了南山北山，给西湖增添了一道妩媚的风景线。

苏堤上的六座拱桥，自南向北依名为映波、锁澜、望山、压堤、东浦和跨虹。苏堤两旁遍植桃柳，另有木兰、海棠、芙蓉、紫藤等四十多个品种的花木，四季景色各异。每逢阳春三月，杨柳夹岸、艳桃灼灼，景色迷人，尤其是晨曦初露时分，青山像披上一层薄纱，桃红柳绿，轻风徐徐，莺声清丽，勾魂销魂，仿佛置身仙境，故得名"苏堤春晓"。

Romanticized as Spring Dawn at *Su* Causeway, the scenery has stayed on the top of the top ten scenes of West Lake since the Southern *Song* Dynasty (1127—1279). It was built in the Northern *Song* Dynasty when *Su Dongpo*, a famous poet and the governor of *Hangzhou*, had the lake dredged. The silt and debris were piled up and formed into a causeway. In order to honour the poet-governor, local people named the Causeway after him. *Su* Causeway, a thin strip of land and 2.8 kilometres long, spans West Lake from *Nanping* Hill in the south to *Qixia* Hill in the north, and connects North Hill and South Hill, which makes the lake more enchanting.

Along the Causeway stand six single-span stone arch bridges by the name of *Yingbo*(reflecting the waves), *Suolan*(locking the waves), *Wangshan*(looking at distant hills), *Yadi*(causeway ballast), *Dongpu*(eastern ford), *Kuahong* (spanning rainbow). Ranged with more than forty species of trees as peach, willow, magnolia, cherry-apple tree, hibiscus, wistaria, etc., the causeway presents different views in different seasons. When spring comes, with the lakeside sparkling in the morning dew, birds cheerfully chirping among swaying willow branches, the surrounding verdant hills shrouded in mist, the scent of peach blossoms wafting through the air, you will question whether you are in the midst of paradise. This amazing scene is romanticized as Spring Dawn at *Su* Causeway.

2)曲院风荷 Breeze-ruffled Lotus at *Quyuan Garden*

曲院风荷,以夏日观荷为主题,承苏堤春晓而居西湖十景第二位。“曲院”原是南宋朝廷开设的酿酒作坊,位于西湖西面灵隐路洪春桥附近,近岸湖面养殖荷花,每逢夏日,和风徐来,荷香与酒香四处飘逸,令人不饮亦醉。公园内大小荷花池中栽培了上百个品种的荷花,笑靥迎宾。

曲院风荷,是西湖环湖地区最大的公园之一,全园分为岳湖、竹素园、风荷、曲院、滨湖密林五个景区,其中尤为迷人的要数风荷景区,水面上分布着名种荷花,架设了造型各异的小桥;人从桥上过,如在荷中行。公园与周边的岳飞墓、郭庄、杭州植物园等景点连成一片,成了西湖北线最具游赏价值的游览区。

Breeze-ruffled Lotus at *Quyuan* Garden features an abundant growth of lotus off its shores in summer and ranks second among Ten Scenes of West Lake. *Quyuan*, located on the bank of West Lake beside the *Hongcun* Bridge on the *Lingyin* Road, where many lotus were planted, used to be an official brewery in the Southern *Song* Dynasty. In summer, the fragrance of the lotus flowers and wine blended by the cool lake breezes was intoxicating. There are plenty of lotus plants of hundreds of species at blossom, which stand gracefully erect in ponds of all sizes, as if they know they have visitors coming to admire their beauty.

Currently, the park is one of the biggest parks around West Lake, including five sections: *Yue* Lake, Bamboo Garden, Lotus Garden, Winding Garden and Lakeside Forest, among which Lotus Garden is the most charming area, with all kinds of lotus and bridges of different styles. With other scenic spots nearby such as General *Yuefei's* Tomb, *Guo's* Villa and *Hangzhou* Botanical Garden, it has become the most charming attractions for the tourists in the north part of West Lake.

3)平湖秋月 Autumn Moon over the Calm Lake

平湖秋月位于白堤西端,面临外湖,背倚孤山,景区面积6000多平方米。平湖秋月景区有其历史渊源,唐朝在此曾建有望湖亭,明朝建为龙王祠。清康熙三十八年(1699)又建为御书楼,并在楼前筑起三面临湖的一座平台,平台向南伸出水面,视线低平,视野广阔,成为临湖赏月的好地方,尤其是在中秋月明之夜,因此后来定名平湖秋月。

平湖秋月是湖边公园,亭台楼阁,蜿蜒桥榭,各式假山,临水平台,缤纷的树木花草点缀其间,美不胜收。尤其在秋季更是绝美胜境。虽然平湖秋月景区的实际面积在西湖十景是最小的,但它的展示面积却是最大的,在这里楼可望,岸可望,水可望。古今皆有赞叹平湖秋月的诗词传世,也有平湖秋月的相关乐曲。

Situated at the west end of *Bai* Causeway, with Outer Lake in its front and Solitary Hill behind, the scenery named Autumn Moon over the Calm Lake, covers an area of over 6000 square metres. The spot can be traced back to the *Tang* Dynasty, when a building known as the Lakeview Pavilion was constructed here. In the *Yuan* Dynasty, it was turned into the Dragon King's Temple. In 1699 during the *Qing* Dynasty the temple was remodeled for use as a study retreat for Emperor *Kangxi* and called the Imperial Book Pavilion, in front of which was a lakeside terrace, considered as one of the best places to enjoy the moon, especially on a mid-autumn moonlit night. Accordingly, it was renamed Autumn Moon over the Calm Lake.

It is a lakeside garden spot with delicate pavilions, zigzag bridges, odd-shaped rockeries, water-hemmed terraces, and trees and flowers of colourful varieties. The lake in autumn has been widely considered as a gorgeous landscape since ancient times. Enjoying the moon at West Lake is a treat full of poetic charm. Though it is the smallest among the top ten scenes in West Lake, one can see the vastest area from here, with almost everything such as buildings, lake banks and water, etc. in sight. Poems and music have been composed to honour the beauty of this scenic spot.

4)断桥残雪 Lingering Snow on Broken Bridge

断桥位于杭州市西湖白堤的东端,背靠宝石山,面向杭州城,是外湖和北里湖的分水点。与西泠桥和长桥一起并称为西湖的三大恋人桥。西湖有三怪:断桥不断,长桥不长,孤山不孤。断桥名字很怪,字面意思是“断了”的桥,即“不完整”之意,但其实不然,断桥和世界上其他桥一样,并没有断。

断桥因为其冬季的独特美景而著名——断桥残雪。此景也是“断桥”得名的缘由。每当瑞雪初霁,断桥的阳面石桥拱面无遮无拦,在阳光下冰雪消融,露出了斑驳的桥栏,而桥的阴面还在皑皑白雪的覆盖下,站在宝石山上远眺,桥面似断非断,故称断桥。断桥地势高,视野开阔,故冬日雪后,站在断桥上,近处皑皑,远山素裹,绝对让你一饱眼福。杭州有句名谚:“晴湖不如雨湖,雨湖不如月湖,月湖不如夜湖,夜湖不如雪湖。”断桥残雪的美景验证了这一说法。

中国著名的民间传说《白蛇传》,为断桥景物增添了浪漫的色彩,吸引了国内外无数的游客。

Broken Bridge is located at the eastern end of *Bai* causeway, between Outer West Lake and North Inner Lake, backed by *Baoshi* Hill and facing

Hangzhou city. It is one of the top three lovers' bridges spanning West Lake, while the other two are *Xiling* Bridge and Long Bridge. The three strange things about West Lake are the Broken Bridge is not broken, Long Bridge is quite short and Solitary Hill does not stand solitary. Broken Bridge has a bizarre name which suggests it is incomplete. However, that's not the case; the bridge is just as complete as any other bridge in the world.

Broken Bridge is noted for its peculiar scene in winter—Lingering Snow on Broken Bridge, which explains the name of this bridge. Standing on nearby Precious Stone Hill, you can see snow on the sunny side of the bridge often melt away to reveal the concrete surface, while the snow on the shady side still lingers and glistens like diamonds. In this case, the bridge appears to be broken. The beauty of this striking scene is deemed as the source of inspiration for the name of Broken Bridge. Situated on high ground, the bridge offers you a great view, which makes it an ideal place to watch the snow. On fine winter days after a snow, you may stand on the bridge to feast your eyes on the snow scene far and near. Distant hills, clad in white, grow more enchanting. It is said that sunny West Lake is not better than rainy West Lake, and rainy West Lake is not better than night West Lake, while night West Lake is not better than snow West Lake. The amazing view of Lingering Snow on Broken Bridge provides a proof to justify this vivid description.

Broken Bridge is also well-known for its role in the popular folklore in China, *Legend of Lady White Snake*, one of China's most famous and popular love stories, which brings Broken Bridge some romance. Thanks to the love story between the human and the immortal, the bridge attracts numerous visitors home and abroad.

5)柳浪闻莺 Orioles Singing in the Willows

柳浪闻莺位于西湖东南岸,前身为南宋时的皇帝御花园,称聚景园。20世纪50年代,经过一系列改造项目,公园恢复了原貌,现在为对外开放的公园。全园分友谊、闻莺、聚景、南园四个景区。今天,公园里堤岸蜿蜒,古树枝繁叶茂,亭台楼榭远,垂柳依依,黄莺鸣啭。人们喜欢来此晨练。它是休闲的理想场所,也是大型娱乐活动和节日庆典的好去处。

Orioles Singing in the Willows, located off the southeast bank of West Lake, which used to be an imperial park named *Jujing* Garden in the Southern *Song* Dynasty. The park came back to life again in the 1950s through a series of refurbishment projects and became a park open to the public. Today, the park includes four parts: Friendship Garden, Listening-to-Orioles Garden, Garden of Composite Views and South Garden. Currently, old trees in the park blossom along the winding bank. Pavilions reveal their ancient romantic style, with weeping willows and singing orioles. People like to do morning exercises here since it is an ideal place for recreation. It is also a good place for large-scale entertainments and holiday celebrations.

6)花港观鱼 Viewing Fish at Flower Harbour

该景点位于花港观鱼公园,地处苏堤南段以西,是以花、港、鱼为特色的风景点。全园分为红鱼池、牡丹园、花港、大草坪、密林地五个景区。红鱼池是全园游赏的中心区域。红鱼池中放养着数万尾金鳞红鲤,每年都吸引大量游人,在观鱼池的曲桥上投入食饵,群鱼就会从四面八方游来,争夺食饵,真是鱼跃人欢,其乐融融。位于红鱼池西面的是牡丹园,牡丹园最高处是牡丹亭,绕亭植有各种牡丹、芍药数百棵,按不同品种分为十多个花境小区块,意趣盎然。

花港的得名可以追溯到南宋时期。西湖边花家山麓下有一小溪,流经此处注入西湖,因沿溪多栽花木,常有落英飘落溪中。南宋时,内侍卢允升在花家山下建造别墅,带有私家花园,故称花港。1699 年清朝康熙南巡时,题有“花港观鱼”四字,后来刻石建碑于鱼池畔。

Located in Flower Harbour Park, west of the southern segment of *Su* Causeway, this site features flowers, harbours and fish. It is made up of five scenic spots, namely, Red Carp Pond, Peony Park, Flower Harbour, Big Lawn, and Grove. Red Carp Pond is the heart of Viewing Fish at Flower Harbour, where tens of thousands carps live and play, attracting thousands of tourists each year. Bending over the rails of the bridge and watching the carps noisily scrambling for food thrown to them is an enjoyable experience. West of Red Carp Pond is Peony Park, with a peony pavilion centered on a rise. Around the pavilion hundreds of peonies and herbaceous peonies are planted, classified into a dozen flower patches.

Flower Harbour dates back to the Southern *Song* Dynasty. According to local history, there used to be a tiny creek that flowed from the nearby Flower Hill into West Lake. At both sides of the creek were trees and flowers. Fallen flowers were floating on water. In the Southern *Song* Dynasty, *Lu Yunsheng* (a palace eunuch) built a villa at the foot of Flower Hill, with a private garden, so the place was named Flower Harbour. In the year 1699 Emperor *Kangxi* of the *Qing* Dynasty visited West Lake and wrote four characters in calligraphy, which means "Viewing Fish at Flower Harbour". The four characters were later inscribed on a stone stele standing near the pond.

7)三潭印月 Three Pools Mirroring the Moon

三潭印月岛又名小瀛洲,与湖心亭、阮公墩均位于外西湖中心,合称为湖上三岛。它是西湖中最大的岛屿,被誉为"西湖第一胜境",湖中有岛,岛中有湖,独具特色。岛南湖面,三座中空小石塔鼎足而立,环塔身分布五个小圆孔。中秋月明之夜,塔内点上蜡烛,人们便可以尽享天上一个月亮,水中多个月亮的奇异景观。第五套人民币的一元纸币的背面采用了三潭印月的盛景。

The island of Three Pools Mirroring the Moon, also named Small *Yingzhou*, together with other two islands, *Huxin* Pavilion, and *Ruan Gong* islet, lie in the center of Outer West Lake. The island of Three Pools Mirroring the Moon is the largest one in West Lake and is considered as its No.1 attraction. It has a unique style of "an island in the lake and a lake on the island". To its south there are three hollow stone pagodas rising from water, each with five openings. On the night of the Mid-autumn Festival, with candle light inside the pagodas, people marvel at the wonderful scenery of the moon in the sky but many reflections in the lake. This magnificent landscape appears on the back of the one *yuan* bill of the fifth set of RMB.

8）双峰插云 Twin Peaks Piercing the Clouds

“双峰插云”碑亭在灵隐路洪春桥畔。双峰指的是南高峰和北高峰。两峰遥相对峙，相距5公里，中间的小山起伏，蜿蜒盘结，春秋雨日，从湖西北眺望，浮云浓如远山，远山淡如浮云，峰顶时隐时现于薄雾轻岚之中，望之如插云天，因而得名。

北高峰位于西湖以北，海拔高度约355米，被称为“天下第一财神庙”的灵顺寺建于山顶上，每逢阳春时节，前来拜求的生意人络绎不绝，香火极盛。南高峰高约257米，位于西湖的西南面，与北高峰遥遥对峙，山上的书画碑廊使其成为一方文化名胜。

The pavilion housing the stele engraved with four Chinese characters which mean“Twin Peaks Piercing the Clouds” is located next to *Hongchun* bridge at *Lingyin* Road, which refers to the Southern Peak and the Northern Peak. At a distance of 5 kilometres, facing each other, the two peaks stand high and magnificent over their neighbouring hills. On a drizzling day in the spring or autumn, the two peaks disappear and appear amongst the drifting rain clouds. The name “Twin Peaks Piecing the Clouds” comes from this convergence of the mountains and the clouds.

The Northern Peak lies north of West Lake at an altitude of nearly 355 metres above sea level, with *Lingshun* Temple, acknowledged as the No. 1 Mammon Temple in China, on its top. When spring comes, many businessmen flock here and pray for good fortune. The Southern Peak, which has a height of about 257 metres, lies southwest of the lake, opposite to the Northern Peak. The Chinese calligraphy stone tablets gallery there makes it a cultural tourist attraction.

9）南屏晚钟 Evening Bell Ringing at *Nanping* Hill

南屏晚钟，指南屏山净慈寺傍晚的钟声。南屏山位于西湖南岸，主峰高不过百米，山体延伸却长达千余米。南屏山是由石灰岩构成，山上石壁如屏，北麓山脚下的净慈寺,是杭州西湖历史上四大古刹之一,是公元 10 世纪时五代的钱弘俶为高僧永明禅师而建,原名永明禅院,南宋时改称净慈寺,并建造了五百罗汉堂。

寺屡毁屡建,现在大部分寺院建筑都是 20 世纪 80 年代重建的。寺内有一口重达一百多公斤的铸造铜钟,钟声洪亮,傍晚的钟声尤其清越悠扬。南屏晚钟与雷峰夕照隔路相对,塔影钟声组成了西湖十景中最迷人的晚景。

Evening Bell Ringing at *Nanping* Hill refers to the bell ringing in the evening from *Jingci* Temple, which is at the foot of *Nanping* Hill. Though no more than a hundred metres high, *Nanping* Hill stretches along the southern bank of West Lake for over a thousand metres. Formed of limestone, *Nanping* Hill contains lots of caves and cavities. *Jingci* Temple, one of the four prominent Buddhist temples in *Hangzhou*, was first built in the 10th Century by *Qian Hongchu* of the Five Dynasties for an eminent monk, Master *Yongming*. It was initially called *Yongming* Temple. In the Southern *Song* Dynasty, its name was changed to *Jingci* Temple, and a Fiver-Hundred-Arhat Hall was built there.

The temple was destroyed and rebuilt several times. The majority of the present temple was rebuilt in the 1980s. One special feature is a cast copper bell, weighing over 100 kilograms. At dusk, with the sun slowly drifting into the lake on the west, a huge bell will ring its farewell to the last sunbeam of the day with the prolonged bell sound reverberating across the lake, with its sonorous sound echoed through the caves and cavities, each reached as far as the other shore of West Lake. The evening bell from *Nanping* Hill and the sunset in *Leifeng* Pagoda make the most charming evening scene among Ten Scenes in West Lake.

10)雷峰夕照 *Leifeng* Pagoda in Evening Glow

雷峰塔位于西湖南面、净慈寺前的夕照山上,是一座八面五层楼阁式塔,为西湖的标志性景点。夕照山这座三面临水、呈半岛状的名山,当年曾为南宋御花园占据。雷峰塔原名黄妃塔,公元 10 世纪时由吴越王钱弘俶庆黄妃得子而建。1924 年雷峰塔倒塌,2002 年重建。

山上遍布许多的樟树、榆树等观赏树木,每到黄昏夕阳西下,水光潋滟,塔影婆娑,晚霞镀塔,令人叹为观止,“雷峰夕照”就此得名。雷峰塔融合了古代建筑和现代技术,站在塔上可观西湖全貌。塔内珍藏有60余件千年宝物。中国四大民间传说之一白蛇传的故事,更是赋予了雷峰塔无以取代的历史意义。

Leifeng Pagoda is located on *Xizhao* Hill which is south of West Lake and in front of *Jingci* Temple. *Leifeng* Pagoda is an octahedron five-story pavilion-style tower and a landmark attraction of West Lake. *Xizhao* Hill, a well-known hill which faces water in three sides and takes the shape of a peninsula, used to be an imperial garden in the Southern *Song* Dynasty. Tradition has it that the pagoda was built in in the 10th century at the order of *Qian Hongchu*, the King of *Wu-Yue* Kingdom, to celebrate the birth of a son by one of his favourite concubines, Lady *Huang*. The pagoda didn't stand the test of time, and collapsed in 1924. In 2002, *Leifeng* Pagoda was reconstructed.

With many ornamental trees on the hill, such as camphor trees, elm trees, etc., the Pagoda looks especially majestic when surrounded by the golden hues of the setting sun. Thus, the scence was named *Leifeng* Pagoda in Evening Glow. With the combination of traditional aesthetic style and modern architecture techniques, *Leifeng* Pagoda affords a view of West Lake in its entirety. There are more than 60 millennium treasures in it.

Leifeng Pagoda has gained its historical importance through its association with one of China's four most popular folk tales, *The Legend of Lady White Snake*.

贰 ◎ 西湖十景(1985)

Ten Scenes of West Lake (1985)

(每一景点名的拼音附在括号里。)

(For each scene, *Pinyin is given in the brackets*.)

1)云栖竹径(yún qī zhú jìng)	Bamboo-lined Path at *Yunqi*
2)满陇桂雨(mǎn lǒng guì yǔ)	Sweet Osmanthus Rain at *Manjuelong* Village
3)虎跑梦泉(hǔ pǎo mèng quán)	Dreaming of *Hupao* Spring at *Hupao* Valley
4)龙井问茶(lóng jǐng wèn chá)	Inquiring about Tea at Dragon Well
5)九溪烟树(jiǔ xī yān shù)	Nine Creeks Meandering Through a Misty Forest
6)吴山天风(wú shān tiān fēng)	Heavenly Wind over *Wu* Hill
7)阮墩环碧(ruǎn dūn huán bì)	*Ruan Gong* Islet Submerged in Greenery
8)黄龙吐翠(huáng lóng tǔ cuì)	Yellow Dragon Cave Dressed in Green
9)玉皇飞云(yù huáng fēi yún)	Clouds Scurrying over Jade Emperor Hill
10)宝石流霞(bǎo shí liú xiá)	Precious Stone Hill Floating in Rosy Clouds

1984年,包括杭州日报社在内的五家单位联合发起举办新西湖十景评选活动。经杭州市民及各地群众积极参与评选,并由专家评选委员会确定,新西湖十景从西湖里外7400多的景点中产生,并于1985年竖立景碑。

In 1984, five organizations including *Hangzhou Daily* newspaper sponsored voting for the "New Ten Scenes in West Lake". Participated by people in and out of *Hangzhou* and confirmed by expert judging panel, New Ten Scenes of West Lake were chosen from among over 7400 places of interest in and around West Lake. They were inscribed on the stone plague set up in September 1985.

1)云栖竹径 Bamboo-Lined Path at *Yunqi*

云栖竹径位于五云山南麓的云栖坞里,西湖之西南,钱塘江北岸,五云山南麓,距西湖12公里,列于新西湖十景之首。据传说,附近五云山上的五彩祥云,常栖留于此,并经久不散,故称"云栖"。此地远离市井,竹林满坡,修篁绕径,素以竹景的"绿、清、凉、静"四胜而著称于世。云栖竹林茂密,还有众多千年古树,周围有回耀峰、宝刀陇、青龙泉、圣义泉、金液泉、壁观峰,合称"云栖六景"。

Yunqi, located in *Yunqi* Valley, at the foot of *Wuyun* Hill, southwest of West Lake and north of the *Qiantang* River, the Bamboo-Lined Path at *Yunqi* is 12 kilometres from West Lake. It ranks first among the New Ten Scenes of West Lake. Legend has it that in an ancient time, some auspiciously colourful clouds swirled around the nearby Colourful Clouds Hill and lingered on, hence the name *Yunqi*, which literally means "lingering clouds". Far away from the city, *Yunqi* abounds in a sea of bamboo and features greenness, clearness, coolness and quietness. Besides dense bamboo grooves, *Yunqi* is also blessed with countless ancient trees over 1000 years old. The bamboo-isined path at *Yunqi* is accompanied by *Baodao* Ridge, *Qinglong* Spring, *Shenyi* Spring, *Jinye* Spring, *Biguan* Peak, which are called "Six Scenes at Yunqi".

2)满陇桂雨 Sweet Osmanthus Rain at *Manjuelong* Village

满觉陇,位于杭州西湖以南,是南高峰与白鹤峰夹峙下的山谷中的自然村落,远离城市,清幽静雅,是隐士和热爱自然人士的天堂,同时是欣赏桂花的胜地,而桂花被冠以杭州市市花之称。自古以来,此地就深得佛教青睐,公园10世纪建有圆兴院,1065年改为满觉院,"满觉"意为"圆满的觉悟",是佛教修行的最高境界。满觉陇因而得名。

满觉陇沿途山道边,植有七千多株桂花,有四个品种,其中树龄最长的约200年。每当金秋时节,珠英琼树,香飘数里,沁人肺腑。当秋风吹过,花瓣随风洒落,密如雨珠,人行桂树丛中,沐"雨"披香,别有一番意趣,故被称为"满陇桂雨",满觉陇也因此成为西湖著名赏桂胜地。

Tucked away in the exuberant forests off the southwest of West Lake, *Manjuelong* Village is a hermits' heaven and a paradise for nature lovers. Nestling within a narrow strip of valley dwarfed by the soaring the Southern Peak and White Crane Peak, this secluded, mysterious and inviting village is a place to appreciate osmanthus flowers, which are crowned as the city flower of *Hangzhou*. Since remote antiquity, this place has held Buddhist flavour. The 10th century saw *Yuanxing* Temple take form. In 1065, it was renamed *Manjuelong*. *Manjue*, which literally means "gaining enlightenment successfully", is the highest state of Buddhist practice. Hence the name of *Manjuelong*.

All along the valley, *Manjuelong* is covered with sweet-scented osmanthus flowers. Now, you will have the privilege to marvel at over 7,000 sweet osmanthus trees roughly falling into four varieties. Among them, the most ancient tree dates back to over 200 years ago. When autumn falls, they will bloom wild and largely in hues of creamy white, golden yellow or shining orange. As balmy autumn breezes blow over them, the tiny blossoms will fall off the trees and cover the ground with an elegant floral carpet. If bathed in the morning dewy flowers, you feel walking in the flowery rain. That's how the scene got its name "sweet osmanthus rain". And that's why *Manjuelong* became a famous place for appreciating osmanthus flowers around West Lake.

3)虎跑梦泉 Dreaming of *Hupao* Spring at *Hupao* Valley

虎跑泉位于西湖西南大慈山麓的虎跑寺。三面被高山包围,形成马蹄形的汇水洼地。泉眼在这洼地中,即使数月无雨,泉水终年不断。泉水自山岩间流出,甘洌醇厚,为杭州三大名泉之首,被乾隆帝赞为"天下第三泉"。相传公元9世纪初,唐代有个高僧住在这里。后因水源缺乏,准备迁出。一夜,高僧梦见一神仙告诉他:南岳童子泉,当遣二虎移来。第二天,果真有二虎"刨地作穴",涌出泉水,故名"虎跑"。

Hupao Spring is located at *Hupao* Temple at the foot of *Daci* Hill southwest of West Lake. Surrounded by hills on three sides, the spring is a u-shaped pool fed by a stream. Because the mouth of the spring is in the pool, it never dries up, even during long droughts. The spring water, filtered through the rocks, is clear and sweetish. It's the first of the three best springs in *Hangzhou*, and was considered to be among the top three springs in China by Emperor *Qianlong*. Legend has it that an eminent monk in the *Tang* Dynasty once living here intended to move out due to lack of water. One night in his dream he was told by an Immortal that two tigers would move *Boy's* Spring from Mount Heng in South China. The next day, he saw two tigers making holes and water coming out. That's how the spring got its name, *Hupao* Spring.

4)龙井问茶 Inquiring about Tea at Dragon Well

龙井,位于西湖之西山林密集之处。古人以为这里与海想通,是龙之所居,故得名“龙井”。龙井泉水清澈甘洌,与虎跑、玉泉合称西湖三大名泉。龙井茶更负盛名,为中国十大名茶之一,尤以产于龙井村地带的为上品。清代乾隆皇帝曾在龙井封过十八颗御树,称为“十八棵御茶”,并题“龙井八景”。

龙井茶外形扁平挺秀,色泽绿翠,素以“色翠、香郁、味甘、形美”四绝著称,有狮、龙、云、虎等品种,尤以狮峰、龙井地之茶为最优,其中奥妙,唯有亲去龙井村品茗问茶方可悟出,因此就有了“龙井问茶”之趣。中国唯一以茶叶为主题的博物馆——中国茶叶博物馆,就坐落在龙井村。

Hidden amid the dense hill forest west of West Lake, Dragon Well, or *Longjing*, keeps attracting tea lovers like a magnet. The water of dragon well is sweet and nice. Dragon Well, Jade Spring and *Hupao* Spring rank as West Lake's top three springs. *Longjing* Village is well-know for *Longjing* Tea, or *Longjing* tea, which is a variety of green tea and ranks among China's top ten teas. *Hangzhou* is one of China's leading tea-producing areas, while *Longjing* is a local village where the finest green tea is produced. During his visit to Fair South, Emperor *Qianlong* granted eighteen of trees here the status of imperial tea, and designated "Eight Scenes of Dragon Well" with his inscription for each scene.

Longjing Tea is well-known for its four special features: green colour, fragrant aroma, refreshing taste and smooth even appearance. West Lake green tea has such varieties as Lion, Dragon, Cloud and Tiger, etc., among which the first two are of the best quality. The charm of *Longjing* Tea is beyond your reach unless you go by yourself, sip a cup of tea and inquire about it right here; hence the name of "Inquiring about Tea at Dragon Well" became famous. The China National Tea Museum, the only one in China with a tea theme, is located in *Longjing* Village.

5)九溪烟树 Nine Creeks Meandering Through a Misty Forest

九溪烟树俗称“九溪十八涧”,位于西湖西边群山中的鸡冠垅下。北接龙井,南贯钱塘江,源发翁家山杨梅岭下,途汇清湾、宏法、唐家、小康、佛石、百丈、云栖、清头和方家九溪,曲折隐忽,流入钱塘江。十八涧系指细流之多,流泉淙淙。一路重峦叠嶂,峰回路转。作为杭州最适合徒步旅行的路线之一,九溪烟树最适合在雾天或雨天游览,正如其名之寓意。该景点以意境深幽的自然景观取胜,青山缥缈,流水潺潺,浓郁的乡村自然风光,荡涤心灵。

As one of the “New Top Ten”, this attraction is situated in *Jiguanlong* among the hills west of West Lake. It is locally called as Nine Greeks and Eighteen Gullies, connecting *Longjing* Village in the north and the *Qiantang* River in the south, is full of rustic flavour. A stream originates from Waxberry Ridge of *Wengjia* Mountain and meander its way through nine creeks, i.e., *Qingwan* Creek, *Hongfa* Creek, *Tangjia* Creek, *Xiaokang* Creek, *Foshi* Creek, *Baizhang* Creek, *Yunqi* Creek, *Qingtou* Creek and *Fangjia* Creek, and then they empty into the *Qiantang* River. During their journey along the verdant forests, they are joined by many streamlets. These circuitous creeks play hide and seek with the mountains. They will pop up unexpectedly or disappear quietly. As one of *Hangzhou*'s top hiking trails, the scenery of Nine Creeks is at its best during misty or rainy days, just as its name hints. This attraction features gurgling waters and misty wooded hills. With serene rustic charms, it remains as natural as ever.

6)吴山天风 Heavenly Wind over *Wu* Hill

吴山,杭州人俗称“城隍山”,位于西湖东南,山势绵亘起伏,伸入市区,由延绵的十余座小山组成,山高均不超过百米,其中以紫阳山“十二生肖石”为最奇,因从一定角度远远看去,这些石头酷似鼠、牛、虎、兔、龙、蛇、马、羊、猴、鸡、狗、猪十二生肖。春秋时为吴西边界,故名吴山。由于伸入杭州市区,俯临河坊街及其他街市巷陌,远眺西湖和钱塘江,登上吴山可尽揽杭州江、山、湖、城之胜,"吴山天风"即由此而得名。

这里古树清泉多,奇岩怪石多,寺观神庙多,民俗风情多,名家踪迹多。其中,位于茗香楼前的"宋樟",已高寿800年以上。中药博物馆位于吴山北麓的百余年历史的胡庆余堂,一派恢宏精美的清代古建筑群蔚为壮观。另外,一年一度的吴山庙会,是每年西博会的重头戏,传承杭州的千年文化。

Wu Hill, also called "*Chenghuang* Hill" by local people, situated at the end of hills southeast of West Lake, is made up of 10 or more peaks, any of which is no more than 10 metres high. It stretches for several miles and extends into the downtown. On *Ziyang* Peak, a strange cluster of rocks which is known as Twelve Animal Stones appears like the twelve animals in the Chinese lunar calendar symbolizing the different years in which people are born: rat, ox, tiger, hare, dragon, snake, horse, sheep, monkey, rooster, dog and hog. In the Period of Spring and Autumn, it was the west boundary of Kingdom *Wu* Hill, and that's why it is called *Wu* Hill. Situated in downtown *Hangzhou*, *Wu* Hill commands a panoramic view of both the bustling *Hefang* Street and downtown *Hangzhou* as well as West Lake and the *Qiantang* River. Hence the name of Heavenly Wind over *Wu* Hill.

Wu Hill is famous for five things: trees and clear springs, grotesque rocks and caves, temples and shrines, engaging customs and rich historical relics. The oldest tree, *Song* Camphor, stands in front of a hilltop tea house which is called Tea Aroma Tower, is more than 800 years old. Moreover, at the northern foot of the hill is China's first traditional medicine museum inside the more-than-100-year-old *Hu Qing Yu* Chinese Pharmacy, also renowned for its very impressive *Qing* Dynasty style architecture. As an important part in West Lake International Expo, the annual *Wu* Hill temple fair expresses centuries-old *Hangzhou* culture to the world.

7)阮墩环碧 *Ruan Gong* Islet Submerged in Greenery

阮公墩是位于西湖中的一座绿色小岛。在西湖三岛即三潭印月(小瀛洲)、湖心亭、阮公墩中,阮公墩面积最小,开发也最迟。但从自然野趣而言,不仅毫不逊色,甚至独领风骚。清嘉庆五年(1800),浙江巡抚阮元疏浚西湖时,民工挖十万四千多吨淤泥堆积而成,为纪念他的功绩,该岛被命名为“阮公墩”。

一百多年来,由于岛上湖泥松软,阮公墩一直都没有营建,俨然成为西湖鸟群栖息的安乐窝。直到1982年,这座岛的旅游资源才真正被开发。整个环境,远山近水,开阔明朗,清逸幽静。远远望去,小岛如漂浮在碧波之上,绿树花丛掩映之下,如碧玉环绕,“阮墩环碧”景名由此而来。

Ruan Gong Islet is one of the three artificial islands in West Lake, i.e., Three Pools Mirroring the Moon (Small *Yingzhou*), *Huxin* Pavilion (North Tower Base) and *Ruan Gong* Islet. Though it is the smallest one among them and the last one to develop, *Ruan Gong* Islet is unique in being natural, rustic. It came to be after the *Zhejiang* Governor *Ruan Yuan* dredged West Lake in the fifth year of Emperor *Jiaqing*'s reign (1800) in the *Qing* Dynasty. To honour his achievement, the later generations address it as *Ruan Gong* Islet.

For more than a century, due to the soft soil, it remained unconstructed and home to birds in West Lake. Its tourism resources began to be developed in 1982. The whole environment, with faraway mountains and nearby water, is bright and tranquil. Looked in the distance, the small island appears to float upon clear, green waves and is hidden away among flowers and clusters of trees, just like crystal emeralds on a jasper plate. The name "*Ruan Gong* Islet Submerged in Greenery" comes from that.

8)黄龙吐翠 Yellow Dragon Cave Dressed in Green

“黄龙”是指位于栖霞岭北坡扫帚坞中的黄龙洞,隐藏于修竹茂林之中,是道教的洞天福地。黄龙洞是傍山垒石而成的假山石洞,是一处独具风韵、明净清幽的庭院式园林。传说南宋时期江西黄龙山有位名叫慧开的禅师来此建庙求雨,有一天突然一黄龙现身,山后一石突然开裂,裂口犹如“龙嘴”,汩汩喷出一股清泉,一时传说黄龙随慧开飞来,因而得名“黄龙”。此外,这里竹林茂密,株株吐翠,故名“黄龙吐翠”。

进入黄龙洞,可见一只黄色大龙头雕塑,龙嘴吐出清泉,下注水池,水声叮咚如琴瑟奏鸣。清泉入池处,一块峥嵘巨石兀立水中,两面分别镌刻唐代刘禹锡《陋室铭》中的名句“水不在深”“有龙则灵”，点出了此地景观的主题。几经历史变迁，黄龙洞起初是佛寺，清朝时变成道观。1985 年，它改建成以“缘”为主题的“圆缘民俗园”，吸引了大批游客。

Yellow Dragon Cave, located at northern foot of *Qixia* Ridge in flourishing woods and tall bamboo bushes, is a Taoist Temple. The Yellow Dragon Cave, integrating both real and artificial hills and both natural scenery and artificial construction, is one of the most elegant and secluded gardens.

Legend has it that in the Southern *Song* Dynasty a monk called *Huikai* from Yellow Dragon Hill in *Jiangxi* Province came here to set up a Buddhist temple and pray for rain. One day, suddenly a yellow dragon appeared and hit the ground strongly. Then, a big rock cracked in the middle like an open dragon mouth and a spring gushed out from it. It was concluded that the monk must have brought a yellow dragon to the site. That's the reason why the cave is called "Yellow Dragon". Moreover, covered with various kinds of green bamboo, Yellow Dragon Cave seems to be dressed in green, so it got its name "Yellow Dragon Cave Dressed in Green".

When you enter the courtyard, you will see a spring issuing from the mouth of the yellow dragon and tickling down into the pool below. In the pool stands a green huge steep rock engraved on both sides with famous quotations from *Liu Yuxi*'s *Ode to the Humble Hut*: "Regardless of its depth" "Divine is the dragon pool". Yellow Dragon Cave was originally a Buddhist monastery and turned to a Taoist resort in the *Qing* Dynasty. In 1985 it was built into a special garden of folk customs, called Good Luck Garden, which features only one Chinese character—*yuan*(缘), attracting tourists with brand-new sights.

9) 玉皇飞云 Clouds Scurrying over Jade Emperor Hill

玉皇山介于西湖与钱塘江之间，海拔 239 米，凌空突兀，衬以蓝天白云，更显得山姿雄峻巍峨。每当风起云涌之时，伫立山巅登云阁上，耳畔但闻习习之声，时有云雾扑面而来，飞渡而去。此处湖山空阔，江天浩荡，云雾缥缈，因此被命名为“玉皇飞云”。

Jade Emperor Hill lies between West Lake and the *Qiantang* River at an altitude of 239 metres. It is towering and dramatic, and becomes even more magnificent and majestic when contrasted by a blue sky and white clouds. When the wind rises and clouds skim quickly across the hill, it is magnificent experience to stand on *Dengyun* Pavilion at the top of the hill to hear the sound of wind around your ears and feel clouds and mist caress your face and fly away. There are always clouds and mist winding around its top, and so this site is called "Clouds Scurrying over Jade Emperor Hill".

10）宝石流霞 Precious Stone Hill Floating in Rosy Clouds

该景点位于宝石山。宝石山为西湖北岸屏障，是当地人周末徒步登山或夏季游玩的好去处。宝石山奇石荟萃，著名的有倚云石、屯霞石、凤翔石、落星石等。山体属火成岩，石色赭红，岩体中有许多闪闪发亮的红色矿物质，尤其是朝阳或落日霞光洒沐之时，保俶奇石披着霞光分外耀目，仿佛数不清的宝石在熠熠生辉，因而被称为"宝石流霞"。

宝石山巅为观赏西湖全景胜地之一，登山远眺，风景如画，西湖美景和市区繁华尽收眼底，令人心旷神怡。

The scenic spot, Precious Stone Hill Floating in Rosy Clouds, is situated on Precious Stone Hill. Precious Stone Hill, a hike-friendly hill perching on the northern bank of West Lake, is one of the locals' most popular weekend jaunts and a favorite summer escape. Odd stones assemble on the hill, like *Yiyuan* Stone, *Tunxia* Stone, *Fengxiang* Stone, *Luoxin* Stone, etc. Therefore, it is named as Precious Stone Hill. The hill consists of rhyolite and tuff rocks which shine dazzlingly bright in the sun like real jaspers. Especially, *Baochu* Pagoda and countless red rocks on the hill sparkle like innumberanle diamonds inlaid in the morning or evening sunlight. Hence, this scenic is named as "Precious Stone Hill Floating in Rosy Clouds ".

Climbing up Precious Stone Hill, you can have bird's view of West Lake and the downtown area of *Hangzhou*. The pictures que scenery will make you soothed and relaxed.

叁◎西湖十景(2007)

Ten Scenes of West Lake (2007)

(每一景点名的拼音附在括号里。)

(For each scene, *Pinyin is given in the brackets*.)

1)六和听涛(liù hé tīng tāo)	Hearing Tidal Bores
2)湖滨晴雨(hú bīn qíng yǔ)	Sunny and Rainy Lakeside
3)岳墓栖霞(yuè mù qī xiá)	*Yue Fei*'s Mausoleum in Dwelling Sunglow
4)灵隐禅踪(líng yǐn chán zōng)	en Aroma of *Lingyin* Temple
5)万松书缘(wàn sōng shū yuán)	Love Story at *Wansong* Academy
6)杨堤景行(yáng dī jǐng xíng)	Strolling Along Scenic *Yanggong* Causeway
7)钱祠表忠(qián cí biǎo zhōng)	Honouring Devotion Stele of King *Qian*'s Temple
8)三台云水(sān tái yún shuǐ)	Suffusing Clouds and Gurgling Waters at *Santai* Hill
9)北街梦寻(běi jiē mèng xún)	Chasing Dreams at *Beishan* Street
10)梅坞春早(méi wù chūn zǎo)	Early Spring in *Meijiawu* Village

西湖是一座美丽的宝藏,人们从未停止过对西湖魅力的探求。不断推出的新整治的许多景点让美丽的西子湖焕发出盛世光彩。除了传统的西湖十景和新西湖十景之外,2007年西湖西博会宣布了三评西湖十景的结果,这就是最新的西湖十景。

The charm of West Lake is endless and people have never stopped exploring on its beauty. A number of old scenic spots have been improved. Apart from the traditional and new Ten Scenes of West Lake, *Hangzhou* has another vote for the latest Ten Scenes of West Lake for the third time.

In 2007, in the *Hangzhou* West Lake Expo, the latest ten views were picked out.

1)六和听涛 Hearing Tidal Bores at *Liuhe* Pagoda

六和塔位于西湖之南,钱塘江畔月轮山上,是杭州的标志性建筑物。该塔结构复杂,呈平面八角形,外观十三层,内分七级,色呈殷红,是中国古代砖木结构的名塔之一,也是游客游览杭州景点必游之地。

关于六和塔名称的由来,有两种说法。其一是取佛教"六和敬"之义,源于佛教典籍:"身和同住,口和无争,意和同悦,戒和同修,见和同解,利和同均"。其二是"六合"之意,取"天地四方"之意。由于以潮水著称的钱塘江位于塔的脚下,在六和塔上可观潮涨潮落,听涛更可以感受万千意象,"六和听涛"因此而名。

To the west of West Lake and on the northern bank of the *Qiantang* River, stands on Full Moon Hill an ancient multi-layered pagoda, one of the landmarks of *Hangzhou*. The dark-red pagoda is made in plane octagonal form, with a rather sophisticated construction style. Although viewed from outside, it appears to be a thirteen-story pagoda, it only has seven interior stories. It's one of the most prominent wood-and-brick structures of ancient China and a must for tourists who come to *Hangzhou*.

Liuhe literally means "six harmonies". There are two kinds of interpretation of "six harmonies". One is that the name is related to six codes of Buddhism, which mean the harmonies of body, mind, speech, opinion, wealth and abstinence from temptation. The other version goes that "six harmonies" refer to the harmony of four directions (east, west, south, west), heaven and earth. Since the *Qiantang* River, which is famous for its spectacular tidal bores, lies right at the foot of the pagoda, one can see every single rise and fall of tide waves, and hear the sound of tidal bores clearly on the top of the pagoda. That's why this scenic spot is named "Hearing Tidal Bores at *Liuhe* Pagoda".

2)湖滨晴雨 Sunny and Rainy Lakeside

湖滨位于西湖和城区的接壤之地,不但是一览西湖三面云山之处,更是品鉴阴晴雨雾的好地方。西湖风景最宜慢慢细品,尤其是多雨时节,漫步湖滨,但见烟雨蒙蒙,水天一色,更加迷人。杭州有句名谚——“晴湖不如雨湖,雨湖不如月湖,月湖不如夜湖,夜湖不如雪湖”,意为西湖景致的四时皆宜。杭州之行,如果没有走过湖滨路,会是一个缺憾。湖滨被称为杭州的客厅,游览西湖的人通过湖滨而走进西湖。

湖滨路上有不少景点,尤为值得一提的是音乐喷泉。西湖音乐喷泉范围长约126米,宽约2米,形状呈弧形。有400多个喷头:其中224个能360度旋转,做出600多种水形变幻;最中间的那个大喷头,可以把水柱喷到60多米高。整个音乐喷泉灯光会随音乐产生不同颜色的转变,美轮美奂,吸引了众多游客。

Hubin, or literally, the lakeside, located in the west of West Lake, between West Lake and downtown, is the best vantage point to view West Lake, on either sunny or rainy days. Seen from *Hubin* Road, West Lake on sunny days is clear, with rippling waves; while on rainy days, it is foggy, full of poetic images. It is said that sunny West Lake is not better than rainy West Lake, and rainy West Lake is not better than night West Lake, while night West Lake is not better than snow West Lake. Without taking a stroll along *Hubin* (Lakeside) Road, your trip to *Hangzhou* won't be complete. *Hubin* Road is considered as the living room of West Lake: it's the first scenic spot to welcome visitors.

There are some scenic spots along *Hubin* Road, while the music fountain is undoubtedly its another highlight. It is about 126 metres long and 2 metres wide with the shape of an arc. There are over 400 nozzles in the fountain, 224 of which can rotate themselves in 360 degrees. And it can produce 600 water effects. The water sprayed from the biggest nozzle in the center can be over 60 metres high. The fountain comes with an enormous number of lights, capable of constantly changing the colourus to make itself attractive and eye-catching.

3）岳墓栖霞 *Yue Fei's* Mausoleum in Divelling Sunglow

岳墓背靠栖霞岭，位于苏堤北面，是南宋抗金英雄岳飞遗体所葬之地。岳飞是南宋最杰出的将领。公元12世纪，他率领南宋军队奋起抗击女真族统领的金朝军队。在宋金议和过程中，岳飞为奸臣秦桧诬陷，被捕入狱，最终在1142年因捏造的罪名，与长子岳云和部将张宪一起被南宋政府所杀害。1163年，岳飞冤案得以平反后，遗体被以礼改葬于此，其长子岳云也葬于此。岳飞成为中国人心目中的，是中国文化忠诚刚烈的化身。

岳庙始建于南宋嘉定十四年(1221)，明景泰年间改称“忠烈庙”，岳庙经历了元、明、清、民国，时兴时废，代代相传一直保存到现在。每当夕阳西下时，岳墓上便有了一道道霞光，非常绚美，因而得名“岳墓栖霞”。

Yue Fei's Mausoleum is located in the southern foot of *Qixia* Hill, north of *Su* Causeway. *Yue Fei* was the most prominent military general in the Southern *Song* Dynasty. He is best known for leading Southern *Song* forces to fight bravely against the *Nuzhen*-ruled *Jin* army in the 12th century. During the peace talks between the *Song* and *Jin* Dynasties, *Yue Fei* was framed by the treacherous minister *Qin Hui* and imprisoned. In 1142, *Yue Fei*, together with his oldest son *Yue Yun* and his subordinate *Zhang Xian*, was executed by the Southern *Song* government for crimes he didn't commit. In 1163, he was proved to be innocent and his corpse was reburied at the present site. Here also buried *Yue Yun*. *Yuefei* is widely seen as a patriot and national hero in China, since, after his death, *Yue Fei* has evolved into an epitome of loyalty in Chinese culture.

Yue Fei's Mausoleum was first built in 1221 (the 14th year of *Jiading* era in the Southern *Song* Dynasty). During the *Jingtai* era in the *Ming* Dynasty, it was renamed “*Zhonglie* Temple” (*zhong lie miao*, which literally means “temple of a loyal martyr”). Throughout the *Yuan*, *Ming*, *Qing* Dynasties and the period of the Republic of China, *Yue Fei*'s Mausoleum was damaged and restored and has been preserved until the present day. Whenever the sun sets, there are colourful clouds resting over the mausoleum, which is marvelous. That's how this site got its name “*Yue Fei*'s Mausoleum in Dwelling Sunglow”.

4）灵隐禅踪 Zen Aroma of *Lingyin* Temple

灵隐寺位于杭州西北角，东晋咸和元年(326)由印度僧人慧理所建，至今已有约一千七百年的历史，为杭州最早的名刹，也是中国佛教禅宗十大古刹之一。在五代的鼎盛时期，该寺共筑有九座多层建筑，十八个亭阁，七十二座大殿，以及供三千多僧人住的一千三百多间居室。历朝以来，寺院屡毁屡建，于今矗立的是一片欣欣向荣的建筑群，包括天王殿、大雄宝殿、药王殿。

地处杭州西湖西的山岭之中，背依北高峰，面迎飞来峰，崖壁雕刻精美。这里佛音庄严，禅意隐现，禅踪乃是灵隐山水的境界所在，故名“灵隐禅踪”，香客和游客云集至此。

Lingyin Temple, also known as Temple of Soul's Retreat (literal translated name), is located northwest of *Hangzhou*. The temple was established in the first year of *Xianhe* era in the Eastern *Jin* Dynasty (326) by an Indian monk called *Hui Li*. With a history of more than 1,700 years, it is one of the earliest renowned temples in Hangzhou, as well as one of "the Top Ten Zen Buddhist Temples of China". At its peak, during the Five Dynasties and Ten States periods (907—978), the temple boasted nine multi-storey buildings, 18 pavilions, 72 halls, and more than 1,300 dormitory rooms, which were inhabited by more than 3,000 monks. Since its construction, it has been restored for many times. What we can see today is a grand group of buildings mainly has three halls, Hall of the Heavenly Kings, Grand Hall of the Great Sage, Hall of the Medicine Buddha.

Situated among the hills at the west end of West Lake, the temple is backed by Northern Peak and confronted with the well-known *Feilai* Peak, famous for its grotto carvings. The tranquility makes the Buddhist melody more solemn, making Zen the essence of *Lingyin* Temple. Today the temple is thriving as a destination for both pilgrims and tourists.

5）万松书缘 Love Story at *Wansong* Academy

万松书院坐落于凤凰山脚的万松岭，建于 1498 年，是明清时杭州规模最大、历时最久、影响最广的书院。明代理学家王明阳曾在此讲学。2001 年 9 月,书院按明代建筑风格复建。

虽然万松书院曾汇集了许多著名的思想家和学者,其名声更多是缘于传说中的人物梁山伯与祝英台,被喻为中国版的罗密欧与朱丽叶。传说中梁山伯与祝英台曾同窗共读于此,梁祝坚贞不渝的爱情,使此处成为男女婚姻一线牵的姻缘之地,故而取名“书缘”。

Wansong Academy, located at the foot of the Phoenix Mountain, was established in 1498. It was the largest and most prestigious of its kind in *Hangzhou* during the *Ming* and *Qing* Dynasties. *Wang Yangming*, a famous philosopher in the *Ming* Dynasty, once gave lectures here. The Academy was was rebuilt in September, 2001 in its original style of the *Ming* Dynasty.

Despite the record number of thinkers and scholars that passed through the stone arches of the academy, the name "*Wansong*" is most famous for a legendary couple—*Liang Shanbo* and *Zhu Yingtai*, or Butterfly Lovers, who rose to literary fame as the Chinese equivalent of Romeo and Juliet. Legend has it that *Liang Shanbo* and *Zhu Yingtai*, once studied here together. Because of their beautiful love story, *Wansong* Academy now has become a place where people try to find their true love.

6)杨堤景行 Strolling Along Scenic *Yanggong* Causeway

西湖杨公堤位于西湖以西,杨公堤是与白堤、苏堤齐名的“西湖三堤”之一。明代弘治十六年(1503),杭州知府杨孟瑛疏浚西湖时筑此堤。后人为纪念杨不畏权势、力排众议,苦求朝廷达 5 年之久始获准许疏浚西湖之功,名堤为杨公堤。2003 年,西湖西进工程中,杨公堤重新建成开放。

杨公堤全长 3.4 公里,北起灵隐路,南至虎跑路,串联起曲院风荷、金沙港、茅家埠和花港观鱼等著名景点,堤上有六桥,原本没有名字,现在的名称是参照田汝成在《西湖游览志》中的命名,自北向南名为:环璧、流金、卧龙、隐秀、景行、浚源。其中隐秀桥、景行桥可供游船通行。“景行”原意指大路,比作崇高光明的德行。杨堤景行,既表达了今人对先贤杨孟瑛浚湖筑堤这一惠及杭州百姓和西湖之行的景仰之情,也点出了杨公堤人行景移、移步换景的特色。

Yanggong Causeway, situated in the west of West Lake, is one of Three Causeways of West Lake along with *Bai* Causeway and *Su* Causeway. In 1503, *Hongzhi* era in the *Ming* Dynasty, in order to dredge West Lake, the then *Hangzhou* Governor, *Yang Mengying* overcame all kinds of difficulties and started the project. The project took five years to complete. *Hangzhou* citizens felt grateful for what he had done and named the causeway after him. In 2003 in the Westward Re-construction of West Lake *Yonggong* Causeway was reconstructed and open to the public.

The present *Yanggong* Causeway is 3. 4 kilometres long, starting from *Lingyin* Road in the north and connects *Hupao* Road in the south. Along the causeway, there are a lot of famous scenic spots like Breeze-ruffled Lotus at *Quyuan* Garden, Gold Sand Harbour, *Maojiabu* Scenic Area and Viewing Fish at Flower Harbour, etc. A stroll along *Yanggong* Causeway is definitely a pleasure. The causeway features six bridges, which are also known as "Inner Six Bridges". There used to be no name for the six bridges. The present-day names were first given by *Tian Rucheng*, the author of *West Lake Travel Notes*. From north to south, the six bridges are *Huanbi*, *Liujin*, *Wolong*, *Yinxiu*, *Jingxing* and *Junyuan*. Boats can pass under *Yinxiu* Bridge and *Jingxing* Bridge. *Jingxing* literally means avenue, and figuratively refers to noble virtue of people in Chinese. The name of this scenic spot, "Strolling Along Scenic *Yanggong* Causeway", expresses people's admiration of *Yang Mengying* whose water project has benefited both local people and West Lake. It also points out their appreciation of the picturesque sceneries along the causeway.

7)钱祠表忠 Honouring Devotion Stele of King *Qian*'s Temple

钱王祠位于西湖东面,涌金池南,邻柳浪闻莺景点。始建于北宋时期,以纪念五代十国时吴越国的开国君王钱镠,在宋代初名"表忠观",清代以后则通称为钱王祠。

钱王祠中最恢宏、最有气势的当数正殿——五王殿。它是整个钱王祠当中最重要的地方,供奉着吴越国三世五王的塑像。来到殿内,坐在中间的就是钱镠，钱镠为吴越国开国国王，称武肃王。两旁是文穆王钱元瓘、忠献王钱弘佐、忠逊王钱弘倧、忠懿王钱弘俶。这三世五王治理杭州八十六载，社会安定，经济发展。钱王祠祠内有苏轼撰书的《表忠观碑记》，是中国书法史上的名碑。碑记叙述并褒扬了历代钱王的事迹。

On the eastern shore of West Lake lies King *Qian*'s Temple. It is situated south of *Yongjin* Pond and is adjacent to the park Orioles Singing in the Willows. It was originally constructed in the Northern *Song* Dynasty in memory of King *Qian Liu*, the founder of *Wu-Yue* Kingdom (907—978) during the Five Dynasties and Ten Kingdoms period. Formerly known as Temple of Loyalty, it has been called King *Qian's* Temple since the *Qing* Dynasty.

In the temple, the most sublime architecture is the main hall—Five Kings Hall. It's the core part of the temple, where are enshrined the five kings of *Wu-Yue*. In the middle is King *Qian Liu*. On its two sides are King *Qian Yuanguan*, King *Qian Hongzuo*, King *Qian Zong*, and King *Qian Chu*. The five kings ruled *Hangzhou* for 86 years, bringing prosperity to *Hangzhou* and were admired widely. In the temple stands the well-known stele with *Su Shi*'s calligraphy, which told the story of the five kings and honoured his devotion and contribution.

8) 三台云水 Suffusing Clouds and Gurgling Water at *Santai* Hill

三台云水以浴鹄湾景区为核心，东靠杨公堤，西临三台山路，北至乌龟潭景区，南到虎跑路。该景点融自然风光和人文景观于一体，景区内曲径通幽，涧水潺潺，最为著名的景点是于谦祠。于谦(1398—1457)生于杭州，葬于杭州，明代(1368—1644)著名的政治家与军事家，与岳飞齐名。1499 年瓦剌军入侵，发生土木之变，明英宗被俘，明王朝危在旦夕，于谦临危受命，率兵保卫京师，在中国历史上抒写了壮烈辉煌的一页。

于谦祠为传统型的祠堂建筑，白墙灰瓦，朱漆大门。始建于明朝 1489 年，1991 年重建。经过多次修缮后，至 1998 年 11 月，面积达 6000 平方米的于谦祠以崭新的面貌重新对外开放。

The scenic spot borders *Yanggong* Causeway on the east, *Santai* Hill Road on the west, Turtle Pool Scenic Area on the north, and *Hupao* Road on the south. The scenic area combines the natural landscape and cultural landscape harmoniously. It is famous for its cultural landscape, especially for the hero *Yu Qian* who resisted against Jin's inva, who was born and buried in Hangzhou. *Yu Qian* (1398—1457) is an outstanding politician, militarist in the *Ming* Dynasty (1368—1644) who enjoyed equal fame with General *Yue Fei*. He is best-known for saving China when Emperor *Yingzong* fought the Mongol Leader Esen Tayisi in 1449 and was taken prisoner at the *Tumu* Crisis.

The temple is a traditional memorial temple with white walls, gray tiles, and big red doors. It's first built in 1489 during the *Ming* Dynasty and was rebuilt in 1991. After repeated renovation, a completely new one with nearly 6,000 square metres opened to the public in November 1998.

9)北街梦寻 Chasing Dreams in *Beishan* Street

北山街东面连着宝俶路,西面连接曙光路,南面就是美丽的西湖,北靠宝石山,全长2600米,是西湖风景区内唯一的历史文化街区。杭州约半数以上的近代中西式著名建筑荟萃这条街上。据不完全统计,整条街会集了近百处人文遗迹,被杭州市人民政府确定为历史文化保护街区。沿途有蒋经国湖畔别墅、抱青别墅、秋水山庄等建筑,是一条名副其实的“名人别墅一条街”。这些大多数是20世纪的建筑,中式和西式建筑辉映,或大厦或私人住所。北山街见证了民国时期杭州的繁华,被称为没有围墙的博物馆,为游客呈现着丰富的历史遗产。

北山街绿荫之下,庭院之间,蕴含着许许多多的理想和情怀——慕才亭下,埋葬着一段刻骨铭心的爱情之梦;武松墓道,刻写了一个游侠四方的英雄梦想;首届西博会工业馆,寄托了富国强民的壮志。“北街梦寻”由此而来。

Beishan Street connects *Baochu* Road on the east, *Shuguang* Road on the west, and faces West Lake on the south, Precious Stone Hill on the north. This 2,600-metre-long street is the only historic street in West Lake Scenic Area. About over half of the modern architectures in various styles in

Hangzhou stand on this street. With roughly 100 cultural relics, this street was designate as the historic conservation block by Hangzhou municipal authority. Along the street scatter many famous villas, like the Former Villa of *Jiang Jingguo*, *Bao Qing* Villa, and *Qiu Shui* Villa, etc. For this, the street is then aptly named "the Street of Famous Villas". Most of the architectures on *Beishan* Street can date back to last century. They are of various types, from mansions to private houses, from traditional Chinese styles to Western styles. The street witnessed the prosperous *Hangzhou* during the period of the Republic of China, and is a veritable museum without walls, showing visitors this history and its legacy.

In the gardens and under the trees on *Beishan* street, there are also places about people who once chased dreams of various kinds. Under *Mucai* Pavillion buried a dream of unforgettable love. In *Wusong* Tomb lied a hero who travelled on every corner of the world in pursuit of his dreams. The first West Lake Expo industrial building holds a dream of making the country and its people wealthier stronger. That's how this site got its name "Chasing Dreams in *Beishan* Street".

10)梅坞春早 Early Spring in *Meijiawu* Village

梅家坞位于杭州市西南部云栖竹径西北两公里、琅珰岭北麓的山坞里。梅家坞四周青山环绕，茶山叠嶂，以生产色绿、香郁、味醇、形美的龙井茶叶著称。梅家坞茶文化村，有“十里梅坞”之称，是西湖龙井茶一级保护区和主产地之一。“春”在梅坞便是茶香之意；早春时节是采茶的最好时机，尤以最早的“明前茶”最为名贵。

梅家坞风景优美，加上独特的茶文化，被称为杭州呈现给世界的一张黄金名片。每年成千上万的游客来此品香茗，赏美景。

Located southwest of West Lake, 2 kilometres to Bamboo-lined Path in *Yunqi* to northwest, *Meijiawu* Village lie in the valley of north *Langdang* Hill. *Meijiawu* village is surrounded by green hills with tea bushes and produces top-quality *Longjing* Tea with green colour, fragrant aroma, refreshing taste and smooth even appearance. *Meijiawu* tea culture village, called "Ten-li

Meijiawu", is the primary protection area of *Longjing* Tea. "Spring" in *Meijiawu* relates to tea aroma. People pick tea in early spring, while the tea picked before *Qingming* Festival ranks best.

For its wonderful natural landscape and unique tea culture, *Meijiawu* Village has become the gold name card of *Hangzhou* presenting to the world. Every year, thousands of people come here to appreciate the best tea, tea culture and the idyllic beauty which is now seldom be seen in urbanized world.

肆◎西湖文化景观列入世界遗产名录
West Wake Cultural Landscape on the World Heritage List

2011年6月24日，在巴黎召开的第三十五届世界遗产大会上，联合国教科文组织宣布将杭州西湖文化景观列入了《世界遗产名录》。联合国教科文组织对西湖的评价是：

“杭州西湖文化景观由西湖及三面环绕的山峰组成。自公元9世纪以来，西湖的湖光山色引得无数文人骚客、艺术大师吟咏兴叹、泼墨挥毫。景区内遍布庙宇、亭台、宝塔、园林，其间点缀着奇花异木、岸堤岛屿，为江南的杭州城增添了无限美景。

“数百年来，西湖景区对中国其他地区乃至日本和韩国的园林设计都产生了影响，在景观营造的文化传统中，西湖是对天人合一这一理想境界的最佳阐释。”

On 24 June 2011, during the 35th session of the World Heritage Conference held in Paris, the United Nations Educational, Scientific and Cultural Organization (UNESCO) announced that the World Heritage Committee had inscribed West Lake Cultural Landscape of *Hangzhou* on its World Heritage List. The official UNESCO description of the Lake is given below:

"The West Lake Cultural Landscape of *Hangzhou*, comprising the West Lake and the hills surrounding its three sides, has inspired famous poets, scholars and artists since the 9th century. It comprises numerous temples, pagodas, pavilions, gardens and ornamental trees, as well as causeways and artificial islands. These additions have been made to improve the landscape west of the city of *Hangzhou* to the south of the Yangtze river.

"The West Lake has influenced garden design in the rest of China as well as Japan and Korea over the centuries and bears an exceptional testimony to the cultural tradition of improving landscapes to create a series of vistas reflecting an idealised fusion between humans and nature."

伍 中国的世界文化和自然遗产项目
World Cultural and Natural Heritage Sites in China

世界遗产是指被联合国教科文组织和世界遗产委员会确认的人类罕见的、目前无法替代的财富，是全人类公认的具有突出意义和普遍价值的文物古迹及自然景观。世界遗产分为四类，包括世界文化遗产、世界自然遗产、世界文化与自然遗产(即双重遗产)，以及文化景观。所有的世界遗产都得到经济资助和和技术指导，同时，世界遗产在全球能够拥有更高的知名度，并且由于来自国际社会的压力，这些地区会得到保护。

《保护世界文化和自然遗产公约》是联合国教科文组织于 1972 年 11 月 16 日在第十七届大会上正式通过的。1976 年，世界遗产委员会成立，并建立《世界遗产名录》。中国于 1985 年 12 月 12 日加入《保护世界文化和自然遗产公约》，成为缔约方。1999 年 10 月 29 日，中国当选为世界遗产委员会成员。中国于 1986 年开始向联合国教科文组织申报世界遗产项目。

自 1987 年至 2014 年 6 月，中国先后被批准列入《世界遗产名录》的世界遗产已达 47 处，其中文化遗产 30 处，自然遗产 10 处，自然和文化双重遗产 4 处，文化景观遗产 3 处，位居世界第二(排在第一位的是意大利，共 50 处世界遗产)。中国的世界文化和自然遗产项目按照批准的时间顺序列举如下：

A World Heritage Site is a place that is listed by the United Nations Educational, Scientific and Cultural Organization (UNESCO) as of special cultural or physical significance, considered to be of outstanding universal value to humanity with unique and irreplaceable property. World Heritage Sites fall into four categories: natural heritage, cultural heritage, the combination of natural and cultural heritage, and cultural landscape heritage. All sites on the World Heritage List receive financial and technical aid. In the meantime, they become better known worldwide and are protected by pressure from the international community.

The Convention Concerning the Protection of the World Cultural and Natural Heritage was organized by UNESCO and officially agreed at the 17th UNESCO's General Conference on December 16, 1972. In 1976, the World Heritage Committee was founded and published the List of World Heritage. China participated into this international organization on December 12th, 1985 and became a Contracting Party. China began to apply for items of world heritage in 1986. In 1999, China became the member of World Heritage Committee.

From 1987 to 2014, the number of sites written into the List of World Heritage in China has increased to 47, of which 30 are cultural heritage sites, 10 are natural heritage sites, 4 are cultural and natural (mixed) heritage sites, and 3 are cultural landscape heritage sites, ranking the second in the world (next only to Italy, which has 50 sites on the List). World Cultural and Natural Heritage Sites in China are listed as follows in chronological order.

World Cultural Heritage Sites in China including (30 items):

世界文化遗产包括(30 项):

1. 明清皇宫 Imperial Palaces of the *Ming* and *Qing* Dynasties in *Beijing* and *Shenyang*

北京故宫(北京),1987.12;沈阳故宫(辽宁),2004.7

2. 秦始皇陵 Mausoleum of the First *Qin* Emperor

陕西,1987.12

3. 敦煌莫高窟 *Mogao* Caves

甘肃,1987.12

4. 周口店北京人遗址 Peking Man Site at *Zhoukoudian*

北京，1987.12

5.长城 The Great Wall

北京，1987.12；辽宁九门口长城（水上长城）2002.11

6.武当山古建筑群 Ancient Building Complex in the *Wudang* Mountains

湖北，1994.12

7.拉萨布达拉宫历史建筑群 Historic Ensemble of the *Potala* Palace, *Lhasa*

西藏，1994.12；大昭寺，2000.11；罗布林卡，2001.12

8.承德避暑山庄及其周围寺庙 Mountain Resort and its Outlying Temples, *Chengde*

河北，1994.12

9.曲阜孔府、孔庙、孔林 Temple and Cemetery of Confucius and the *Kong* Family Mansion in *Qufu*

山东，1994.12

10.平遥古城 Ancient City of *Ping Yao*

山西，1997.12

11.苏州古典园林 Classical Gardens of *Suzhou*

江苏，拙政园、网师园、留园和环秀山庄，1997.12；艺圃、藕园、沧浪亭、狮子林和退思园，2000.11

12.丽江古城 Old Town of *Lijiang*

云南，1997.12

13.北京皇家园林——颐和园 Summer Palace, an Imperial Garden in *Beijing*

北京，1998.11

14.北京皇家祭坛——天坛 Temple of Heaven: an Imperial Sacrificial Altar in *Beijing*

北京，1998.11

15.大足石刻 *Dazu* Rock Carvings

重庆，1999.12

16.皖南古村落——西递、宏村 Ancient Villages in Southern *Anhui*—*Xidi* and *Hongcun*

安徽，2000.11

17.明清皇家陵寝 Imperial Tombs of the *Ming* and *Qing* Dynasties

明显陵（湖北）、清东陵（河北）、清西陵（河北），2000.11；明孝陵（江苏）、

十三陵(北京),2003.7;盛京三陵(辽宁),2004.7

18.龙门石窟 *Longmen* Grottoes

河南,2000.11

19.青城山和都江堰 Mount *Qingcheng* and the *Dujiangyan* Irrigation System

四川,2000.11

20.云冈石窟 *Yungang* Grottoes

山西,2001.12

21.高句丽王城、王陵和贵族墓葬 Capital Cities and Tombs of the Ancient *Koguryo* Kingdom

吉林,辽宁;2004.7

22.澳门历史城区 Historic Centre of Macao

澳门,2005

23.殷墟 *Yin Xu*

河南,2006.7

24.开平碉楼与村落 *Kaiping Diaolou* and Villages

广东,2007.6

25.福建土楼 *Fujian Tulou*

福建,2008.7

26.登封"天地中心"历史建筑群 Historic Monuments of *Dengfeng* in "The Centre of Heaven and Earth"

河南,2010.8

27.元上都遗址 Site of *Xanadu*

内蒙古,2012.7

28.红河哈尼梯田文化景观 Cultural Landscape of *Honghe Hani* Rice Terraces

云南,2013.6

29.丝绸之路:长安—天山廊道的路网 Silk Roads: the Routes Network of *Chang'an—Tianshan* Corridor

陕西、河南、甘肃、新疆,2014.6

30.大运河 The Grand Canal

北京、天津、河北、山东、河南、安徽、江苏,2014.6

World Natural Heritage Sites in China include (10 items):

世界自然遗产包括(10 项):

1.黄龙风景名胜区 *Huanglong* Scenic and Historic Interest Area

四川,1992.12

2.九寨沟风景名胜区 *Jiuzhaigou* Valley Scenic and Historic Interest Area

四川,1992.12

3.武陵源风景名胜区 *Wulingyuan* Scenic and Historic Interest Area

湖南,1992.12

4.云南三江并流保护区 Three Parallel Rivers of *Yunnan* Protected Areas

云南,2003.7

5.四川大熊猫栖息地—卧龙、四姑娘山和夹金山 *Sichuan* Giant Panda Sanctuaries— *Wolong*, Mt *Siguniang* and *Jiajin* Mountains

四川,2006.7

6.中国南方喀斯特 South China *Karst*

云南、贵州、重庆,2007.6;广西,重庆、贵州,2012.6

7.三清山国家公园 Mount *Sanqingshan* National Park

江西,2008.7

8.中国丹霞 China *Danxia*

贵州、福建、湖南、广东、江西、浙江,2010.8

9.澄江化石遗址 *Chengjiang* Fossil Site

云南,2012.7

10.新疆天山 *Xinjiang Tianshan*

新疆,2013.6

World Cultural and Natural Heritage Sites in China include(4 items):

世界文化自然双重遗产包括(4 项):

1.泰山 Mount *Taishan*

山东,1987.12

2.黄山 Mount *Huangshan*

安徽,1990.12

3.峨眉山风景区及乐山大佛风景区 Mount *Emei* Scenic Area, including *Leshan* Giant Buddha Scenic Area

四川,1996.12

4.武夷山 Mount *Wuyi*

福建,1999.12

World Cultural Landscape Heritage Sites in China include(3 items):

世界文化景观遗产包括(3 项):

1.庐山国家公园 *Lushan* National Park

江西,1996.12

2.五台山 Mount *Wutai*

山西,2009.6

3.杭州西湖文化景观 West Lake Cultural Landscape of *Hangzhou*

浙江,2011.6

陆 文化注释索引
Cultural Notes Index

柒◎参考文献
Bibligraphy

[1] Izabella Horvath. *Tales of West Lake*[M]. Hang Zhou: Xiling Yinshe Publishing House,2009.

[2] Wang Huiming. *Folk Tales of the West Lake* [M]. Beijing: Foreign Languages Press, 1982.

[3] 辞海[S]. 上海:上海辞书出版社, 1980.

[4] 陈刚. 西湖诗赞[M]. 杭州:浙江摄影出版社, 1996.

[5] 陈刚. 新大杭州指南[M]. 杭州:浙江摄影出版社,2012.

[6] 陈建一. 西湖民间故事[M]. 杭州:浙江摄影出版社, 2009.

[7] 郭沫若. 西湖民间故事[M]. 杭州:浙江文艺出版社, 2009.

[8] 顾军,苑利. 文化遗产报告:世界文化遗产保护运动的理论与实践[R]. 北京:社会科学文献出版社,2005.

[9] 莫高. 白蛇传传说[M]. 杭州:浙江摄影出版社,2008.

[10] 杭州市民间文艺家协会. 三江两湖传说集[M]. 杭州:浙江人民出版社,1988.

[11] 杭州市文化局. 西湖民间故事[M]. 杭州:浙江人民出版社,1978.

[12] 杭州市文化局编. 西湖民间故事[M]. 杭州:浙江文艺出版社,2000.

[13] 洪尚之. 西湖传说[M]. 杭州:杭州出版社,2006.

[14] 蒋水荣. 大杭州名胜古迹民间故事集[M]. 杭州:浙江摄影出版社, 2002.

[15] 庞学铨. 品味西湖三十景[M]. 杭州:杭州出版社, 2013.

[16] 山海经故事丛书. 乾隆下江南的传说[M]. 杭州:浙江文艺出版社,1983.

[17] 山海经故事丛书. 八仙的故事[M]. 杭州:浙江文艺出版社,1983.

[18] 孙克勤. 遗产保护与开发[M]. 北京：旅游教育出版社,2008.
[19] 孙琦, 陈勤. 白娘子传说[M]. 北京:中国社会出版社, 2006.
[20] 王国平. 西湖全书[M]. 杭州:杭州出版社, 2006.
[21] 王建华. 钱镠与西湖[M]. 杭州:杭州出版社, 2005.
[22] 吴一舟,陶琳,沈少英. 浙江省非物质文化遗产代表作丛书:西湖传说[M]. 杭州:浙江摄影出版社, 2012.
[23] 谢先泽. 旅游英语读本:中国的世界遗产概览[M]. 北京:外语教学与研究出版社,2011.
[24] 许渊冲(译).白居易诗选[M]. 石家庄:河北人民出版社,2006.
[25] 许渊冲(译).苏轼诗词选[M]. 长沙:湖南人民出版社,2007.
[26] “西湖天下”丛书编辑部. 西湖民间故事[M]. 杭州:浙江摄影出版社,2011.
[27] 郑土有,胡蝶. 梁祝传说[M]. 北京:中国社会出版社,2006.
[28] 周航,王全吉. 浙江民讲故事[M]. 杭州:浙江文艺出版社, 2010.
[30] 周静书. 浙江省非物质文化遗产代表作丛书: 梁祝传说[M]. 杭州:浙江摄影出版社,2009.
[31] http://en.gotohz.com/discoverhangzhou/wheretogo/attractions
[32] http://en.wikipedia.org/wiki/Main_Page
[33] http://www.chinaculture.org/focus/focus/cities
[34] http://www.chinaheritagequarterly.org/
[35] http://english.cntv.cn/program/documentary/20120626/114420_2.shtml
[36] http://whc.unesco.org/en

后 记

“上有天堂、下有苏杭”是人们对杭城之美的由衷赞叹。杭城之美,美在西湖。西湖依杭州而名,杭州因西湖而盛。自古以来就盛传,“天下西湖三十六,此中最美是杭州”。

西湖之美,不仅美在其秀丽的湖山景色、丰富的文物古迹,更美在其悠久的历史文化、丰富的人文景观。千百年来,许许多多动人的“西湖传说”将西湖美丽的自然风光融汇到其丰厚的文化底蕴中。漫步在西湖山水间,几乎每一步都能踏出一段优美的传说。

萌发译介西湖传说的念头始于几年前。我领着几位来杭的外国友人欣赏西湖的自然美景,讲述着景点的故事。他们不仅流连于巧夺天工的西湖美景,更痴迷于美妙悠久的西湖传说,返程之际仍意犹未尽,向我索要英文版的西湖传说译介。此时我才发现各大书店竟然都找不到英文版的西湖传说。译介西湖传说,向外国游客译介西湖自然和人文之美,是生活在西子湖畔的高校外语工作者义不容辞的责任。

2013 年我以“关于西湖传说的译介”为选题,申报了浙江省社科联科普课,并有幸立项,因此有了汉英对照版的《西湖传说文化探微》。在此对浙江省社科联课题评审专家们的支持深表谢意。如果没有他们的慧眼,我的设想也不可能这么快得以实现。

这一年多的时间里,我全身心投入这项工作,搜集了大量的资料,听从了诸多专家和学者的建议,没有他们的支持,就没有这部书稿的问世。尤其要感谢的是浙江科技学院陈亚轩女士自始至终的指导,从选题的敲定、大纲的拟定到格式的选择、语言的推敲,她都给予了热情的关注和有益的建议。尤其是她在美国访学期间,还心系书稿,并担任了全书的审校。

本书稿译介工作还有幸得到了浙江工商大学外国语学院几位同事的鼎力支持。本书翻译工作的分工如下:张英女士翻译了第一章名胜传说部分除“明珠”以外的六个传说;李莹莹女士翻译了第二章物产传说部分;章瑜女士翻译了第三章人物传说;朱肖一女士翻译了第四章爱情传说;郭宏宇女士一直献计献策。同时，武汉大学外国语言学院崔璨女士翻译了第一章中关于“明珠”的传说以及附录部分西湖三十景的所有内容。李莹莹女士负责大纲的拟定、全书的统稿、所有诗歌部分的收集整理等工作。

引领我走入翻译殿堂的是我的恩师山东大学博士生导师孙迎春教授。孙老师不仅治学严谨，待人宽厚，而且对我耳提面命，传授我为学之道与为人之道。即使在我毕业后，他也对我一如既往的关怀与支持。当我将这本书的初稿寄给恩师，请他为书稿赐序，他欣然应允，并提出了许多宝贵的修改建议。在此，请允许我向恩师表示深深的敬意与谢意！

我还将书稿寄给了曾经未能如愿得到西湖传说英译本失望而归的几位外国友人。他们读完书稿后，对我的书稿大为肯定：“读着这些传说，就像是在给孩子讲故事，这些故事非常生动有趣，读着读着就被故事感染了”。他们的肯定给了我极大的鼓舞与信心。其中，尤其要感谢的是来自英国的 Pamela 女士以及 Calum Boyle 先生，他们认真研读了整部书稿，提出了许多宝贵的建议。

回想在完成本书稿一年多的时间里，自己常常因为沉迷于传说而幻化，会不由自主地游离于现实和传说之间，并因此会时常冷落了家人。感谢家人的理解和支持！

本书稿在译介过程中，还参阅了许多学者的相关研究成果，从中获得了珍贵的资料和启迪。对引用的资料，有的注明了出处，有的由于种种原因，如资料时间久远，资料索取的途径不完全是我本人，来自于网上的部分资料出处不全等，所以在注释中可能有遗漏，特此说明，并对被引用资料作者的智慧与贡献表示诚挚的感谢！

译无止境，拙作只是一块引玉之砖。由于我们的水平和时间有限，加之也受限于手头所能获得的文献资料，书中缺点错误之处在所难免，敬请各界专家和广大读者不吝赐教，以便再版时修订。

李莹莹

2014 年 6 月

于西子湖畔

AFTERWORD

As the Chinese saying goes, "there is a paradise in heaven, while there are *Suzhou* and *Hangzhou* on earth", people marvel at the beauty of *Hangzhou*. The fascination and allure of *Hangzhou* lies in West Lake. In the ancient times, there was a saying stating that "there were 36 beautiful lakes in China, among which West Lake was the top one".

The beauty of West Lake lies not only in its elegant natural landscape and historic relics but also in its long standing historic culture and humanistic landscape. It carries with it a certain aura that makes you feel as if you are touching a folk story with every step you take alongside the waterfront. West Lake legends are a harmonious combination of both the profound historic culture and the charming natural landscape, which has become a bright pearl in the human heritage and brings credit to *Hangzhou*.

I came up with the idea of translating West Lake legends a couple of years ago, when I had friends from other countries and I showed them around West Lake. They were so fascinated about the legends I shared with them that they asked for the English versions of those exciting folk stories. To our disappointment, no English versions of those legends could be found in *Hangzhou* bookstores. As an English teacher working in *Hangzhou*, I felt it my duty to translate West lake legends into English.

Fortunately, after years of collection and research work, in 2013, my research project about West Lake legends was approved by *Zhejiang* Federation of Humanities and Social Sciences Circles. That is the main reason how this book eventually came together. Above all, I'd like to express my gratitude to the support of *Zhejiang* Federation of Humanities and Social Sciences Circles. It would have taken much longer to turn my dream into reality without their support.

I am much obliged to many experts and scholars for their valuable suggestions and help, esp Mr. *Xu Hairong*, the Chairman of the board of Hangzhou Publishing Group, and Ms Chen Yaxuan from *Zhejiang* University of Science and Technology. Mr. *Xu* suggested me to focus on the cultural connotations of legends and offered a preface to this book. Ms. *Chen* provided unselfish support and did the proofreading work.

Thanks to the research atmosphere and high level team work of *Zhejiang Gongshang* University, this book can be completed in due time. The work of this book has benefited a lot from the support from Prof. *Chai Gaiying* and Prof. *Jia Aiwu*, as well as "Going Global Cultural Strategy and Cultural Transmission Collaborative Innovation Center" of *Zhejiang Gongshang* University. Additionally, this book has been co-translated by Ms. *Zhang* Ying, Ms. *Li Yingying*, Ms. *Zhang Yu*, Ms. *Zhu Xiaoyi* and Miss *Cui Can* (Ph.D candidate of Blaise Pascal University in France). *Li Yingying* took charge of the whole work, including producing the outline, data collection and other issues. Ms. *Guo Hongyu* contributed her wisdom and inspiration to the improvement of this book. Thanks go to all of them for their support in many ways.

Mr. *Sun Yingchun*, professor and Ph.D supervisor in *Shandong* University, taught me not only how to do academic research but also how to be a decent person. He put forward constructive suggestions to the book after going over the manuscript and gladly wrote a preface to this book. I must express my heartfelt gratitude to him.

The manuscript was also sent to my international friends who left *Hangzhou* without finding any English book of West Lake legends years ago and thus motivated me to do the research and translating work related to West Lake legends. They spoke highly of the manuscript and shared with me their feelings and comments of reading the version. Ms. Pamela and Mr. Calum James Boyle went over the whole book with great care and gave valuable suggestions from the perspective of international readers. Their wisdom and inspiration means a lot to this book. Thanks also go to Ms. *Liu Yun* and Miss *Shen Xian*, both from *Zhejiang Gongshang* University Publishing House, for their patience and effort in making this book look better.

This book has also benefited from a lot of papers and books related to this field, whose help cannot be ignored. As to the reference data, the source was indicated where possible. For some data, due to limit of time and space, the source cannot be properly targeted and might not be indicated in detail. However, the wisdom and contribution of all the previous researchers is highly appreciated.

Translation is endless work. This book is just a tentative attempt and hopefully more work will be done in this area. Admittedly, due to the limit of time and literature, the book is far from perfect. We look forward to comments and suggestions from experts and readers so that we can do better in further research in the future.

Yingying Li

June, 2014

West lake, *Hangzhou*